REFUSAL AND THEN . . . SURRENDER

Abruptly his arms were around her, and she felt a rush of panic. His mouth was hard and angry, and his kisses were a brand of shame. Holding her prisoner, with his fingers through her pale gold hair, he kissed her deeply again and again.

She tried desperately to stop herself from making obvious the inevitability of her own response, but when his hand found its way inside her shirt and began to caress her warm, rounded body, she gave a long moan of desire . . .

GLORIOUS DAWN

Dorothy Garlock

FAWCETT GOLD MEDAL • NEW YORK

A Fawcett Gold Medal Book
Published by Ballantine Books
Copyright © 1982 Dorothy Garlock

ISBN 0-449-14492-5

Manufactured in the United States of America

First Ballantine Books Edition: October 1982

10   9   8   7   6   5   4   3   2   1

To ADAM—for being wonderful and always loving.

CHAPTER ONE

THE SMALL PLATFORM at the end of the Wild Horse Saloon seemed miles away to Johanna. Paused in the doorway, she tried to collect herself, to somehow contain the conflicting feelings that swam in her mind. What was she doing in a place like this? she asked herself again. She was a schoolteacher, daughter of a schoolteacher, reared with a love of learning and a sense of purpose. She was used to standing before her students giving to them the knowledge that would help prepare them for life. And here she was in a dingy saloon with people who had little interest in books, or in any of the things she cared about. These men were here to get the dust from their lungs and the smell of cattle from their nostrils. They were drovers, drifters, gamblers, and soldiers, from nearby Fort Davis, from which the town got its name.

Still, she thought, her father did use to say that no work was disgraceful, so long as you did it well. And she did sing well, and as for purpose, Lord knew she and Jacy needed the money she could earn here.

Johanna braced herself, shut out thoughts of her parents' murder, her sister's rape, the consequent baby the now mute Jacy carried. As she swept through the room a sudden hush fell. The loud voices ceased, as did the scraping of boot heels on the plank

1

floor and the clinking of glasses; even the tinkling of the piano that stood near the bar. Every head turned toward Johanna, every eye focused on the lovely face, framed in silvery blond hair.

Johanna seated herself on a chair, adjusted her guitar, and the dress that covered her slender figure from chin to toe, a costume she'd insisted on despite the owner's plea that she at least show a bit of cleavage for the men.

"How about singin' 'Sweet Kate McGoon'?" a slurry young voice came at her.

Johanna's cheeks turned scarlet at the mention of the well-known bawdy song. There was a censorious murmur and a chair crashed to the floor as the offender was silenced.

"Sing 'Believe Me If All Those Endearing Young Charms.' " The voice was that of one of the young soldiers. Johanna smiled at him gratefully, again adjusted her instrument, and began the introductory bars.

The audience was attentive, almost reverent, as she sang. Even the bartender stopped pushing the wet cloth over the grimy bar. When she ended the song her audience pounded on the tables with whiskey bottles and beer glasses. Johanna acknowledged their "applause," then swung into a lively tune, her lips curved in a smile, her slender fingers moving rapidly over the strings. The men stamped their feet to the music and the room was filled with rollicking gaiety. Her next offering was about a Spanish dancer with flashing eyes. It was sung in perfect Spanish, which delighted the Mexican customers, who joined in the chorus, loud and off-key. When she began a ballad, her azure eyes took on a dreamy faraway look. Her voice was soft and husky and ideally suited to the songs. These were her favorites, and always worked their magic on her as well as her audience. If only she could sing until the stroke of midnight, she thought. Then she would be free to return to the rooming house. But that was not part of the bargain she'd made with the saloonkeeper. She had agreed to serve drinks to Wild Horse patrons once she had entertained them with her songs.

Finally the performance was over and she laid down her guitar on the piano. She moved toward the tables to refill empty glasses, cringing as she passed between the tables, aware of being the only woman in the room.

For the most part customers were respectful, although some did try to engage her in conversation. Fortunately, she was not assaulted by lewd or suggestive remarks, probably because Johanna's every movement pronounced her a good woman.

Johanna approached the bar with a tray of empty glasses. "I'll be going now, Mr. Basswood."

"Stay another hour and I'll pay another dollar," he said hopefully.

"It's almost midnight," she said firmly.

"You'll be back tomorrow night?"

"I'll be back."

"Introduce me to the lady, Basswood."

The gray-haired, portly man who had spoken moved down the bar to stand beside Johanna. She glanced at him, taking in everything about him in one glance: his carefully brushed silver hair, the dark suit, and the gold watch chain draped across his ample chest.

"Sure, Mr. Cash." The bartender looked pleased. "This here is Miss Doan. Miss Johanna Doan."

Johanna nodded coolly and turned to the piano to pick up her guitar. "Excuse me. I've got to be getting home."

"Miss . . ." The bartender leaned toward her. "Will you go out the back way? When they see you leave, they'll all go over to . . ." He jerked his head in the direction of his competitor.

"No. I'll not go into that dark alley." Her hackles rose at the thought of slinking out the back door.

The portly man finished his drink and set his glass on the bar.

"I can understand that, Basswood. I'll escort the lady, with her permission, of course."

"That's right kind of you," the bartender said before turning to Johanna. "Mr. Cash is the lawyer here, Miss Doan. You'll be safe with him."

The lawyer followed Johanna through the back door and down the dark alley. He didn't speak until they stepped on the boardwalk fronting the stores on the main street.

"I'll walk you to your door, Miss Doan. I'm rather surprised Mrs. Scheetz is allowing you a room in her house, considering your . . . er . . . profession."

"Mrs. Scheetz has already given us notice to move."

"This is your first experience singing in a saloon, isn't it?" Not waiting for her to reply, he went on, "You were fortunate to pick Basswood's saloon. He runs as decent a place as is possible in this lawless town."

"I visited every respectable business in town asking for work before I approached Mr. Basswood." Her voice was taut, strained.

They walked along in silence, the heels of their shoes tapping on the walk. The lawyer glanced covertly at the girl beside him. He marveled at the beauty which nature had bestowed upon her: fine-boned, yet delicately curved; flawless skin; wide-apart azure eyes. Her exquisitely shaped face was crowned with soft-spun hair of a curious mixture of silver and gold. She was slender to the point of appearing fragile. But the set of her mouth and chin, the candor in her eyes, and her bearing all showed strength of character. Of course he had no proof of this, but he felt instinctively she was the right person for the proposition he intended to make.

They reached the gate leading to the porch of the boarding-house, and Johanna turned to the man.

"Thank you." She smiled politely. "Goodnight."

"Are you interested in other employment, Miss Doan?"

"What kind of employment?" Her eyes looked unwaveringly into his.

"Perfectly respectable employment," he said evenly. "That is, if you have no objections to living out of town."

"My sister goes where I go." It was a flat statement.

"I've taken your sister into consideration, and also the fact that she is . . . pregnant."

Surprise flickered across Johanna's face, and her lips tightened.

"I know quite a lot about you and your sister. I watched you get off the stage a few weeks ago. I went to Fort Stockton and talked to the banker. He told me you were asked to leave your teaching job; asked to leave town and take your sister with you."

Johanna drew herself up rigidly. Irate sparks flared in her eyes.

"Did they tell you," she snapped, "that the renegades who murdered my father and mother also carried off my seventeen-year-old sister and kept her for three days? Did they tell you that she is mute; that she hasn't uttered a single word since she was found wandering on the prairie?" Johanna paused to collect herself, but could not still her temper. "The good people of Fort Stockton turned us out. They wouldn't believe Jacy's pregnancy was the result of her ordeal."

"I believe it."

Johanna was, for a moment, taken aback by the statement. "Why would you believe it when practically every person in Fort Stockton didn't believe it?"

"Because I took the trouble to find out why you left San Angelo. You wanted to get your sister away from the place where your parents were killed, where she suffered . . . violation. You left San Angelo and found the teaching job in Fort Stockton, but the Mrs. Scheetzes of Fort Stockton didn't believe your sister had been raped. You were too honest, Miss Doan. You should have said she was a widow." He waited for her to speak, and when she did not, continued, "It will be difficult for you to find decent lodgings here, and your money must be almost gone." He added the last apologetically.

Her mind was racing. No use pretending; the money *was* almost gone and the landlady had given her two days to find another room.

Johanna's straightforwardness slightly unnerved the lawyer, and he felt a pang of indecision about offering her the job in Macklin Valley, but he shrugged it off. He had looked too long for the right woman to go soft over this girl.

"My office is above the dry-goods store, just west of the bank. Will you come there in the morning? About midmorning, if it's convenient?"

"I'll be there." She started to turn away, then turned back and thrust out her hand. "Thank you," she said softly.

The lawyer looked into the young woman's face, so open, so

beautiful, and felt again a slight twinge of conscience. He shoved it aside.

"See you in the morning, miss. Goodnight," he said in his reserved-for-the-office voice and quickly walked away.

Johanna felt her way up the darkened stairway and down the hall to the small room in the back of the house. Quietly she opened the door and let herself in. She frowned when she saw that the oil lamp was still on. Mrs. Scheetz would have found that still another flaw in her and Jacy's character, had she known. She put her instrument down and walked over to the bed where her sister lay sleeping, her light-brown hair spread over the pillow, her dark lashes shadows on her pale cheeks. Her face was so young, so stirringly beautiful, and her body so slight it hardly seemed to make a depression in the big bed.

"What a cruel twist of fate." She said the words softly, her mind months and miles away; a whole lifetime away for her and Jacy. She usually tried to block the events from surfacing as if it had all been a bad dream, but it was real, it had happened, and she would never forget a second of it.

Her father had sent her to the shack in the grove to fetch the old black man who worked for the family. They were returning when the sounds of the shots and the screams reached them.

Eyes wild with shock, Johanna fought the hands that held her. Her father lay dead in the yard and her stepmother lay nearby; the flames from the burning cabin were already licking at her body. Every nerve in Johanna's body screamed with terror at the sight of her sister spread on the ground thrashing uselessly as each man took his turn spending his lust on her.

The old black man's strength was too much for Johanna. He dragged her into the thick brush and held her fiercely against him. There was nothing they could do but wait in the murky darkness for the renegades to leave. A barking dog alerted the men to possible capture, and one of them picked up Jacy's limp body and threw it over the neck of his horse and rode away.

The citizens of San Angelo had formed a posse to hunt down the murderers of their schoolteacher and his wife, but the area was vast and almost impossible to cover fully. Three days later they returned with Jacy, mute, and teetering on the brink of insanity.

Thankful beyond words for her sister's return, Johanna set about trying to make a normal life for Jacy, to restore her health and help her to regain her speech. She took her father's teaching job in San Angelo, but after a month decided it would be best to remove Jacy from the scene of the tragedy. They moved to Fort Stockton.

Then the calamity of Jacy's pregnancy! Knowing that she carried the child of one of her parents' murderers deepened her depression. She began to sit for hours staring into space. She seldom smiled, and at times Johanna would find her pounding her small fist on her already protruding abdomen.

Johanna blew out the light, undressed in the dark, and slipped into bed beside her sister. She closed her eyes and tried to sleep, to forget for a while the problems that faced her. But there was no relief. Her thoughts continued to flow. It was plain now that the biddies in this town were no different from those in Fort Stockton. Only this time their prejudices were directed toward her, for she had, indeed, told Mrs. Scheetz that Jacy was a widow. Perhaps, Johanna reasoned, Mr. Cash would provide the solution. Whatever he offered would be better than attempting to stay on here at Fort Davis.

Johanna was up and dressed by the time Jacy awoke. "Get up, sleepyhead. Get up and get dressed. I have an appointment to see about a new job."

Obediently Jacy got up, but remained expressionless and showed no interest in what Johanna had said. She dressed, washed her face and hands, brushed her hair, and coiled it into two buns over her ears.

Johanna chattered on as though Jacy had been eager to hear what she had to say. "There was a crowd at the saloon last night, Jacy. The men liked 'Rosewood Casket.' You could have heard a pin drop in that saloon while I was singing it. Oh, how those big, rough cowmen like a sad song! It's hard to believe unless you see it. Big men with guns strapped to their waist, whiskey in their hands, and tears in their eyes over a sad song.'' Her voice trailed away. She had failed, once again, to engage Jacy's interest. She tucked a handkerchief into her sister's pocket. ''Come along—we've got to get down to breakfast before Mrs. Scheetz clears it away.''

Johanna put a protective arm across Jacy's shoulders as they entered the dining room. Mrs. Scheetz was sitting at the head of the table, her grim mouth pressed into a tight line of disapproval. The other two occupants at the table, middle-aged male store clerks, acknowledged the young women's entrance by half rising from their chairs, but upon seeing their landlady's disdain they quickly sat down. Soon they finished their meal and left.

The three women sat in silence, the tension gradually building. Finally the stout woman pushed herself from the table and stood up.

''You be out of that room this afternoon.'' The words were hissed at Johanna. ''This is the last meal you'll have at my table. The idea . . . a saloon singer living in my house and eating at my table. I'll never be able to hold my head up in this town again!''

Johanna calmly continued to eat. ''Our rent is paid until tomorrow. We'll not be leaving until then.''

''You will leave today!'' The words burst from the tight mouth, reverberating in the small room.

Johanna wanted to laugh. The woman's face had turned a plum red, and she suddenly felt a vengeful need to further antagonize her.

''We'll stay until tomorrow, and if you make any trouble for us,'' she said softly, ''I'll tell the men at the saloon you're sleeping with Mr. Rutledge.'' She glanced up to meet the woman's astonished eyes. ''I know it isn't true, but they won't know, will they?''

Mrs. Scheetz seemed to swell up, her face took on an even deeper color, and her eyes rolled back in her head. For a moment Johanna almost regretted what she had said. Perhaps she had gone too far and the woman would have a stroke.

''But . . . but . . . you, you . . .''

"I was sure you would allow us to stay, Mrs. Scheetz. Thank you."

The woman gasped and walked unsteadily from the room.

Johanna turned to see Jacy looking straight at her, an unmistakable glint of amusement in her eyes. Johanna could have cried with joy. Jacy had finally reacted.

At a few minutes before nine o'clock the girls left the boardinghouse. Johanna had dressed carefully for the meeting with the lawyer. She wore a light-blue cotton dress that fit snugly over her tiny waist and full breasts, but was demurely styled. Her one and only hat, a stiff, natural-color straw, decorated with a pink satin rose, sat squarely on top of her soft piled hair. Jacy wore a dark-brown dress attractively brightened by a white collar and cuffs and a light shawl which she draped about her shoulders.

Satisfied that they were presentable, Johanna looked about the street with interest. Several wagons were standing in front of the mercantile store. The horses, with blinders attached to their bridles, stood patiently, their long scraggly tails swishing away at the pesky flies that tormented them. Two cowboys sauntered toward the young women, their high-heeled boots beating a hollow tattoo on the boardwalk. They lifted their wide-brimmed hats and murmured, "Mornin'."

Jacy turned her eyes away, but Johanna nodded a greeting.

They walked to the corner and across the dusty street, dodging a whirling tumbleweed, and past the bank, where they stopped under the sign that read: SIMON CASH, ATTORNEY AT LAW. Johanna took Jacy's hand and they walked up the wooden stairway.

Cash rose from the chair beside the massive rolltop desk. "Good morning, ladies."

"Morning. This is my sister, Mr. Cash. Miss Jacy Doan."

"Morning, miss."

Jacy ignored the greeting. The man gave her a puzzled glance.

"Is there a place where my sister can wait for me?"

"My living quarters are in the next room. She can sit there by the window."

9

Johanna took Jacy by the hand and followed the lawyer into the next room.

"Look, Jacy. You can see the whole of main street from here." Jacy sat in the chair, her eyes reflecting a hopelessness that tore at Johanna's heart.

Cash offered Johanna a chair by his desk, then seated himself.

"Is your sister always like this?" he asked kindly.

"Since we found out about her pregnancy. But this morning I was quite encouraged—she smiled at me after Mrs. Scheetz and I had a little tiff."

Cash didn't react. He leaned back in his chair and absently took out a gold watch, flipped open the case to glance at it, then returned it to his pocket. He smoothed his hair, which was already slicked down. He sat up straight in the chair and looked sternly at Johanna, but did not speak. A wave of despair swept over Johanna. It was obvious he was skeptical about offering her the job.

To her relief he finally spoke. Johanna leaned forward eagerly.

"I have been debating with myself. I had almost decided not to offer you the position, but knowing you are in need of work away from this town . . ." He paused. "Oh, yes, I know the ladies are going to ask you to leave. Mrs. Scheetz has a powerful influence with the ladies. If you were a different type of woman you could move to the other side of town, but then if that were the case I wouldn't be considering you for the job."

Johanna's hopes began to rise, not only because of what he said, but because she sensed a softening in his stern face.

"Let me put the facts to you, Miss Doan, and then we will talk about it. My client lives quite a distance from here, in a valley he found over thirty years ago. Mack Macklin fought Indians to get the valley. He fought Indians, outlaws, and Mexican renegades to keep it. While other men were dreaming of the California gold fields, he dreamed of building an empire in that valley. He worked hard and carved himself that empire. He built a house and a dam, built irrigation ditches where he wanted them. Built bunkhouses for his drovers. He drove a herd of cattle west when there were no cattle in this country. It was not an easy chore to drive cattle to New Mexico, but he did it. He turned the cattle loose, and now they have bred into some of the biggest herds in the Southwest." He paused and rocked for a moment in the desk chair. "He's old now. His foot was taken off a few years back and he gets around on his sticks. He's ornery and cantankerous, but I figure he's earned it."

Cash ceased talking for a moment and looked directly into Johanna's eyes. "Macklin has asked me to find him a housekeeper. A pretty young woman with blond hair and blue eyes. Seems he had a woman once who looked like that, and in his old age he would like to have one around to look at and to care for his home." His voice trailed off, but he continued to look at Johanna, who sank back in her chair relieved.

"Oh, saints be praised! You were so stern. I was afraid it was going to be something I couldn't do. A housekeeper! It's perfect for me. I love to keep house and I'm a good cook."

"Miss . . ." Cash looked really stern. "The valley is a long way from here. A very long way."

Johanna's spirits were too high to falter; no matter how far away it was, she'd be willing to make the trip. Laughter bubbled up in her throat. "I'll work hard," she said. "I'll work very hard. Oh, you don't know how relieved I am." Impulsively she reached across the desk and clasped his hand strongly. "When do we go? How do we get there?"

The lawyer studied the young woman, and a smile played about the corners of his mouth. He liked her. Liked her quiet determined spirit. She had courage. He hoped enough courage to cope with old Mack. The tough old man had told Cash, "By God, I don't want no milk-and-water lass. No milksop that'll weep and cringe. I want a strong lass with guts. Guts! Guts is what made Macklin Valley."

Old Mack would be madder than sin when he first saw the girl. She wasn't the big-boned, hefty type of woman he wanted, but she did have the blond hair and the blue eyes, and she wouldn't fold up under the first attack of the old man's wrath. The thing that bothered the lawyer most was the sister, who looked part Mexican. Old Mack hated Mexicans with a cruel passion that

Cash had never understood. That was something Johanna and Jacy would have to work out with Mack, he finally decided.

"Every six months a train of ten to twelve wagons comes in from New Mexico. The valley is closer to El Paso, but it is easier to bring the freight wagons over the plains than to cross the mountains. It will take about three days for the men to blow off steam and to load the wagons. Besides their usual load of supplies, this time they're taking back lumber to build a windmill. I suggest you and your sister stock up on whatever you'll be needing for the next few months. You'll be going back with the train. You realize, Miss Doan, that you'll be traveling over very rough country? You'll cross over three hundred miles of every type of terrain imaginable. It will be a hard trip for any woman, and doubly so for one in your sister's condition. I'll talk to Mr. Redford, the head teamster, and see if he can fix up something a little more comfortable than a freight wagon for you to ride in."

"I was assured that Jacy is in good physical condition, Mr. Cash. I wish you could have known her before. She was so lively, so bright and pretty. The doctor in San Angelo said that there's a good chance she'll be well and speak again. He said sometimes a second shock can loosen the vocal cords. She's terribly frightened of men, especially Mexican men, and justifiably so."

"They'll be at least two dozen men on the train, and a good part of them will be Mexican. You have nothing to fear from them. The danger will come from outlaws, renegade Apaches or Mexican bandits—although it would take a good-sized gang to risk attacking a dozen wagons and two dozen men." Cash looked at her sympathetically. "I told you exactly what you will face because I want you to know it won't be easy."

"I never expected it to be easy," she said simply. "If I've learned one thing, Mr. Cash, it's that the good things in life seldom come easy."

CHAPTER TWO

T HE BIG COVERED wagon rolled down the dusty street, past curious bystanders lounging in front of the stores, then began the long curve out of town. Ahead of them the freight wagons waited to fall in behind the lead wagons. Johanna acknowledged with a warm smile each driver as they passed the wagons, and the men in turn tipped their broad-brimmed hats. Several riders were in the trail ahead, some beside the train, and a few more leading strings of mules, replacements for those hitched to the heavy wagons.

Johanna sat on the high seat beside the driver, a ranch hand named Mooney. Redford, sitting astride a powerful sorrel, waved them on, and the pace picked up. When the wagon swerved, Johanna clutched at the seat, then turned to look back at Jacy lying in a hammock stretched between the stout sides of the wagon. Redford had suggested the hammock with heavy springs on each end to cushion the jolts of the rough trail. He said he had seen it work before and was sure he could fix up the contraption.

There had been a rough moment when Mooney attempted to lift Jacy onto the wagon seat. She struck his hands and cringed behind Johanna. The incident stiffened Johanna's resolve to ask Mr. Redford to explain Jacy's situation to the others and perhaps avoid a repetition of the scene with Mooney.

The days since her meeting with Cash had sped by. He had brought Redford to meet her. He was a short but heavily shouldered man with iron-gray hair and a drooping mustache. His face was brown and seamed with wrinkles. The flannel shirt he wore was ragged and sun-faded, and his boots were even dustier than the hat he held in his hands.

Johanna told him everything, beginning with Jacy's ordeal and ending with the possibility of being asked to leave the so-called decent part of town because of her job in the saloon. The kind eyes turned cold with fury, then softened when she told him about her hopes for Jacy's recovery. The night before they were to leave, Redford acquainted the women with Mooney. He told them, with a twinkle in his eye, that the man was his oldest driver and far more trustworthy than the young scutters he had. Mooney laughed and hit Redford on the back with his dusty hat.

"By gol, I ain't that old!" he said.

Johanna untied the strings of her stiff-brimmed sunbonnet and took it off. The breeze stirred her hair and felt cool on her neck. The sun had begun to climb over the horizon and promised the kind of warm early-September day that Texas settlers knew well. She watched the slow, rhythmic steps of the horses and the cloud of fine white dust they stirred, dust that soon covered them all with an almost suffocating film. The miles stretched before them, and to Johanna, on the swaying wagon seat, they seemed endless and timeless.

She smiled at the driver, who sat with one booted foot on the guard rail, his hat pulled low over his brow.

"Have you made this trip many times, Mr. Mooney?"

"More times than I could shake a stick at, I reckon."

"Mr. Redford said it would take about two weeks to get to the valley."

"Yup. Red got it figured 'bout right."

"Please don't be offended at what my sister did this morning, Mr. Mooney. She suffered a terrible shock, and it will take time for her to get over it. I'll ask Mr. Redford to explain so you'll understand."

Mooney leaned out over the side of the wagon and let loose a stream of tobacco juice into the dusty trail. "Don't let it worry your head none. Red done gathered us all 'round and told us 'bout what happened to your sister. He didn't want any of us to be a-scarin' her, you see. It was just pure-dee old ignorance on my part what I did. If I'da give it a thought I'da knowed better."

Johanna smiled, relieved. "I'm glad he told you, Mr. Mooney."

"You don't have to be addin' a mister to my name, ma'am. I'm just plain old Mooney." He looked at her and his leathery face creased with his grin.

"All right. Call me Johanna. Tell me about the valley, Mooney."

"Big valley. Pert nigh fifty miles long."

"Does the ranch cover the whole valley?"

"And then some."

"Mr. Cash said Mr. Macklin lost a foot a few years back. It must be difficult for him to oversee such a large spread."

"Old Mack don't oversee nothin' much 'cept a few things."

"Well . . . who does?"

Mooney shifted uncomfortably in his seat and adjusted the reins in his hands, evidently thinking about what he was about to say. Johanna wasn't quite sure why he hesitated, and his answer did not make things any clearer.

"Burr runs things," Mooney finally said. "Goddam good at it, too. Better'n old Mack ever done."

"Tell me about Mr. Macklin," Johanna prodded, anxious to know more about the man for whom she would work.

"Ain't much to tell. He's an ornery old coot."

His description made her laugh. "Ornery or not, it took courage to build a ranch way out there."

"He's got grit, all right. He was good at fightin', gettin', and holdin', but he ain't no good atall at managin'. Burr's got him beat all hollow."

Johanna already knew Mr. Macklin was difficult and that the ranch was huge. She hadn't known, however, that he had a ranch manager. If she had stopped to think about it at all, she would have known. After all, he was an old man.

The day went quickly. The sun arched high overhead and then

moved in a relentless path until it was a glowing orb hung low over the western edge of the world. When finally it was no more than a faint, rosy tinge, the freighters circled the wagons for the night. Mooney stopped the big covered wagon under the fanning branches of a huge old pecan tree. The drivers leaped from their wagons and stretched, then unhitched their teams and led them to the water wagon. Lids were removed from the wooden barrels, and each horse was allowed to drink before being turned inside a roped area to roll in the dust and eat the sparse prairie grass. Minutes later a fire was built in the center of the circle of wagons and over it was hung a huge iron pot. On one side of the fire a squat, very black coffee pot was already sending up a plume of steam.

Johanna helped Jacy climb down over the big wheel of the wagon. "I'll help get the supper if you'll tell me what to do."

"Ain't no call for you to do that, ma'am," Red said with a grin. "Old Codger over there is about to bust a gut a tryin' to fix up a good meal for you ladies. Don't know when I've seen him get so high behind."

She laughed, and the men, unaccustomed to a woman in their midst, paused to look at her.

"There's something you *can* do, ma'am, if you're a mind of it. You can sing tonight. The men heard you at the saloon, and they was mighty taken with what they heard."

"I'll be pleased to sing for them, Mr. Redford." Her voice must have carried in the stillness of the evening, because from several wagons away came a wild yell.

Red shook his head. "I'll swear," he said. "They ain't got no manners atall."

The light disappeared from the sky while they ate. Codger brought the young women each a plate of smoke-flavored beans and bacon, then returned with two tin cups and the squat coffee pot. Surprised at her hunger, Johanna attacked the meal with relish. The food was wholesome and filling. Jacy, too, seemed to enjoy the meal. They emptied their plates and sipped at the hot black coffee. Night sounds filled the air with pleasant and familiar harmonies, and Johanna relaxed, enjoying the rustle of the leaves in the pecan tree and the crackling of the burning wood of the campfire. It was comforting, too, to hear the quiet rumble of masculine voices keeping up a steady stream of talk while they finished off their second and third helpings of food.

Johanna heard the sound of running horses and looked up in alarm. The men continued to eat and showed no concern. The riders pulled their mounts to a sudden halt, leaped from the saddles, and draped the reins over the wheel of a wagon. They were laughing and teasing each other as they approached the campfire.

Jacy stood up and looked wildly about. Her eyes were huge with fright. She crouched, like a small animal, ready to spring away into the safe darkness. Before Johanna could stop her she leaped up onto the crate and tried to crawl into the wagon.

"Jacy, no!" Johanna pulled her back and into her arms, where she stood trembling. "It's all right. There's nothing to be afraid of."

The three cowboys stood stone-still, a bewildered look on their dusty faces. They started to back away.

"Please stay," Johanna urged. "Jacy," she said gently to her sister, "look at them. They work for Mr. Macklin, just as we will. Turn around and look at them." Firmly she took Jacy's shoulders and turned her to face the men.

The only sound to be heard, while the men stood still allowing Jacy to look at them, was the blowing and stamping of the horses. Two of the men turned their eyes away, but the taller one of the three stared at her. Johanna thought he was the handsomest man she had ever seen. He was tall, whiplash-thin, his features finely chiseled. His hair was as black as a raven's wing, and his eyes, between a fringe of black lashes, were as blue as the sky on a summer day. He was dressed in tight black pants and Mexican boots and wore a loose vest over his shirt. A black sombrero, held by a cord about his neck, rode on his back. He had two silver-handled pistols strapped about his slim hips.

Johanna turned her attention back to Jacy. She was looking directly into the man's eyes. She was quieter, and Johanna drew her back down to sit once more on the box beside her.

The tall man didn't move. He stood still and looked at Jacy.

"Thank you," Johanna said quietly.

He tilted his head and walked away. Red detached himself from a group of men by the fire and came to squat down in front of the two young women.

"Ma'am," he said earnestly to Jacy, "there ain't a man jack here what wouldn't lay his life right down on the line for you. You don't have nothin' to be a feared of long's you're with us, and that's the God's truth."

His kind, homely face and sincere manner must have got through to Jacy, because she timidly held out her hand to him, and he gripped it with his big, rough one. A lump came up in Johanna's throat that threatened to choke her. To hide her emotions she reached into the back of the wagon and brought out her guitar. Red carried the crate closer to the campfire. When Johanna began to strum the strings of the instrument all conversation stopped. She flashed a sudden friendly smile and began to sing.

> "Two little children, a boy and a girl,
>   stood by the old church door.
> The little girl's feet were as brown as the curls
>   that lay on the dress that she wore."

She sang the ballad in English, then repeated it in Spanish. She sang song after song, and never had she had a more attentive audience. She let her eyes roam over the faces of the men. Most of them were of Mexican descent, as was the tall, handsome man with the silver pistols. He had moved back in the shadows and was sitting very still. The brim of his black sombrero was pulled down over his eyes, but he was facing in their direction, and Johanna could almost feel the impact of his sharp, blue eyes. There was something about his manner that gave her a moment of uneasiness, but she pulled her thoughts away from him and gave her attention to the song.

That night, for the first time in her life, Johanna slept in a covered wagon. Although tired, she felt strangely more content than she had since her parents' death.

"H'yaw! Hee-yaw!" Mooney shouted at his team and cracked the bullwhip over their backs. The yell was echoed down the line as the drivers started their teams and the wagon train began to move. The camp had been stirring since an hour before daylight when Codger had banged on the iron pot. "Come 'n' git it!" he'd hollered.

This was the fifth day on the trail. About them lay vast, immeasurable distances, broken by a purple tinge, the hint of the mountains ahead. Overhead the sun sent its heat waves shimmering down on the train, moving like a sluggish river, in the desert of sparse prairie grass and baked earth.

Johanna fastened her eyes on the notch in the mountains toward which they were heading. Mooney pointed out that they would have to cross the river before they reached the mountain pass. All travel on the plains, he said, was governed by the need for water. They would fill the barrels with river water, and it would have to last until they reached the mountain pass, where there was a waterhole. Between the river and the mountain pass was the meanest stretch of country God's sun ever shone on. Mooney told her, "It ain't fit fer nothin' but tarantulas, centipedes, and rattlesnakes."

Later in the afternoon they encountered one of the latter.

They were rolling along at a steady pace, Johanna drowsing on the seat beside Mooney, Jacy in her hammock, when suddenly the two lead horses swerved off the trail, bringing the wagon to an abrupt halt.

"Right there must be the grandpappy of all rattlers," Mooney said.

Johanna's eyes followed his pointing finger. In the middle of the trail was a large snake, coiled in striking position. Its head was up and swaying, its beady eyes looking straight at them. The rattles on the end of its body were in constant motion. Johanna shuddered, but couldn't take her eyes off the snake. Jacy, standing behind her, clutched her shoulders and stared with horror at the squirming monster, whose rattles could be heard by the teams pulled up behind.

Mooney was having difficulty holding the badly frightened team. Johanna turned her eyes to them for only an instant, then heard the shot. She looked back to see the snake, now missing its head, uncoiling in its death throes. A rider astride a horse as black as midnight was shoving his silver pistol back into the holster. He turned in the saddle, and the somber blue eyes slanted across Johanna to rest on Jacy's pale face and shiny brown hair.

"Thanky, Luis." Mooney let loose a stream of tobacco juice. The horses ceased their restless movements and stood trembling in their harnesses, so Mooney wound the reins about the brake lever and jumped down from the wagon.

The two men walked over to the dead snake. Its body was as thick as a man's leg, and stretched out it would have measured over six feet. Mooney grabbed the snake by the tail and pulled it off the trail.

"Make good eatin', Luis, if Codger'll pick it up."

"*Sí*—I will tell him." In one easy motion he mounted the black horse and looked at the girls once again before he whirled the animal around and headed back down the line.

It was the first time Johanna had seen the slim, good-looking cowboy in the daylight. He always came into camp after dark and was gone by morning when the wagons rolled out. She wanted to ask Mooney about him, but decided to wait until the time was right. She turned to him now.

"That was real shooting, Mooney."

"Yup, but that warn't no chore fer Luis. I seen him shoot the eye outta a jackrabbit at full gallop."

Johanna expected him to turn and grin at her as he did sometimes when he was exaggerating, but his face remained serious.

"Is he a gunman?" She didn't know why she asked the question and wished she could rephrase it.

Mooney let loose another mouthful of tobacco juice. "Depends on what you call a gunman."

"You know what I mean. Was he hired by Mr. Macklin because he's good with a gun?"

"Ain't hired," came Mooney's clipped reply.

Before she realized it Johanna let out a sigh of exasperation. Mooney grinned.

"Iffen you want to know 'bout Luis, why don't you just come right out and say so 'stead of beatin' around about it?"

"Mooney, you are the beatinest man!" Johanna laughed. "All right, tell us about Luis."

"Luis is just Luis. A breed all his own."

"Why is he with the train if he isn't hired?"

"He makes the trip once in a while. Likes to look over the horseflesh in town. Got a lot of knowhow 'bout horses. Hates cows."

"Does he live in the valley?"

"Yup. He lives there." Mooney waited, but Johanna decided not to ask any more questions. "Built a nice little hacienda down the valley a ways. Got a string of horses, all good stock. Right steady feller, Luis, but in a fight he ain't got no quit atall."

Now that Mooney had started, Johanna held her breath for fear he would stop talking.

"Once I recollect the time when Jesus Montez—he was a powerful mean Mexican—come a-raidin' up and cross Texas and got into New Mexico. He raided and burned out Mex and gringo alike till he come to Macklin Valley. Hit the Mex village when most of the men was out gettin' strays fer the roundup. Men what was left turned tail and run for it. All but Luis. He stood alone till Burr got there and the two of them cleaned out the whole kit and caboodle. Them two birds together could lick their weight in wildcats."

He glanced at the young women to see if they were impressed. They were.

"I didn't realize there was a village in the valley."

"Ain't exactly a village. All the Mex what work fer Burr kind of live together like. Burr got it fixed up real nice. Women got a place to wash, even. Them Mex women are the washingest women. Always got clothes a-dryin' on the bushes. Good folks, I'd say, even if old Mack do hate 'em like poison."

21

"But . . . why?" Johanna asked the question almost as soon as the words left Mooney's mouth.

"Its a long story and an old 'n and I ain't sure it's even the real one, but its the only one I know of. Old Mack wrestled this range out of Indian country. He talked peace when he could, fought when he had to. Twice all the Mex deserted him and all he had left was Calloway, and him green as grass for all his book learnin'. Old Mack, he say he ain't got no use for a goddam Mex. Allus worked hell outta 'em, give 'em a little corn for tortillas and a lot of cussin'. Burr see it different. Treat 'em decent, he says, and they'll more than likely stand by you when the goin' gets tough." He pulled his hat down, and Johanna knew Mooney wanted to drop the subject.

"Thank you for telling us about Luis and about Mr. Macklin. It's good he's got a kind and thoughtful foreman. Burr sounds like a nice man."

"Jesus Christ!" Mooney said. "I never said nothin' 'bout Burr bein' kind and thoughtful. He ain't got hardly a kind bone in his body. Get right down to it, he's 'bout as ornery as the old man, but different somehow. He'd jist as soon knock ya down as look at ya. Do you're job, shut up, stay outta his way is the way to get along with Burr. Any kind thing Burr does is fer the good of the valley, and that's 'bout the size of it."

Johanna looked at him sharply, seeming to measure his sincerity in one comprehensive glance.

"You . . . you don't like him?"

"Hell, yes, I like him, but that don't mean he's soft. He's hard as nails and rougher than a cob, and there ain't no reason why he'd be anything else." Mooney gave her a disgusted look that shut off all further questions.

Johanna had a lot to think about. For the first time since she had accepted Cash's offer she felt somewhat apprehensive. She pushed the feeling aside. No matter how disagreeable Macklin was, she would be able to handle it. Jacy would have her baby in Macklin Valley, and when they left the valley it would be with most of the wages she earned. This job in the valley was going to give things time to work out.

Jacy climbed onto the seat. Johanna put her arm around her sister, and gave her a little hug. Jacy smiled at her. The change in Jacy during the past week was almost a miracle. She was eating better than she had for several months and was taking an interest in things around her. Johanna no longer had to coax her to wash or to comb her hair. The doctor had said to treat her normally, not to urge her to talk but to give her time to get used to her pregnancy. Johanna had obeyed the doctor's instructions and added an abundance of love and devotion. Suddenly she was almost happy. The sky was bluer, the breeze cooler, the country more beautiful. Things would work out. They were just bound to.

CHAPTER THREE

THE "SETTLEMENT," WHEN they came to it, was a couple of adobe houses and a lean-to shed. Farther out there were several abandoned dugouts. It was in low land and near the river. This was where they would cross the Pecos. Mooney explained that the riverbed, at this point, was solid rock and one of the few places within a hundred miles that the heavily loaded wagons could cross. There was a plume of smoke coming from the chimney of one of the houses, and Johanna was disappointed when Red circled the wagons some distance away from the settlement.

"Who lives here, Mooney? Who would want to live so far out on the prairie?"

"That's a mean outfit, Johanner. Small-caliber, but mean. We don't usually have no truck with 'em."

It had been a long day, and evening began to settle its purple darkness about them when the hot cook fire was built and the large pot containing beef and potatoes was swung over it, as well as the ever-present black coffee pot. The young women sniffed appreciatively.

When the pot of stew was ready and the plates passed around, Red brought his plate to where Johanna and Jacy sat on the wooden box.

"We'll cross the river come mornin'. Luis was across and back. Says the rains up north has raised it a mite, but still ain't nothin' to worry 'bout.''

Across the campfire from them Luis sat back in the shadows, as he did each night, silently watching, his face expressionless. Tonight his face was turned away from them as he visited with his companions, and they could see his profile clearly in the flickering firelight. Jacy's eyes dwelled on the man often, and Johanna wondered if she was attracted to him or just curious about him, as she herself was.

Red adjusted the dusty hat on his head nervously. "Ma'am, I been a-wantin' to tell you this, and I guess now's as good a time as any. Iffen you get to the valley and it ain't what you all thought it would be and iffen you want to leave it and go back to town, all y'all got to do is say so. There ain't a man jack here what wouldn't sign on to take you and the young miss back, and that means Luis, too.''

While his craggy face showed no emotion the sincerity of his words conjured images of doubt within Johanna.

She was quick to respond, a challenge for Red to explain himself clearly visible in her eyes. "What makes you think we will want to leave?''

"Well . . . I just thought you might. These lawyer fellers can paint a pretty good picture with their smooth words, and I . . . just thought . . . well . . .'' his voice trailed off, and then he added, "You might not want to stay.''

Johanna laughed with relief. "I'm used to hard work, Red. I know it won't be easy to get along with Mr. Macklin, but I can do it. Surely he can't be so mean as to not want me to have my sister with me. Don't worry about us.'' She put her hand on his arm. "But . . . thank you.'' Their eyes met and he looked away, embarrassed.

Red was taking their empty plates back to the cookwagon when the horsemen approached the camp. They stopped outside the circle of light and called out, "Hello the camp!''

"It's Burris and a couple of Mex, Red.'' The soft slurry voice of the night guard came out of the darkness.

"Come on in, Burris." Red's voice held a touch of annoyance.

The men dismounted and tied their horses to the wheel of a wagon. One of them came forward and shook hands with a reluctant Redford.

"Just thought I'd ride over and say howdy and see iffen there was anything I could do fer you all. Anything atall."

"Thanky," Red said, "but we're makin' out just fine. You're welcome to some coffee before you ride out." Red turned his back and walked away.

Codger set three tin cups on the ground near the coffee pot and motioned the two Mexicans toward the fire. None of the men sitting around the campfire made any attempt to get up or to greet the visitors. It was obvious they were not welcome, but the unwritten law of the prairie demanded they offer the minimum of hospitality.

The man called Burris was bearded, heavyset, and gray-haired. It was difficult to tell where his hair left off and his beard began. His clothes were typical range clothes, dirty and ragged. The two Mexicans looked much like hundreds of men Johanna had seen lazing around the saloons in San Angelo, unkempt and shifty-eyed. These two had guns strapped about their hips with the holsters tied down.

The evening was cool, and after a glance at the men, she turned to the wagon to fetch a shawl for herself and Jacy. Johanna was about to climb into the wagon when she heard the mournful cry.

"Maa . . . maaaa . . . !"

Turning, Johanna saw Jacy standing with her hands clasped tightly over her ears, her gaze riveted on the two Mexicans squatted by the coffee pot, their features clearly outlined in the flickering light of the campfire. They were staring at the girl with something like disbelief on their faces.

The plaintive cry came again.

"Maa . . . maaaa . . . !"

The wail broke from Jacy's throat, and her eyes widened with terror. For an instant the scene around the campfire was suspended in silence, although the echo of Jacy's hopeless cry hung on the evening's stillness.

The two men stood up in unison, mesmerized by Jacy's stare.

"Madre de Dios! La hija, la virgen!" Mother of God, the daughter, the virgin. The words tumbled from the man's lips.

It was a moment before Johanna realized exactly what was happening.

"It's them, Johanna!" Jacy babbled. "It's them! They did it. They shot Papa . . . and hurt Mama . . . and Mama begged them not to hurt me. And oh, Johanna, it was so terrible what they did. I wanted to die . . . I prayed to die . . . Johanna, I'm sick! I'm sick and I'm going to throw up!"

Johanna pulled her sister into her arms as a black-clad figure, moving with incredible speed, emerged out of the shadows.

The Mexicans shifted their attention to the man, awareness of their desperate predicament plainly visible on their faces. The cowboys behind them faded into the background, stood alone beside the fire. Luis faced them, feet apart, his body bent slightly forward, his face expressionless but for his narrowed eyes. His hands hovered over the twin guns strapped to his waist.

"Perros!" Dogs—the word, when it came, was hissed through tight lips.

The two men hesitated, knowing in an awful instant that they were going to die. Their eyes flicked to the men standing alert, then to the slim, black-clad figure facing them. The feeling was on them that they were the ones facing great odds from this single challenger. In desperation they reached for their guns.

Luis's hands flashed down with a blurring movement, and his guns sprang up. The muzzles were rising toward him when he fired. One of the men staggered and fell back. The other went to his knees, his face wolfish, teeth bared in a snarl. He lifted his gun and Luis fired again. A hole appeared between the man's eyes and he fell backward, the back of his demolished head disappearing in the short prairie grass.

The roar of the guns was so unexpected that Johanna and Jacy were shocked into paralyzed silence. Then from the end of the wagon they gazed with horror at the two dead men and at Luis as he shoved the pistols into their holsters. The reality of what they had just witnessed began to take hold.

Burris stood rooted to the ground, then slowly lifted his hands, palms out.

"Where do you stand?" Luis waited, his stance loose, eyes missing nothing.

Burris shook his head and his hands at the same time. "I stand alone, *señor*. I stand alone."

"When I see you again I'll kill you." The words were softly spoken, but the import was plain.

"Now see here . . . I ain't never saw them afore they come a-ridin' in a few days back. I don't know nothin' 'bout them, hear?" Burris looked at Red. "I ain't never had no trouble with Macklin riders, Mr. Redford, you know I ain't."

Red looked at him coolly. "Only 'cause you was afeared to, Burris."

"But . . . this here's my place and . . . I ain't no gunfighter."

"Then you better go. Luis ain't one to repeat hisself."

Holding her sobbing sister in her arms, Johanna bathed her face with a wet cloth and talked quietly to her. Then they climbed into the wagon. She lit a candle, after lowering the canvas flap, and helped her sister undress for bed.

"Darling, keep talking. Please keep talking. I'm so afraid you'll stop. Tell me everything. We'll talk it all out and then it will be over. We need never mention it again."

"How can you say that?" Jacy sobbed. "You know I can never forget it. I've got this . . . thing growing in me. I hate it, Johanna! I hate it! Why won't it die? I'm ruined, and you know it. Everytime anyone looks at me they'll . . . know." Jacy turned her face into the pillow and sobbed.

Johanna sat beside her, searching for comforting words to say.

"Jacy, dear." With gentle fingertips she turned the tear-wet face toward her, and a pain of anguish shot through her heart. There was such futility in Jacy's eyes. "We'll face what comes together," she said. "Our parents are gone, but think about this, Jacy. You're going to have an extension of Papa and Mama. They'll live on in the baby."

28

"No." Jacy shook her head, and Johanna saw in the forlorn look the death of a young girl's dreams. "Johanna, I'm so ashamed I can hardly look anyone in the eye. Oh . . . I miss Mama so much!"

"I know you do, and so do I. Mama wouldn't want you to hate the baby. She was a wonderful mama to me. I owe her so much. She took me to her heart and loved me when my own mama deserted me and Papa."

Tenderly she pushed Jacy's brown hair back from her face. It had been a long day and one full of emotions. Jacy was exhausted and soon fell asleep, her hand still holding tight to her sister's.

Johanna sat beside Jacy for a long while before she blew out the candle and left the wagon. The moon was up and flooded the camp with light. The small fire in the center of the circle of wagons burned low under the coffee pot, put there for the night guard. The silence was absolute except for the sounds of the horses cropping the prairie grass and an occasional blowing and stamping. Without these familiar sounds, Johanna thought, one might think the world had gone away, except for herself, a tiny island, in a sea of prairie grass.

Slowly she sank down on the crate and leaned her head against the wagon. She was weary and closed her eyes for a moment. When she opened them she saw a figure come out of the shadows and walk across the center of the camp toward her. As he passed the campfire she saw the gleam of the silver-handled pistols. She got to her feet and stood waiting for him to reach her. He approached to within a few feet of her and stopped. She could see only his silhouette as he stood with his back to the fire.

"The señorita? Is she all right?" His voice was soft but masculine, his accent Spanish.

"She's had a terrible shock, but it was for the good. She'll be all right now." Johanna spoke to him in fluent Spanish. "Thank you for what you did." She added the last hurriedly, because he had turned to walk away. He looked back at her now.

"Goodnight, señorita."

"*Buenas noches*, Luis."

Johanna watched the tall, slim figure slip back into the shadows and disappear. She sat down again. The silence of the night made itself felt after he left her, and she knew, without diagnosing it, that here was someone who shared only a small part of himself with other people.

They were moving toward the mountains where purple shadows promised cool breezes and relief from the relentless sun and the continual cloud of dust that hovered over them.

The crossing of the Pecos began with the first faint streaks of red over the eastern hilltops. The air was alive with excitement, and for Johanna and Jacy, so long under their own dark cloud, the sense of adventure, the challenge to reach Macklin Valley across miles of desolate and dangerous terrain, was a thrill they could not have imagined.

At the point of their crossing the riverbed was solid rock, and though the water barely came to the bottom of the wagon, the current was swift enough to be a real danger. Even with Luis guiding them and the extra precaution of heavy ropes secured to either side of the wagon and outriders alongside, the vehicle skidded on the moss-covered stones. Finally, though, the wagon rolled safely onto the riverbank and Luis wheeled his black stallion to plunge back across for the dainty sorrel mare that had been tied to one of the freight wagons. It was evident from the way he handled her that he was immensely proud of the horse. He led her up to the wagon where Jacy and Johanna sat as they watched the heavier wagons make their crossing, then swung out of the saddle and approached the excited mare. He talked to her softly, gently stroking her nose and neck.

Jacy watched the man and the horse, and when he saw her looking at him, he smiled. He led the mare over to her and held out the lead rope.

"She's beautiful!" Jacy's face came alive, and she forgot completely her earlier inhibitions toward him. When she laughed, Johanna felt tears spring in her eyes. The sound was so familiar and so . . . dear.

"*Sí*, she is!" Luis gave Jacy so searching a look, so penetrating yet filled with understanding, that she was compelled to meet his eyes.

As the significance of his words dawned upon her, the color came up to flood her cheeks. Her breath seemed to stop and her pulse to accelerate. For what could have been eternity, their eyes held, and then he smiled. It was as if they had reached an understanding that needed neither words nor action to make it any more real.

He mounted the stallion and looked at Jacy once again before he splashed back across the river, leaving her holding the mare's lead rope.

"Wal, now." Mooney tugged at his dusty hat. "Luis sets a mighty big store by that mare, missy."

Jacy gave the rope a tug. The mare bobbed her head up and down and moved close to smell the hand that reached out to her. The young woman turned a beaming face to Mooney.

Johanna couldn't believe the change in her sister. Just twenty-four hours ago she had been a silent, brooding girl whose spirit appeared completely broken. Now it seemed as if the floodgates had been opened by last night's tears and at least a portion of the dark depression that gripped her had been washed away.

The wagons and the horses had all crossed the river, and still Luis didn't come for the mare. Mooney climbed down and led the horse to the rear of the wagon and tied her rope securely to the tailgate. Jacy moved to the back so she could be near the mare. She talked to her in a gentle voice, and occasionally laughed, so taken was she with the animal. After the months of silence every sound that came from her sister's lips was one that Johanna treasured.

The trail followed a tortuous route. This was the mean country Mooney had talked about at the beginning of the trip. It was a baked and brutal land, sun-blistered and arid. The trail snaked its way through the stands of organpipe cactus, prickly pear, and cat's claw. Bleached bones lay alongside the trail, grim reminders of those who had gone before and lost the struggle with the land. The desert allowed no easy deaths, only hard, bitter and ugly deaths . . . long and drawn-out. They traveled on in silence, while the sun grew hotter as it rose higher in the sky.

Jacy lay in the hammock, her face turned toward the mare trotting along behind the wagon. When Johanna was sure she was asleep, she turned abruptly to Mooney.

"Does Luis have a family in the valley?"

Mooney said nothing. He shifted the cud of tobacco from one cheek to the other and kept his eyes straight ahead.

Johanna turned in the seat in an attempt to search his face, but he continued to stare straight ahead.

"Don't you want to talk about Luis?" she asked in a rather strained voice and waited patiently while he flicked the backs of the sweating team with the long whip.

"It ain't that . . . exactly."

"Well, go on, Mooney. Don't stop now." She said it lightly and with a small laugh so as to ease the tension between them.

"Luis is old Mack's son," Mooney said directly, and looked into her face to judge her reaction. She was smiling.

"Is that all? I thought he might be an outlaw, or something worse, the way you hesitated."

"It ain't nothing to joke about. The old man hates him worser than a rattlesnake."

Johanna looked startled. "I find it hard to believe a man hates his own son." And remembering their meeting beside the campfire the night he had killed the Mexicans, his concern for Jacy, and his quiet dignity, she added, "He can't be that bad, Mooney."

"Wal, it's true enough, and you'll find out once you get to the valley. Old Mack's a hard case. He hates most things he don't understand. Guess that's why he hates the Mexicans."

"And Luis is definitely Mexican," Johanna said, now aware that Mooney had more to tell. "That is obvious to me despite the blue eyes and his height. But why would Mr. Macklin marry a Mexican if he dislikes them so much?"

"He ain't never married." It was obviously something he didn't want to say.

It was something she hadn't thought of, and it shocked her into remaining silent for a moment. Why did she suddenly think of

Jacy's baby? There could be no comparison in the situations, she was sure, because Luis knew his father, something Jacy's baby would never know.

"Poor Luis," she said at last.

"Ain't no call to feel sorry for Luis, Johanner. It's the old man what's got his tail in a crack. He never did have no use for Luis, 'cause his ma was a Mexican, but after him and Burr took off his foot to keep the old fool from dyin', he ain't got no use for nobody, 'specially Luis and Burr. They don't seem to pay it no never mind. Luis keeps the ranch supplied with horseflesh and Burr does the ramroddin'."

Johanna's mind was swimming. "Are you saying that Burr is Mr. Macklin's son too?"

"Yup. You'll know soon's you clap eyes on him. Spittin' image of the old man."

"And," she went on, though she hesitated to ask, "Mr. Macklin didn't marry his mother, either?"

"Nope. Said he never married."

"I don't think I'm going to like Mack Macklin very much."

"It ain't all that bad. Don't seem to set very heavy on Burr. Luis is a mite shy, but could be his nature. The only thing about it is . . . nobody goes around a callin' nobody a bastard. It just ain't done in Macklin Valley. 'Course now, the old man . . . wal, he ain't got no sense atall when he gets riled, and that's the first thing he says. Don't bother the boys none, leastways they don't let on."

Johanna was by now convinced she would not like Mack Macklin and told Mooney so in the plainest language possible.

"Never figured you'd take to him," the crusty driver replied.

"I need this job, Mooney," she said slowly and sincerely. "I'll work hard for Mr. Macklin, but I'll not tolerate any abuse of Jacy because of her mixed blood." Johanna lifted her head, and the defiant look in her eyes brought a chuckle from Mooney.

"Glad to hear it. You'll need spunk to stand up to the old man." He punctuated the statement with a grin that showed his tobacco-stained teeth.

* * *

That night they made camp in a narrow, oddly shaped arroyo. It was an easy place to defend, Mooney explained. This was Apache land.

"Nope," he said, when asked if they expected an attack. "But where 'paches is concerned they don't never do what you think they're goin' to."

The wagons were drawn in a tighter circle and the horses staked out closer to the camp, and the cook prepared the pinto beans and chilis quickly so the fire could grow small. There was a feeling of tension in the damp, though the sisters seemed not to notice it. They excused themselves as soon as they finished their meal.

In the privacy of their wagon Johanna related to Jacy all the information Mooney had given her about the Macklins. Jacy's interest centered around Luis, and she questioned Johanna for any details she could remember from her conversation with the driver.

"I've told you everything I know, Jacy."

"Don't you think Luis is handsome?"

"Yes, dear, I do," Johanna said after a short pause. "He's very handsome, and brave. Facing two armed men takes exceptional courage, but . . . we don't know anything about him except that he's Mr. Macklin's son. He may be a gunman for all we know."

"He isn't anything bad, Johanna. I know that. I think he's been alone a lot and he is shy. He didn't say a word to me when he came for the mare. He just looked into my eyes the way he did before, untied the horse, and went away."

The sound of hoofbeats broke the stillness of the night. Johanna lifted the canvas flap and peered out. An outrider was talking to Red. It wasn't Luis, because this man sat low in the saddle. The conversation was in Spanish.

"There are three of them, señor. The same ones Luis saw before we cross the river. All gringos. Got good horses, one pure Arab, Luis say. Black as midnight, got deep chest and strong legs. Luis say he ain't seen a horse to compare."

"Sounds like an Arab. Not many like that in this part of the country. The gringos are a-ridin' in our dust, Paco, 'cause they are feared of the 'paches. If they want to trail us, ain't nothin' we can do 'bout it but keep our eyes peeled. Where's Luis?''

"He make sure they bed down." The man laughed. "Luis hate like hell to have the Apaches get that horse."

Luis left the camp before daylight and headed in a westerly direction toward the hills. He rode cautiously along the dim trail. It was rugged, lonely country where stunted cedars and gnarled oak clung to the ridges of the canyon and where the low-spreading shrub with its peculiar hooklike thorns thrived. He was tired and the sun·was hot. He went off the trail and into the rocks, careful to give himself a background where he would not be outlined against the sky.

He had come to this place for two reasons. He could see along the trail for almost two miles, and he was accessible if Gray Cloud wished to contact him. The unpredictable Apache had been trailing the train for the last two days. This puzzled Luis. He knew Gray Cloud didn't have enough men to attack the wagons, and he supposed his own surveillance of the three gringos following discouraged him from attacking that camp.

Settling himself into a comfortable position against a rock, he lowered his head and waited. Soon there was movement on the trail below. Luis recognized both mount and rider. Gray Cloud and two of his men were headed toward him.

His own horse scented the wind, skittish at the intrusion.

"It's all right," Luis said softly to the horse. "It's all right."

When the Indians reached the spot where the trail started upward again, the two braves stopped and Gray Cloud came on alone. The mare the Indian was riding lifted her head, and her nostrils flared when she became aware of the big black. Unhurriedly, Luis left his observation post and stepped into the saddle, keeping a firm hand on the reins of the excited stallion.

He held up his hand in greeting and spoke in Apache dialect.

"Greetings, Gray Cloud. My brother is far from his lodge."

The Indian stared at him silently with dark, fierce eyes. Luis knew the man had strength and courage. He was also a shrewd trader, but for the last few months Luis had found trading with him distasteful. Gray Cloud had changed, become difficult, bitter. Luis suspected he was not receiving the recognition from his people that he felt he deserved.

"Why does my brother bring whites onto Apache land?"

"We promised to bring no whites into the valley of the stone house, and we bring none."

"What of the women who sit on the wagon? I will barter for the one with hair like a cloud."

Luis was surprised, but his face and voice didn't register the feeling. "The woman is not mine to trade."

The Indian stared into his eyes. "Whose woman?"

"My brother's woman." Luis knew the Indian was testing him, and he never took his eyes from the stern face.

The Apache glared at him with burning intensity. "He can have other woman," he spat out bitterly.

"Other woman is my woman. I keep my woman," Luis said, matching his tone with the Indians.

Gray Cloud turned his eyes down the trail where the freight wagons had raised a dust that drifted against the cloudless sky. The dark eyes moved back to Luis and glittered with hatred.

"I could take pale woman." His expression changed to one of arrogance. "Mescalero wait in hills."

Luis watched closely and chose his words carefully.

"A Chiricahua Apache brave has need of the Mescalero to take a woman?" He put a touch of scorn to his words.

"Because of Gray Cloud the Mescalero stay in hills." A look of cunning came into the dark eyes. "I will trade mare for rifles and talk to my brothers the Mescalero."

Luis had no doubt he could draw and kill Gray Cloud and at least one of the braves. But if there were Mescaleros in the hills and if Gray Cloud did have influence with them, there was a chance they would seek revenge on the train. He studied the situation carefully before he spoke.

"I thank you, my brother Gray Cloud, for holding off the Mescalero. Come to the place near my lodge and we will trade horses for food, blankets, tobacco. We have traded together many times. Your chief is a friend to the whites of the stone house. We will be friends and barter as before." Luis purposely omitted mention of the rifles.

The expression of hatred appeared again on the Indian's face.

"Soon we will kill all whites and take your pale-skinned women. I, Gray Cloud, will lead my braves against the stone house and take what you have." He paused, but Luis knew he was not finished and waited for what he knew would come. "I will kill Sky Eyes and take his woman to be my slave."

Without waiting for Luis to speak, the Indian wheeled his horse around and trotted back down the trail. His braves fell in behind him.

Luis waited a full five minutes before moving his horse out. Gray Cloud and his men didn't worry him, but the information about the Mescaleros did. He headed his horse into the hills, scouting the area with care until he found where six ponies had been tied to a few clumps of brush. The leaves on the brush had been freshly cropped, Luis determined, and indicated that the Indians, riding unshod ponies, had definitely been trailing the wagons.

Mounting up, he took the most direct route to the train, to warn Red of the possibility of an attack. He considered it would be no more than harassment if only the six riders were involved, but there was the chance they were part of a larger party.

The freight wagons circled once again for the night. Johanna and Jacy had kept up a steady flow of conversation all day, and the time had passed so quickly they couldn't believe that night had fallen.

The drivers squatted around and ate the meager meal the cook prepared over the bare mention of a campfire. They talked in hushed tones. Johanna and Jacy's wagon had been drawn closer inside the circle, and gradually Johanna came to realize that something peculiar was happening. As time passed, she became more and more uneasy.

"Mr. Redford?" Her voice was low, but managed to reach him.

"Yes, ma'am?" He had passed her, but turned and came back.

"Is something wrong?"

The old cowboy took off his hat and scratched his head before answering.

"You might say that, ma'am. Luis spotted Mescaleros in the hills. Might be they'll try to steal horses. If it should be, and I ain't a sayin' it will, I want you ladies to stay down in the wagon, keepin' your heads below the sideboards."

"Are the men still following us, Mr. Redford?" Johanna felt a sudden spurt of worry for the three white men and their Arabian horse.

"They've pulled up a mite closer." Red grinned. "They be all right. You all go on to bed and don't be worryin' none."

"It's kind of hard not to worry, Mr. Redford."

Johanna glanced at her sister, expecting to see fear in her face. To her surprise Jacy was calm.

"We'll be all right, Johanna."

"That's right, little lady," Red said gently. "We'll all see to it that nothin' happens to you."

It was dawn before the sound of gunfire woke Johanna from a sound sleep. Her first instinct was to jump up and see what was going on, but remembering Red's words she hugged Jacy to her and lay flat on the floor of the wagon. Her heart pounded and she felt a flash of guilt for having brought her sister into yet another danger. She prayed silently that God would protect them, and the men who were fighting to keep them safe.

Off in the distance a shrill cry broke through the roar of the guns and she felt Jacy's hand, tightly held in hers, tremble. A horse whinnied and a man, close by, cursed. But they heard nothing more.

The gunfire stopped in a matter of minutes, and the waiting became almost unbearable.

"Do you think it's over?" Jacy whispered.

"I don't know."

"Can we get up, Johanna? Oh, I hope Luis is all right!"

"Johanner?" It was Mooney's voice just outside the wagon. "Ya can come on out iffen you want."

Both of them stuck their heads out through the canvas flap.

"Was anyone hurt?" Johanna asked.

"None of us," Mooney said dryly. "Rag-tailed bunch of Mescaleros a-tryin' to steal the mules. We be a-gettin' started soon's coffee's been had. Gettin' in the valley today, and they ain't goin' to follow us in there—that's Chiricahua country."

CHAPTER FOUR

T HE LONG, MAGNIFICENT sweep of the valley was green and glistening in the morning sun. Johanna could hardly believe the beauty of the place as the horses moved through rich green grass that stroked their bellies and caught in their harnesses. Along a stream, birds flitted from bush to bush, a startled deer raced into the trees, its white tail standing straight up as it fled. Johanna caught her breath and laughed with sheer pleasure.

The slopes on either side of the valley were blanketed with stately pine trees, and beneath their branches was an abundance of wild flowers and ferns. The green was a startling contrast to the snow-capped ridges that towered above the valley.

To Johanna it was breathtaking, overpowering, and beyond anything she could have imagined. This was Macklin Valley!

She turned her head quickly, sharply, and looked at her sister's glowing face.

Jacy's voice was joyous. "Look at it! Isn't it magnificent?"

Johanna looked at the valley again and became suddenly uneasy. Silent as the wagon made its way down into the valley, she kept turning over in her mind what she had learned about Mack Macklin. Thinking about it now gave her a twinge of doubt, but she quickly put it from her mind.

The outriders prodded the plodding work mules and galloped past the wagon waving their hats and shouting.

Mooney chuckled. "They'll all know 'bout you before we get to the ranch. The scutters are just a-dying to tell it. Yup, by granny, you'll be looked over by the time we get thar."

"How long have you been in the valley, Mooney?" Johanna asked.

" 'Bout five, six years." Mooney let go a mouthful of tobacco juice, a sure sign he was about to say more. "Red and me met up with Burr and Luis in El Paso just after the war and we liked their way of doin' things. Burr, he told us 'bout the valley and we hired on 'cause we didn't have nothin' else to do. Red, he tied up with a Mex woman and they got a little young'un and another on the way, so I guess he ain't never gonna leave. Me, I don't have nobody nowhere, so I'll stay long's I can work."

Jacy had been quiet. She turned often and looked back at the string of wagons behind. Most of the outriders had gone on ahead when Luis rode up beside the wagon leading the sorrel mare. He tipped his hat and smiled.

"Señorita, you like?" he asked, indicating the mare.

"Yes, very much," and with the uninhibited frankness of youth, she asked, "Are you going to breed her to the black?"

"No, señorita. He is too big for her. I have the perfect mate at my hacienda. Would you like to see him?"

"Yes, very much," she said again.

"Then I will come for you. *Adiós*." He tipped his sombrero to Johanna, then swung his eyes back to Jacy. His face was different, more alive. He spurred the black horse and raced down the trail, the flowing mane and tail of the mare standing out as she sped along behind the powerful black.

Johanna looked at Jacy's beaming face and glowing eyes. She's smitten with him! she thought. Please, God, don't let her be hurt. Don't let him break her heart all over again.

Involuntarily she reached for her sister's hand, and Jacy squeezed it tightly.

The wagon topped a rise, and Johanna caught a glimpse of the buildings. A cluster of sun-bleached adobe dwellings, surrounded by a patchwork of garden plots, shone brilliantly in the afternoon sun. Even as she watched, the houses emptied and people ran out toward the trail. There were women in brightly colored skirts with small children clutched in their arms, while older ones ran alongside, laughing and chattering. They lined up beside the wagon track, heads turned toward the approaching train. They waited quietly, shyly, for a look at the strangers. Dark, solemn eyes gazed at Johanna and Jacy. Some of the children hid behind their mother's skirts.

"Buenas tardes," Johanna called out gaily. A few smiles appeared at the use of their language. Most of the two dozen or more women who lined the trail smiled back at the newcomers, and a few answered their greetings.

Johanna remembered her hat and reached for it. She placed it squarely on top her high-piled flaxen hair. She felt better. Somehow the hat gave her courage.

The trail curved around the adobe houses, and the rest of the ranch buildings came into view. And Johanna's heart fell.

The place looked like an army post. The buildings and the ranch house made of stone blended with the land as if they and the mountains that framed them had been created together. The peaked roof of the house extended down and out to form the roof of the porch, which was supported by the husky posts that fronted the house. Several hide-covered chairs stood along the wall. There were three doors at the front of the building and three glass-paned windows. Stone chimneys, one emitting a weak plume of smoke, protruded high above the roof on each end of the squat stone structure. While the place looked permanent, there wasn't a bush, flower, fence, or anything at all to lend warmth or humanity. Several large trees stood in the yard, and under their spreading branches was the hitching rail.

Mooney stopped the wagon and waited while the freight wagons veered off toward the buildings behind the bunkhouse, which was as long as the house, but not quite as deep. Beyond that was a network of split-rail corrals and several small stone buildings. All the activity was around the bunkhouse. The outriders who had arrived earlier were turning the tired horses into the corral. There was much shouting and backslapping as the men were greeted by those who had stayed behind.

Red rode up beside the wagon. "Take 'er on up, Mooney. I'll go on ahead and tell the old man. I see he's a-waitin' for us."

Johanna gripped Jacy's hand and smiled reassuringly. She had steeled herself for the meeting with Macklin, and despite the uneasiness she felt she was determined to face the man boldly.

"He didn't know I was coming, Johanna," Jacy said nervously.

"Don't worry about it, dear. Mr. Cash thought it all right for you to come. You stay with Mooney and I'll go speak to Mr. Macklin."

"That's a good idey, missie. You stay with me till Johanner gets the lay of the land."

Mooney pulled the horses to a stop beneath the trees. Johanna glanced nervously toward the house, where Red was talking to a man sitting in a huge chair. She patted Jacy's hand, straightened the straw hat on her head, and turned to climb down over the wagon wheel.

She made one step and was about to jump lightly to the ground when the horses suddenly lurched forward. She fell heavily, her straw hat bouncing off her head and rolling under the wagon. She sprang up quickly, and out of the corner of her eye she saw a small boy disappear behind the house. Badly shaken from the fall, her face flooded with color, she smoothed her skirts and patted her hair into place. Jacy leaned over the side of the wagon and looked at her with horrified eyes. Johanna felt like a fool and wished the ground would open up and swallow her.

"Jo! Johanna, are you hurt?"

"That goddam Bucko!" Mooney cursed and held the frightened horses. "I'll get me some skin off his butt!"

"I'm all right." Johanna tried desperately to compose herself. "I'm not hurt, just kind of embarrassed." She laughed nervously and glanced at her hat under the wagon; the lovely satin rose was crushed and dusty. She refused to bend her dignity still further to retrieve it. Her legs were unsteady, but her shoulders were square and her back straight as she walked up the path to the ranch house. Red turned to look at her. Another wave of color flooded her face when she realized both men had witnessed her inelegant sprawl in the dust.

The big man seated deep in a cowhide-covered chair had thick white hair. His mustache, stained with tobacco juice, curved down on each side of his mouth. Closer now, she could see in his lined face a lifetime of struggle against man and the elements. His bright-blue eyes were compelling and tinged with hard impatience. She met his hard discerning stare and started to look away, then forced herself to return his appraisal with a measuring look of her own. He had on a faded flannel shirt with rolled-up sleeves, and wore a high-heeled boot beneath one pant leg while the other pant leg flapped emptily in the breeze. The hands that gripped the arms of the chair were huge and gnarled, but the flesh on his large forearms was loose and sagging. His sunken blue eyes were cold, and Johanna met them unflinchingly.

"I'm Johanna Doan. I—"

"I know who the hell you are," he broke in rudely. "Got a letter here from that goddam Cash. I told him I wanted a woman, a real woman, not a prissy miss that can't get outta a wagon without fallin' on her arse!"

Johanna drew in her breath, but never allowed her eyes to waver from his. His hard words hit her like stones, and she stiffened her back and answered him sharply.

"I assure you, sir, I am a real woman and I know how to work like one. And as far as my . . . ungraceful descent from the wagon is concerned, the child that threw the stone at the horses should be thrashed."

"I doubt if the bastard was aimin' at the horses, miss. 'Twas that silly thing atop your head he was goin' for."

Johanna was speechless. His attack was unsettling and unwarranted. She could feel her knees weakening again, but not from terror. The anger started down in her stomach and surged up, but before she could retort Red broke in, a questioning frown on his face.

"We'll unload the trunks, Mack."

44

The old man grunted noncommittally and his gaze swept up and down the slender figure standing before him.

"You got all the parts of a woman and you got the hair and eyes and you're here and I ain't got much more time to be a-dallyin' round. I wish to God you wasn't such a skinny bitch."

Her emotions in check, Johanna looked at him with disbelief. "I'm not going to like working for you, Mr. Macklin."

The man's eyes were cold, but there was a strange sort of smile at the corners of his mouth. He nodded in Red's direction.

"Wal . . . bring in her gear."

Johanna forced herself to appear calmly contemptuous of his rudeness, and soon her anger gave way to pity for the man whose heart was so corroded with bitterness.

"Cash says your sister's going to whelp and it'll be a bastard. One more bastard in the valley ain't gonna matter none. Does she have your hair and eyes? Is she heftier than you?"

Bluntly Johanna answered him. "No, she is small, and no, she doesn't look like me because her mother was Mexican." She said the last deliberately, then clamped her mouth shut and waited for an explosion.

"Another bastard!"

"No," Johanna said firmly. "My father and I loved her mother dearly, and I want you to understand this: I'll not allow you to mistreat her because of her mixed parentage. I insist that she not be subjected to any unpleasantness. She is the dearest thing in the world to me, and if she isn't welcome in your home, now is the time for you to say so."

The look on his face was surprise, then smoldering anger.

"I ain't got no use for a goddam Mex, and you better swaller that and keep 'er outta my way!"

Johanna answered calmly, "That will be impossible, living in this house, so I suggest you learn to control your prejudice."

His eyes narrowed and he glared at her. It seemed he was taking a second look at the slender young woman, aware now of her defiant stance, the eyes that met his unafraid. He had sent men scampering off the porch with his roar, and this woman stood firmly in front of him and gave *him* an ultimatum. The silence was heavy between them as they took each other's measure.

Still looking at her, the old man opened his mouth and bellowed, "Calloway!"

A door opened at the end of the porch and a small man came toward them.

"This here's the woman," old Mack said in way of introduction.

As she offered her hand, Johanna's eyes roved the lean features of the small man. His eyes were piercing and showed slight surprise, but his clean-shaven face was kind. In his youth his snow-white hair would have been black, the brown eyes daring. His body was slim but wiry. She waited for him to speak.

"Call me Ben. Only Mack insists on calling me Calloway."

Johanna looked into the faded brown eyes that were on a level with her own. "My name is Johanna."

"Johanna," he repeated, and his eyes flicked at old Mack. "Lovely name," he said softly.

Red came to the porch holding Jacy by the arm. It was obvious he wasn't sure about the reception she would receive. Johanna came forward and put her arm about her sister and led her to the old man.

"Good afternoon, sir," Jacy said timidly.

Old Mack grunted, turned in his chair, and looked off toward the mountains.

Paying no attention to his rudeness, Johanna introduced her to Ben, who smiled and bowed gallantly.

"Two lovely ladies in the house," he said. "I'm overwhelmed."

He led them through the middle door and into a hall running the length of the house. There were two doors on each side of the hall and a small, steep stairway at the end. A door to the back of the hall opened onto what appeared to be another porch. The first two doors in the hall were closed, but looking into one of the last doors, Johanna saw a large kitchen with a black iron stove and a long trestle table with two benches. On the other side of the hall was a room with several chairs, a table, and a huge fireplace full of cold ashes. The place was stark and bare and dirty. The floors were the same as those of the porch patio and were covered with dust so thick it looked as though it had been there for years. She glimpsed several lamps, their chimneys black with soot.

Ben painfully climbed the steep stairway to a room tucked under the roof. Johanna could walk upright only in the middle of it, because of the sharp slant of the ceiling. It looked large because its only furnishings were a bed, a table, a ladder-backed chair, and an old trunk. Pegs for hanging clothes lined the wall at one end. A faded quilt that Johanna recognized as being pieced in the "flower garden" pattern covered the straw mattress on the rope bed. Jacy looked at the room in dismay.

Forcing a lightness in her voice, Johanna said, "After a good cleaning we'll be very comfortable here."

Ben smiled, but his voice was anxious. "This house needs a woman. I'm glad you're here."

"Thank you," Johanna said, then asked hesitantly, "Is Mr. Macklin always difficult, or is this just one of his bad days?"

Ben's brows went up. "I'm sorry to tell you this, Johanna, but Mack is always difficult. He's an unhappy, unfulfilled man, and perhaps this is one of his better days. If you can do it, close your mind to his cruel remarks, for he's to be pitied. He's never allowed himself to be happy. He cares for no one and nothing but this valley. He feels it's a sign of weakness to show either mercy or compassion to another human being."

When the sisters were alone, Jacy came to Johanna and rested her head on her shoulder.

"That old man is horrible, Johanna. I can't believe he's Luis's father."

"Neither can I," Johanna said. She took hold of her sister's shoulders and held her away from her so she could look into her face. "We won't be discouraged, Jacy, and we won't let that old man think he's smart enough to get our goat!" She laughed, and Jacy couldn't help but smile.

"Oh, Johanna, you're just like Papa. You can paint a silver lining on the blackest cloud."

"We can make this dreary, dirty room livable," Johanna said with determination. "You get out our sheets, towels, dresser set, and mirror. I'll go down and get a pail of water and a broom.''

Later, in a faded brown dress, an apron tied snugly around her slender waist, her blond hair secured in a topknot, Johanna took her first tentative steps down the stairway. She entered the kitchen and stopped short. Wrinkling her nose at the offensive odor coming from the spittoon by the hearth, she stood in the middle of the room and gazed in despair at the disorder. The cooking range and a very long work counter were both covered with piles of earthenware plates, pots, and an assortment of cutlery. The floor was constructed of smooth stone slabs and littered with grease and scrapes of food embellished with chunks of dried mud that, Johanna assumed, had been tracked in by the men. Soot hung like Spanish moss behind the cookstove, and cobwebs floated from the ceiling beams. A flicker of anger burned in the corner of her mind as she realized the ashes in the hearth had probably been there for months.

As she hesitated, hard footsteps, accompanied by the jingle of spurs, resounded on the stone floor outside the house, then into the hall. Seconds later there came a murmur of voices that escalated into a storm of angry words, unintelligible and rumbling. She could distinguish the cold, harsh voice of the old man, and a second, equally cold voice rising in argument. Johanna was gripped with curiosity. Who would dare raise his voice to the formidable old man?

The hail of angry words grew louder until the unknown antagonist and the old man were shouting at each other. The old man's angry words reached into the kitchen.

''You do as I say, you bastard, or you ain't gonna get one foot of this valley!''

The words were cut off by the sound of a door that slammed so viciously the walls of the house shuddered. Silence fell, a silence into which she drew a long breath of relief for the end of the barely restrained violence.

She moved to find the broom and the pail, and then she heard the hard steps and the soft jingling of spurs coming down the hall. She stood, apprehension holding her motionless, wishing desperately she didn't have to face another difficult Macklin. It was too soon. She needed time to adjust to the violent tempers and the drab, unfriendly atmosphere of the house.

A huge man with hard blue eyes and white-blond hair filled the doorway. Speechless, Johanna stared, her startled eyes questioning his apparent anger at her for being here. His face was twisted with bitterness and smoldering anger.

Arrogantly her stare was returned. He stood, with feet apart, balancing on the high heels of his boots. His long legs seemed to stretch up forever before reaching slim hips about which were strapped a wide gunbelt. His shirt, opened at the neck, revealed a chest tanned toast-brown and a head of curly, wind-tossed flaxen hair. Piercing blue eyes gleamed diabolically over a blade of nose. Tightly compressed lips opened and he bit out:

"You're the one! You're the one that's come to stud!"

Johanna had no idea how many seconds went by while she stood and stared at him, his words echoing through her mind. The seconds could have been hours, so timeless did the spell between them seem, until she broke it by saying,

"What did you say?" The words were forced from her tense throat.

"With outraged virtue, too!" he sneered. "A saloon girl with outraged virtue!"

Surprised by his attack, Johanna felt faintly giddy. His voice and face moved back to the sphere of her consciousness, and his words . . . Her face, framed by the blond hair almost exactly the same as that of the man standing before her, paled.

"Why are you talking to me like this?" A movement in her throat betrayed the fact that she was swallowing hard. "Who are you?"

He strode forward until she had to arch her neck to see his face. He searched her distraught face for a hint of duplicity. Without softening his expression, he said cuttingly, "Is it possible the old man hasn't told you about the bastards of Macklin Valley? I'm surprised! Let me introduce you to one of them. Burr Englebretson Macklin. My mother's name was Englebretson, but I've taken the name of Macklin for my own, just as I'll take this valley for my own by the right of having been unfortunate enough to be sired by that old man. And because I've ridden hard, driven hard, and worked until calluses stood out on my hands and I almost dropped in my tracks. That's my right of ownership, and I'll not have a scheming woman shoved down my throat in order to keep what's already mine!"

He was angry! There was no doubt he was so angry he was oblivious to her except that she was the one chosen to bear the heir for Macklin Valley.

Johanna gasped at the onslaught. "I don't understand any of what you're saying."

He looked down at her with cold, interested eyes that narrowed to mere slits, and his voice was sharp and harsh.

"Don't tell me you didn't know of the old man's plans! We're pawns. Pawns, in his plan to populate the valley with legitimate grandsons made in his own image. Look at yourself and you'll know why you were chosen for this honor. Blond hair and blue eyes, same as mine. He'll see to it we are wed, all proper and legal. No more bastards . . . Macklin Valley will never be left to a bastard." His chin jutted and softly he taunted, "How does it feel to know you have been brought here solely to act as brood mare?"

"No! I don't believe you!" Johanna was bordering on the edge of hysteria.

"Believe it!" Savagely he glared into her rebellious face, his jaw muscles pulsing as he fought to contain his anger. "The old man's devious as the devil, but bastard or not, I'll have a woman of my own choosing and I'll not give up what's mine."

He was gone before she could ask him to explain. His giant strides swallowed up the length of the hall, and the sound of the door, when it slammed, echoed throughout the house.

Clasping her arms around her shuddering body in an effort to dispel the effect this overpowering man had left on her, Johanna almost collapsed onto the bench by the table. He was every bit as rancorous as the father he so obviously despised. How could Mr. Cash have sent her to this place knowing what the old man had in mind? This man was so far removed from her imaginings of the man she would someday marry that she felt she would prefer to face plague, pestilence, or starvation rather than become tied to him for life. He was cold-eyed, uncivilized, and savage; and there was not a speck of difference between him and old Mack Macklin, who had sired him.

CHAPTER FIVE

S O YOU'VE MET him."

Johanna spun around, a picture of flagrant outrage, her classic beauty highlighted by the high color in her cheeks and the sparkle of unshed tears in her eyes. Ben hesitantly came through the doorway.

"Yes," she said, anger still in her voice. "And there's not an ounce of difference between father and son."

His reply, as he took a seat opposite her, was no more than a sigh. "I'm sorry," he said gently. "It's unfortunate you had to meet him just now. He—"

"To meet Burr Macklin under any circumstances would be unpleasant," she retorted. "He is detestable—uncivilized, boorish, and . . . self-centered! I'm no meek little mouse, Ben, and I refuse to be intimidated by a loud voice and crude language. I resent that man's implying that I came here for any reason except to do the job I was hired to do. And from the looks of this pigsty, a housekeeper is sorely needed!"

"Lass, Burr was as unaware of Mack's plans as you were. It's natural for him to be resentful." For a brief moment a small flicker of pain showed in his eyes.

Johanna tried to steel herself against softening, but it wasn't her nature to stay angry for long.

"Ben, what can I do?" She looked pleadingly at him. "We have almost no money left. My sister—"

He interrupted. "Red told me about your sister. He thought that perhaps she should stay with him and Rosita."

A lump of fear came up into her throat. "Do you think that he . . . that Mr. Macklin will be unkind to her?"

"I'm sure he will, if the opportunity presents itself. We must try and keep them apart."

His use of the word "we" had a soothing effect on Johanna. She reached across the greasy table and clasped his hand. His fingers were long and slim and his nails trimmed and clean. It struck her how out of place he was in this house, but for now, her mind was too crowded with impressions to wonder why he was here; it was enough to know she had a friend.

"She mustn't know about this other thing, Ben. This reason Mr. Macklin wanted me here. She's just beginning to accept her . . . condition, and I don't want her upset."

"We'll do all we can to keep her from knowing. I'll speak to Burr."

Johanna got up. "I'd better get back upstairs. I came down to get a broom and a pail of water," she said with a smile, "and what I got was a blow, right between the eyes."

Back upstairs she set to work with vigor, making as little noise as possible lest she wake Jacy, who was curled up on the end of the bed. She swept down the walls with the broom before sweeping and mopping the floor, using strong lye-soap water. When she finished she was exhausted, but the room was clean and smelled of soap and scrubbed wood.

After giving the room a satisfied glance, she carried the pail of dirty water down the stairs and out the back door. She stopped, then moved on when she saw a small boy, with his back against the house, watching her. He lowered his eyes when she looked at him. Appearing to ignore him, she walked to the end of the porch and threw the water out into the yard. The boy didn't move. She started toward the door, then veered off toward him. Johanna loved children, and missed the contact she'd had with them in the schoolroom. She was particularly curious about this child, anxious to know why he disliked her so.

When she greeted him the boy neither looked up nor answered.

"Hola," she tried.

He continued to look down. His dark-brown hair was long and looked freshly washed. She couldn't see much of his face, for his chin rested on his chest, but he was rather light-skinned and his features were sharp. The bright flannel shirt, obviously new, was much too large for him, and the sleeves were turned up at the cuffs. She reached out a finger and lifted his chin.

"No English? No *español*?" she asked gently.

The boy jerked his head away from her hand and looked up at her. She almost recoiled from the venom that shot from the child's cold blue eyes. The shock of seeing the blue eyes between a fringe of dark lashes left her speechless. Quickly she concealed her surprise and smiled at him.

"You gave me a fright when you threw the stone at the horses," she said in Spanish.

"I no want hit horses!" His small face was tight and he looked at her defiantly.

Still smiling, Johanna said, "You didn't like my hat?"

"I no like you!" The words burst out as though he couldn't hold them back.

The smile left Johanna's face. "How do you know you don't like me? You don't know me."

"Old Mack want you be Burr's woman. He said to Ben when wagon come. Burr don't want no woman." The little boy's lips were trembling and he was trying hard to stare her down and keep the tears from his eyes.

Johanna heard a door open at the far end of the porch.

"And that's the reason you don't like me?"

The boy didn't answer.

"Well, then there's no reason why we can't be friends. I'd rather be most anything than be . . . Burr's woman. I wouldn't have your precious Burr if he were served up to me on a silver platter." She laughed lightly.

Still the boy said nothing.

"You believe me, don't you?"

"Bucko!"

The boy jerked around at the sound of the sharp voice. He turned back to Johanna.

"Burr say to me to say I sorry."

Johanna looked steadily at him. "But you're not sorry, are you?"

"No."

"Then I don't think you should have to say so."

The boy glanced at the man, then back to Johanna. He moved away from the wall and went toward the man, who was waiting at the end of the porch. He lurched as he walked, and Johanna noticed for the first time that he had a clubfoot. The man was watching her over the boy's head, waiting to see her reaction to the boy's deformity. She didn't allow her expression to change until the man turned his back and, taking the boy's hand, went toward the bunkhouse. Only then did she let the disgust she felt for Burr Macklin reflect in her face. He expected her to show revulsion. Because he lacked compassion he did not believe such an emotion might be found in others.

"Like his father!" she hissed under her breath.

Ben came out from the kitchen. "You've met Bucko." It was a statement. "Both of them are quite a dose to take in one day, eh, lass?"

"Are there any more hostile members in this family, Ben?" she asked wearily.

"Don't you think those two are enough?" His eyes twinkled.

"I'm not worried about the child—he's young enough to be won over. It's the father and the grandfather that worry me."

"Burr's protective of the boy and keeps him out of Mack's way as much as possible."

Not wanting to get on the subject of Burr Macklin, Johanna asked, "About the evening meal, Ben. Will I be expected to prepare it?"

"No, lass, you've done enough for today. We can eat over at the bunkhouse."

*   *   *

Johanna slept badly that night. Physically and mentally she was exhausted. After the bewildering meeting with old Mack, climaxed by the meeting with Burr Macklin, her mind was plagued by an even greater turmoil than that which she'd experienced at Fort Davis. When sleep did finally claim her, nightmares came to torment and confuse her.

Once in that deep blackness she had awakened to a strange unnerving feeling that brought her to full awareness. A poignant loneliness possessed her for the first time in her life. Mindful not to wake Jacy, she pushed herself up and out of bed and went to the window. Far away a coyote called to his mate, and her answer echoed down the hills. Johanna was filled with uneasiness, and thoughts raced around in her head. Had the scene with Burr Macklin really happened? Did old Mack really think she would marry that overbearing, arrogant man? Thank God the idea didn't appeal to Burr. And the little boy whose eyes were so like Burr's . . . she wondered how many more children in this valley had blue eyes. She would ask Red to take her and Jacy back to town, but she thought the trip would be harmful to Jacy. So she would stay, because of Jacy's condition, until the next supply train went into town. That thought held, and she resigned herself to it. But she wouldn't allow these loathsome men to imtimidate her. Maybe it would be best for Jacy to be with Red and his wife, but, oh, she would miss her! Ben had promised to help keep her and old Mack apart, so maybe she would wait and see how things worked out.

Johanna paced the room restlessly. When finally she lay down beside Jacy, she closed her eyes wearily. She dozed eventually and fell again into an uneasy sleep.

When dawn brushed the sky with the first faint streaks of light, Johanna got up and went down to the kitchen. She found Ben bent over a tub of dishes.

"Sit down, lass." He picked up two of the freshly washed cups. "Let's have some coffee."

Johanna sat down at the trestle table, and Ben set the coffee in front of her, then slowly eased himself down onto the bench opposite her. The grimace of pain that crossed his face caused her to say, "Ben, you shouldn't have been bending over that tub."

"It's been a long time, lass, since I've been chided by a woman. Sounds kind of nice." His eyes twinkled, and he reached into his pocket for his pipe. "Burr ordered this tobacco all the way from South Carolina. I was surprised when it came on the train, and I'm like a small boy with a bag of stick candy."

"I know," Johanna said. "My father was the same with his favorite tobacco."

"You haven't always lived in Texas, have you, lass? I don't recognize your accent."

"I should have a Texas drawl, Ben. I've lived there since I was five years old. My father and I came from St. Louis. He was a teacher and pronounced his words very distinctly, and I probably acquired the habit from him." She sipped her coffee, her face thoughtful. "Are there any more surprises waiting for me, Ben? This is a very strange family." She gave a nervous little laugh.

Ben sat and puffed on his pipe for a moment, saying nothing, his expressive features sobering. When he answered her his voice was without warmth.

"It isn't a family, Johanna. There's Mack, and then there's Burr and Bucko and Luis."

"And you, Ben?" she asked softly and felt a lump in her throat when she looked into the faded eyes suddenly filled with pain.

"Ah, lass, there's me. It's natural that you would wonder why I stay on with this tyrant. There is not an ounce of friendship between us, no respect and no liking."

"It's obvious you're an educated man, Ben," she said, feeling the waste of his life.

Once again Ben paused before he spoke, his lips curved over the pipestem, his eyes alight with admiration for her.

"Educated in every way except in how to take care of myself in this savage and unpredictable land. When I was a lad I left my home in Massachusetts. I had become involved in some unpleasantness, and my family felt that I had disgraced them. I arrived in El Paso as green as grass and completely unequipped for the life in the lawless, brawling town. To make a long story short, Mack saved me from being stomped to death by a bunch of drunken cowhands. It was a purely selfish act on his part; he needed me to guard his back. Nevertheless, I was grateful and came back to New Mexico with him. I've been here ever since, except for a few trips I've made outside.''

"But . . . but why do you stay?''

Ben stirred uncomfortably and knocked the ashes from his pipe. ''Well, I stayed at first because I had no other place to go. Then Mack went out with a mule train and came back with a young girl.'' His face closed and he looked away. ''Mack had only contempt for her.'' He paused. ''She was never strong enough to leave the house after Burr was born.'' A wistful note crept into his voice. ''Anna died when he was four years old and I stayed on.'' Then he added softly, almost under his breath, ''I promised her I would.''

For a moment Johanna said nothing, then she put her hand on his. ''You stayed because of Burr?''

''Yes, I stayed because of Burr,'' he said.

Johanna refilled the coffee cups. She felt a sadness, and it reflected in her eyes.

Interpreting the look, Ben said cheerfully, ''You're not to feel sorry for me, lass. I had more in a few short years than most men have in a lifetime. And I've had the pleasure of seeing Anna's son grow up to be a fine man.'' His eyes twinkled at her. ''Despite what you think now, he is a fine man.''

Johanna decided it would be wiser not to argue the point at this time.

''Why do he and his father hate each other so?'' she asked.

''Always have,'' Ben said matter-of-factly. ''As a little fellow, Burr was scared to death of him—not that Mack came near him very often. There was a time when Burr was about fourteen that Mack took sort of an interest in him. Took him out to El Paso, and, I found out later, to a sporting house. At fourteen he was a man, and one day he found Mack laying a horsewhip on Luis and he fought him like a tiger. 'Course, Mack almost beat him to death. Ever since that day there's been open antagonism between them.''

So many things crowded into Johanna's head and she found it incredibly hard not to keep asking questions.

"Why did Burr stay?"

"He left after a while," Ben said slowly. "He was gone a few years, fought in the war, and saw a lot of the world. He came back about five years ago and found Mack with a crushed foot turned putrid with rotting flesh. He and Luis took off the foot and saved Mack's life. Not that they ever got any thanks for it; just the opposite. Mack's cursed them every day since then. But Burr says he's set on staying. He says he's never seen a place to compare with the valley. Luis feels that way, too. Nothing Mack can do will run them off. They've worked hard and made a lot of improvements these past five years."

"What will Burr do, Ben, if Mr. Macklin doesn't leave the land to him?"

"He'll fight for it," Ben said simply.

The statement gave Johanna food for thought as she worked beside Ben and finished washing the tub of crockery. Perhaps Burr did have a reason to feel bitter, but her opinion of him remained the same. Fine man indeed! Fathering children the same as his father before him. And the boy, Bucko, would undoubtedly do the same.

"Ben, does Mr. Macklin spend most of his time in his room? Shall I make breakfast for him?"

"Mack gets up at dawn and sits on the porch and watches the men get saddled up for the day's work. Codger brings him coffee and, later, breakfast if he wants it. I don't know what the arrangements will be now that we have a housekeeper." He smiled at her mischievously.

Johanna smiled back. She could really become fond of this slight, gentle man. He had lasting qualities, like her papa, a calm confidence, sense of humor, and compassion.

It was midmorning. Jacy had come down, had breakfast, and helped with some of the lighter cleaning before Johanna suggested she go out and look around. Ben offered to accompany her, and she went readily enough. Johanna suspected Jacy sensed she was unwelcome and was glad to leave the house, if only for a while.

Alone in the kitchen, Johanna found the work satisfying. She placed the freshly washed dishes on the trestle table and filled a large wooden bowl with hot water from the kettle on the cookstove. After rubbing a chunk of hard lye soap between her hands to build up suds, she laid it aside and scrubbed the shelves before replacing the dishes. The cupboard at the end of the room held few supplies, but she scoured it and replaced those foodstuffs that were still edible. The tin of flour was full of weevils, so she dumped it and washed the tin, leaving the lid off so the can would become thoroughly dry. She scoured the trestle table and the benches before she poured the soapy water into a tub to use on the floor. She felt she was making progress and hummed softly under her breath, almost forgetting the brooding, hate-filled household. The call, when it came, couldn't have startled her more if the man had come upon her with bared vicious teeth.

"Girl!"

Johanna straightened and caught her breath. The old man's roar filled the house. Taking her time, she dried her hands and smoothed back her hair. After pausing in the hall to make sure her features were composed, she calmly walked out the door and confronted the old man sitting in the cowhide chair.

His gray hair was long, hanging almost to his shoulders. His mustache drooped on either side of his mouth. The rest of his face was covered with a stubble of beard. He had once been a powerful man. The shoulders were broad, the torso long, but age and inactivity had thickened his waist, and his soiled shirt barely came together over his protruding stomach. However, his eyes were sharp and penetrating and his lips set defensively.

"Did you call?" Johanna asked cheerfully. "By the way, my name is Johanna."

The old man was still. Only his eyes were alive, and examining her from head to toe.

When he didn't say anything Johanna continued, "You should

have a small bell, Mr. Macklin. So you needn't shout." She smiled at him, determined not to let him think he frightened her.

"Hush your foolish prattle and sit down," he snapped.

"Thank you, I'll be glad to sit and rest awhile." Johanna turned one of the chairs so she would be facing him and sat down, calmly adjusted her skirt, and waited.

He slumped in his chair and stuck out his booted foot, deliberately, she thought, but she refused to look at it and continued to look him straight in the eye. Finally he turned his eyes away and looked out over the valley.

"Do you like this place, girl?" he asked begrudgingly, as if it pained him to ask.

"I've been here only two days, Mr. Macklin. Hardly time enough to decide if I like it or not," Johanna said innocently.

He glared at her. "You've been here long enough to know if you like the valley and the house," he said impatiently.

"It's a lovely valley." She smiled pleasantly.

"Speak up," he ordered sharply. "Do you like it or don't you?"

Johanna turned her eyes from him and looked out around the ranch buildings before she answered.

"Yes, I like the valley very much. It's a beautiful place. I don't like the house; I'm sure a woman didn't design it. But then, I'll make do while I'm here, which won't be for long." She looked him straight in the eye, determined not to back down, to meet him on an equal basis whether he liked it or not. She needed to stay in the valley awhile, but not at the expense of her pride or humanity.

Anger tightened the muscles in old Mack's face, and instinctively Johanna knew he was holding back his rage at her criticism of the house.

"What's wrong with it? It'll last. It's every bit as strong as when I built it thirty years ago."

Johanna smiled sweetly. Somehow she knew her smiles irritated him.

"Oh, yes, it's built to last. I'll grant you that. But it's an unhandy house. I will say it has potential. Water could be piped

61

into the house from the spring, and it would take only rugs on the floor and curtains at the windows and a few more lamps to make the house more homelike. And, oh, yes, one more thing . . . an outhouse. This ranch could certainly use an outhouse.''

He didn't say anything at first, and Johanna thought maybe she had stunned him with her frankness, but she saw his lips quirk at the corners, and although she was sure he hadn't smiled in years, he seemed very close to doing so.

"An outhouse, aye? Can't a gal from town go out in the bushes and do her business like the rest of us?'' he jeered and spat a stream of golden tobacco juice into the can beside his chair.

Keeping her face composed as though this were an everyday topic of conversation, Johanna retorted, "Oh, yes, and I'm sure I can manage it easier than, say, an . . . older person. I was thinking of your convenience, Mr. Macklin, as well as my own.''

They stared at each other, and suddenly Johanna felt good. This arbitrary old man knew she was no spineless creature who would scurry away when he bellowed.

"You ain't got no folks to go back to. You ain't got nothing,'' he said suddenly. "Stay here and the valley can be yours.'' His probing eyes scoured her face, but she showed no reaction to the statement.

She smiled and got to her feet. "Thank you, but no. My sister and I will be leaving when the next supply train goes to town. Mr. Redford tells me the trip is made every six or eight months.''

Stung to anger by her blunt refusal, he threw back his head and spat out, "Ain't good enough for ya, aye? You don't need to be acting so uppity with me, gal. I know you ain't got a pot to piss in, and you got that Mex gal what's gonna whelp. I'm offerin' you a chance to own the best valley in the Southwest and money to fix the house the way you want it. I'll give it all to you and not to that bastard you'll have to wed to get it.''

Johanna crossed her arms and lifted her head. Sparks of anger danced in her eyes.

"No!'' she said firmly. "When I wed, if ever I do, it will be under circumstances entirely different from the ones you offer. I want no part of your son or your valley.''

Her scorn cracked like a whip across his pride. He jerked erect and gritted out viciously, ''Yer goddam bitch! Yer goddam whorin' saloon gal!''

Johanna backed away from his vehemence, and opening the door, walked away from him. The hall was dark and cool, and she placed a hand over her madly thumping heart and leaned against the wall in an effort to compose herself.

''So the old man put the proposition to you, did he?'' The cold voice broke the stillness of the hall.

Johanna lifted her chin and a fiercely defiant glint glittered in her eyes. It seemed her ordeal was not yet over. Burr Macklin lounged in the kitchen doorway.

''He offered you the valley. Why didn't you accept his offer? Of course, the gift would include his bastard son served up on a silver valley!'' His cold blue eyes pinned her glance. ''Now that I think about it, it might not be such a bad idea. It would save me a trip to El Paso to visit the whores.''

Johanna would have gone past him and into the kitchen, but his bulk filled the doorway and barred her path. Coldly she stared at him, taking her time, her contempt no less obvious because it was mute.

''It doesn't appear to me that you've deprived yourself, Mr. Macklin,'' she said stiffly, and turned to walk up the stairs.

He gripped her wrist so viciously that she barely withheld a pained cry as he spun her around.

''What do you mean by that remark?'' he said through lips taut with suppressed anger. ''You, a saloon gal. A whore, if the truth were known!''

Her heart hammered wildly. The fingers that circled her wrist tightened their grip, discouraging any attempt to break away. They stood like that for several seconds, saying nothing, her expressive features giving some indication of what was going on in her mind. Then she shook her head slowly.

''That's the second time that you've called me a saloon girl,'' she said frigidly. ''Are you waiting for me to defend myself? All right, I did work in a saloon for a while. It was honest work and I was paid for services rendered.''

He threw her hand from him in a gesture of contempt. ''I bet you were,'' he snarled.

Johanna's control snapped. Her hand flashed up and she struck him a resounding slap across the face. She was as stunned by her action as the man who stood before her. It was the last thing she ever expected to do; something she had never done in her entire life. These Macklins were far different from the men she had known. They seemed to bring out traits in her that had never surfaced before.

''Damn you!'' His arms were around her and she was pulled forcibly against him even before he finished speaking, and one large hand entwined itself in the hair at the nape of her neck pulling her head back. ''I'll teach you not to bait the bear, Miss Prissy!'' Using the hand in her hair to hold her head, he covered her mouth with his, hard and angry.

Johanna struggled to free herself. She wanted only to strike out at him, to treat him as violently as he treated her. Burr, however, was too much for her and she was forced to abandon the struggle and yield to the fierce, cruel demand of his mouth. His arms held her so tightly against him that she could feel the wild beating of his heart against her breast. She was aware of the tangy smell of his freshly shaved face, and his mouth, as it ground into hers, tasted of tobacco. He released her mouth at last and for a moment she stood locked in his embrace, breathing deeply and erratically as though she'd run too far too fast.

''Let me go!'' Her voice had a husky, breathless quality. ''I said, let me go!''

Slowly he let his arms slide from around her, and she saw a hint of a smile on his face that did not quite reach the cold eyes.

''Now you can say you've been kissed by a bastard,'' he said softly.

Johanna's throat felt choked with bitterness that almost matched his. She allowed her lips to form a contemptuous sneer and at the same time she realized the futility of the gesture, for he had turned away.

"Being a bastard is no excuse for bad manners," she informed him in as cool and steady a voice as she could manage.

"Bad manners?" He laughed. The sound was short and dry and owed little to humor. He turned and reached out one hand and touched her cheek lightly with his fingertips. "I might point out that bastards are not supposed to have manners." He tapped her cheek and laughed again, and went on before she could retort, "Do you think you deserve the niceties, coming here as you did?"

Johanna felt her heart throbbing under her ribs in a strange and urgent way that alarmed her. Almost unconsciously, she raised her hand to wipe it across her lips, still warm and tingling from his kiss.

"Are you making a bid for my sympathy, Mr. Macklin?" she asked quietly, rashly uncaring that she could arouse his anger again. "You have so much to be grateful for, and yet you're bitter and angry because . . . because your father didn't marry your mother."

It took her only a moment to realize that this time she had gone too far. She stepped back when she saw his mouth tighten and the twitch of the muscles in his strong jaw. His eyes bored into hers and his large hand tightened into a fist. He shook his head sharply as if to clear it, and the harshness in his deep voice chilled her.

"You little fool! Don't you ever pity me, do you hear?"

Johanna was not aware, as was he, that Ben had come into the hall from the back of the house and had caught those last few words. He came up to them, his face creased in an uneasy grin, his anxious eyes going from one to the other with the unasked question of why they were standing so closely together.

"Burr, did you tell Johanna her sister is going to spend the evening at Red's and that he wants her to come down later with her guitar and the violin?"

Burr swung around on him, his features still hard and unrelenting.

"No," he said without preliminary, his mouth tight-lipped. "I have only one more thing to say to our . . . housekeeper, and

65

that is, Bucko and I will take our meals in the ranch house, as is our due, from now on!''

He wheeled and strode out the door, his steps hard, his spurs leaving a musical sound trailing him as he crossed the stone floor of the porch and headed in the direction of the corrals.

CHAPTER SIX

B EN WATCHED BURR leave, then swung around to face Johanna. She shook her head. Nothing would stop the tears that came to her eyes, and Ben would probably misinterpret their meaning.

"That is the most detestable, uncouth man I have ever met!" She turned swiftly and went into the kitchen. It was ridiculous to cry, she told herself, but there was nothing she could do about the tears that rolled down her cheeks.

Ben followed her, his face full of concern. "What did he do, Johanna? What in the world did he do to make you cry?"

She turned on him, not wishing to include him in her anger yet unable to subdue it. "I'm just so mad, Ben, that's all. I'm just so mad!"

"Sit down and we'll have coffee," he said soothingly.

Johanna wiped her eyes on her apron and gulped back tears.

"I'm sorry, Ben. This must be embarrassing for you. I don't know what's the matter with me. I don't usually give in to my emotions like this—I've never been a weepy person."

"It's perfectly understandable, Johanna," he told her quietly. "Beauty in a real woman is the capacity to feel things deeply, and that includes the pain as well as the joy." He clasped her

67

hand warmly. "Don't judge Burr too harshly, He's had so lass.little of what really matters in this life."

Her cheeks warmly pink, she looked at him with eyes that shone brightly through the tangle of wet lashes, and her brain whirled with emotions from the verbal and physical contact with Burr. She couldn't bring herself to pour out her feelings of disgust for the man Ben so obviously loved like a son.

"But . . . but he's so crude, Ben, and so . . ."

"He is that, lass, but it's due to his battling all these years with Mack. He resents his beginning, girl, and who can blame him? Anna wanted me to tell him the circumstances of his birth as soon as I thought he was old enough to understand. She never wanted her son to think she had willingly submitted to a man like Mack. I told Burr as much as I knew, but there is a depth to Mack that none of us will never know. He's not a man who explains his actions. I only know he came riding in one day with Anna and my life took on a different meaning."

It had been an unusually wet spring in the year 1843. Mack Macklin was tired. He had been away from his valley for two months. It had been almost that long since he had had a woman, and the ache in his loins added to his discomfort, made him impatient and irritable.

He hugged the rifle against his shoulder, took careful aim at the rock, and fired. The rock splintered and the boulder tilted. At the bottom of the slope the Indians were grouping for the next, more than likely final, assault on the wagon train.

Carefully, Mack Macklin took another sight and fired. He never knew if the second shot was necessary, because the instant his finger squeezed the trigger a pile of rocks broke loose from the wet hillside and came thundering down. There was a startled yelp, then another and another. Two Indians raced into the open, and Mack Macklin calmly drilled the first through the chest, and dropped the second with a bullet in the head. The stones tumbled down, bouncing off a shoulder of rock, then down into the arroyo.

Swiftly, before the Indians had time to adjust themselves, the big blond man positioned himself so that he had a view of the short gully leading into the main canyon. He grinned. A shrewd, experienced Indian fighter, he knew just exactly what the Indians would do. They would be on the trail and fast, and he'd get them one by one.

Grinning with satisfaction, he leaned against the rock, reloaded, and methodically fired into the canyon. He picked off four men, being careful not to hit the horses, then he stopped firing and waited until one of the Indians commenced to crawl toward the brush, leaving a trail of dark, wet blood on the sand of the dry creekbed. The giant man smiled wryly.

"Bastard," he muttered and squeezed off a shot. The Indian's body jumped, then lay still.

Mack Macklin took off his hat and wiped the sweat from his brow with his shirtsleeve. He checked his rifle, replaced his hat, and with catlike agility moved across the rocks toward the horses. His blue eyes narrowed, bringing sun-bleached brows together over a beak of a nose. His wide, thin-lipped mouth twisted in a sneer as he gazed with contempt into the canyon.

He shoved his rifle into the holder on the saddle bow and mounted the big sorrel, who carefully picked his way among the rocks as he descended. The man who had just calmly killed a dozen or more men felt his pulses quicken. If his eyes hadn't deceived him, and it wasn't likely they had, there was a woman with the wagon train. He had seen the sun shining on her blond hair as he peered over the rim of the rise after hearing the shots. It was then he had decided to take a side in the skirmish between the Indians and the greenhorns, who had formed a half-assed circle with their wagons and were, in his opinion, doing a piss-poor job of defending themselves.

As he rode toward them he removed his hat. He didn't want the sons of bitches to think he was an Indian and open fire. One thing he had learned in his almost five years in the territory was that greenhorns were unpredictable. He squinted his eyes against the sun and searched the site for a glimpse of the girl. He saw her bending over a figure sprawled in the dirt beside an overturned wagon. A look of smugness settled over the hard features. From the looks of things it wasn't going to be hard, not hard at all, to get her.

Now that he had spotted what he had come for he took his time riding toward the train and looked around. They had about ten poorly equipped wagons and hardly any know-how at all. If they got out of New Mexico territory it would be a miracle. Good thing he had come along when he had or the woman's long, shiny hair would be hanging from an Apache belt by now.

A group of pilgrims were waiting for him. All farmers looking for the promised land, he thought sarcastically. One of the group moved toward him and held out his hand. Mack ignored it until he had looked the man up and down, then shook it uninterestedly. The man was thin, and his pointed beard bobbed up and down on his chest as he talked.

"We sure do thanky, mister, yes sirree, we sure do thanky," he blabbered. "We'da probably got ourselves together and got the heathens, but you comin' like you done helped. Yes sirree, with God's help we'da done it, but he saw fit to . . ."

Mack Macklin stared coolly down into the man's face. "You'da shit, too!"

"I ain't a-takin' nothing away from you," the man hastened to say. "I ain't a-takin' nothing away atall. It was God's will, was all I was a-sayin'."

Mack's look dismissed him, and after hesitating the man lifted his shoulders and stood aside. The big man urged his horse into the circle of wagons and dismounted. His sharp eyes missed nothing. Two horses and two oxen had been killed. Three men lay dead with arrows in their backs, and a fourth lay dying. The blond girl, his reason for being here, bent over him. Mack went to her and without preliminaries squatted down beside the wounded man.

"You this girl's pa?"

"Uncle," he gasped.

"Yore done for, you know that," Mack said coldly.

"Aye." The word was whispered.

"You know the Indians'll be back. Too many braves died here. There'll be weepin' and wailin' in the village and they'll have a need for revenge. You a-wantin' this girl here to stay and get scalped or to come with me and live?''

The man's eyes were beginning to glaze, but with an effort he said, ''Go, Anna. Go with him.''

Mack got to his feet. He motioned to the leader of the group. ''Tell this man what you want,'' he said to the dying man.

''Anna, go with him and . . . live,'' he gasped and his eyes swung to the girl's tear-wet face, then glazed over. The girl's bowed head rested on his breast and she sobbed.

Mack turned to the group standing behind him. ''You heard him,'' he said curtly. ''Get me a shovel.'' Mack's almost forty years had brought him a better than average acquaintance with fools, and he had no patience with them.

An hour later he lifted the crying girl to the back of a horse, strapped her trunk onto a mule, and rode off without a backward glance. He wanted to be as far away as possible when the second Indian attack started, because with or without his help those people didn't stand a chance.

For the first time in a long time Mack felt a sense of well-being. He had his valley and he had a woman to produce the sons he wanted. The girl was younger than he had first believed, and thin, but with luck and good food he could fatten her up. God, he wished she would hush that damn bawling. What was done was done, and no good could come from whining about it. He'd give her the rest of the day and the night before he started using her. He felt a stirring in his loins. Jesus Christ, it'd been a long time since he'd had a white woman.

The morning after their first camp, Anna Englebretson lay exhausted. The emotional shock of the Indian attack, her uncle's death, and her sudden departure from the train with this silent, overpowering man had left her physically and spiritually fatigued. He was up before first light, and after a cup of coffee, they broke camp and headed toward the rising sun. Anna had not ridden a great deal, and never astride. As the morning progressed, pains began to shoot through her body until the struggle not to cry out consumed her every thought. Despite her efforts an occasional cry did escape her lips. When finally the man turned to look at

71

her she saw in his cold, angry eyes a threat that so filled her with terror that she pressed her lips together and determined never to do it again.

Anna hadn't wanted to leave her home in upper New York State to come west with her uncle. Her life on the small farm, if uneventful, had been pleasant. She had a small circle of friends, her house to keep, and her needlework. But when her uncle, her only living relative, had caught the fever to go west and sold their farm, she had no choice but to go with him. Anna was a gentle person who had led a sheltered life. Nothing in all her sixteen years had prepared her for the violence and hardship she experienced during their trip.

It was on Anna's second night with Mack that she came to the realization that she was at the complete mercy of this strange man, who had not even bothered to ask her name. A feeling of foreboding froze her heart as she crawled into her bedroll, outside the circle of light. She watched as Mack added a piece of mesquite root to the small blaze, and when it flared he got to his feet and came toward her, his intentions perfectly clear even to the naive young woman.

"You ever been with a man, girl?" the rough voice asked.

Anna felt a rush of heat in her face, and she looked up at him, her eyes pleading.

"I see you ain't," he said curtly, "but it makes no never mind."

He unbuckled his gunbelt, laid it on the ground, and placed his hat over it. His big hand commenced to work at the buttons on his breeches.

"No," Anna pleaded. "Please, no!"

His eyes held hers and his fingers continued working until they released the swollen, rigid member between his legs. He stood gazing down at her for a few minutes, his hands on his hips, his legs braced apart, allowing her the full view of his sex, rising straight and hard out of a thatch of blond curls that matched the curls on his head.

Anna gasped, her entire body shaking violently.

"I ain't saying yer gonna like it," he said harshly, "but yer gonna have it. It's the way of things."

She whimpered, feeling like a small animal caught in a trap. Dimly she was aware that he was pulling down his breeches, and that his hands were pulling up her skirt and forcing her legs apart. Something hot, hard, and throbbing pushed into her.

She lay under him, feeling his crushing weight on her breast and the hot searing pain of the rod he was thrusting so rapidly into her. He grunted, and his large body arched and heaved, then jerked in spasm. His breathing was loud in her ear, and an acrid smell of perspiration came from him as he stirred and lifted his weight from her slight body. Closing her eyes tightly, she wished fervently she could die.

When he removed himself, the night air felt cool on her wet thighs, and she painfully brought her legs together and covered them with her skirt. The pain between her legs was excruciating, and her lower legs and ankles smarted from the contact with his rough boots.

"That's the worst of it, girl," he said and strapped on his gunbelt. "You'll get used to it in time. Ain't saying you'll like it. Never heard of no woman a-likin' it but a whore. I aim to get sons outta you for my valley. Sons, big like me with yeller hair and blue eyes. If you breed for me, I'll wed you. If you don't . . . wal, I'll sweat on it when I come to it."

He kicked dirt onto one side of the fire to dim the blaze, stretched out, and was soon snoring.

In the days that followed, Anna was used each night. Once when she protested he gave her a resounding smack that threw her head to one side and sent a flashing pain through her jaw. Her life took on a pattern of unreality. When the man came to her, she docilely spread her legs and detached her mind from the act being committed upon her body.

By the time they reached the valley, Anna's slight body had become even thinner and so weak that her heart pounded from the slightest exertion. Mack seldom looked at her. Days went by without a word spoken between them but each night he poured his seed into her. His contempt was obvious as he drove her

73

relentlessly across the sea of barren arroyos, thirsty creeks, and sandy gullies.

They arrived at the stone ranch house in his high green valley late one afternoon. Anna was sick. Her head throbbed and her body ached. She had thrown up while still on the horse because she didn't wish to bring attention to herself by asking to stop. She vaguely knew when they reached their destination, but sat on the horse dazed, looking at the stark stone house.

"Get off the horse," Mack commanded sullenly.

Anna fought back the tears. "I don't know if I can."

"Calloway," he bellowed, "where the hell are you?"

A small, slight young man came toward them with quick sure steps.

"I'm here, Mack. If you had looked you could have seen me coming."

"Get her off the horse. She's sick, I reckon. Emptied her guts a ways back."

The young man came to her and put his hands on her waist and gently lifted her down from the horse. His soft brown eyes were filled with compassion, and at the sight of the first sympathetic face she had seen in weeks, Anna's eyes flooded.

"Name's Annie, I guess," Mack growled and started unsaddling his horse. "Got her off a wagon train afore she got her hair lifted by the Apaches. Was gonna make her my woman, but she ain't any stronger than a pissant, and I can't abide a whimpering, puking woman. If she don't shape up you can have her." He stomped off toward the bunkhouse.

"Please," Anna whispered, "can I lie down?"

The room to which he led her was cool and clean, and Anna's pain-dulled eyes found a row of books on a shelf by the bed. She looked at him; his dark crisp hair framed a serious young face, and his voice was gentle and his accent reminded her of . . . home. Tears filled her eyes again.

"I'm afraid I'll throw up," she whispered.

"Don't worry about it," he said. "I'll get a bucket and leave until you can get into bed, then I'll be back with something to make you feel better."

74

Later he sat beside her and placed a damp cloth on her fevered brow. She smiled her gratitude and reached out a thin hand. The man took it in his and immediately lost his heart to her. Anna's eyes closed. It all came flooding back, and she began to shake with dry sobs. The man held her close, smoothing her hair back from her face. The tears came and her body shook convulsively. He held her tightly, and she buried her face against his shoulder, clinging to him to give her some sanity in a world that had suddenly gone insane.

In the weeks following, he devoted himself to her, stayed with her night and day. They talked for hours, revealed their every secret thought, and their love and devotion for each other grew until it was all-consuming and the only world they knew existed in that one room of the stone house.

"Ben," she said one evening as she sat by the fire, her feet puffy and cold and a light shawl draped about her shoulders, "if your name is Burnett, why are you called Ben?"

"Because, my lovely," he said teasingly, "my name is Burnett Nathan Calloway. My father called me by my initials, B.N., and it just worked into Ben."

"I think Burnett is a lovely name for a boy," Anna said softly. She looked at him with glowing eyes. "What would I have done without you, Ben?"

"After you have the babe," he said, ignoring the question, "we'll leave and find a place of our own."

"Do you think he'll let us go?" she asked wistfully.

"I don't know, Anna. We'll just have to wait until the time comes and see."

"I don't care where we are, my love, as long as I'm with you."

"You'll always be with me, Anna. Always."

The baby was born on a cold windy night. Ben sent down to the Mexican quarters for a woman to help Anna. The women were afraid to come, because the Mexicans were never allowed near the house. With the help of a ranch hand, a woman was brought up and slipped into the room where Anna lurched and screamed in the agony of childbirth.

It was a long night for Ben as he watched his beloved give birth to another man's child. Her suffering was his suffering and her pain was his pain, until at last the woman held out a wet, wriggling mass of humanity for him to hold.

With her son, clean and wrapped, lying beside her, Anna smiled weakly as Ben touched her lips with his.

"I'm going to call him Burnett," she said. "Burr for short. A burr that will stick in the craw of that . . . of that man. Don't ever leave him to Mack Macklin, Ben. Promise you'll stay with him and teach him that brawn alone won't make him a man."

"We'll teach him, my darling. We'll teach him together."

She closed her eyes, and Ben gazed at her fragile beauty and then at the red-faced baby in the curve of her arm. His heart quickened and a lump rose up in his throat. She was so weak, he thought, so weak!

Anna lived until her son was four years old. She seldom left the room, but she was content, basking in Ben's love and tender care. Her son was the joy of her life, a strong, bright boy with a mass of blond, curly hair. During the day she used most of her strength to teach and play with Burr, and in the evenings Ben would read the stories he most loved to both mother and child. It was a peaceful, comforting life, though obviously confined, since their time was spent solely in Ben's room. By now Ben and Anna were resigned to the fact that she would never survive the trip out of the valley.

Mack's activities kept him away from the house much of the time, but when he was there he seemed to accept the relationship between Ben and Anna. For the most part the strange master of Macklin Valley ignored them. He maintained a grudging civility toward Ben. He needed him. Ben kept all the ranch records and acted as buffer between him and the Mexican workers. Furthermore, he was reliable and could be left in charge while Mack was away. Ben knew this, but he suspected Mack also allowed Anna and himself to stay because of the boy. Occasionally he caught Mack watching the miniature of himself, a quiet, solemn expression on his face, as if he were remembering events from his own childhood.

On a bright summer day, Ben held the cold hands of his beloved and kissed her serene lips for the last time. Holding tightly the hand of the small boy, he followed her blanket-wrapped body to a grassy knoll above the ranch house. The men lowered the body, then stood with hats in hand while Ben read from Scripture. Somberly and silently they covered the thin body with the warm earth and walked away to leave Ben and the boy alone.

The breeze that came down from the mountains stirred the boy's blond curls and rippled the wild flowers he clutched in his hand. Ben took the flowers from him and scattered them on the grave. He and the boy got down on their knees. Ben put his arms about the bewildered child, and they wept together.

Ben's depression was deep. No one could know what the lovely, frail woman had meant to him. For days he could not eat, and at night he walked the floor. After a while he began to realize his life with Anna had been beautiful and fulfilling but it was time to get on with those things that needed doing. Anna had left with him her most precious possession, her son, and through him Anna would live. With quiet determination he went about the task of raising Burr. He committed himself wholly to the boy's welfare and education, all the while planning revenge for what Anna had suffered. Someday he and Burr would wrest from Mack Macklin this valley—the only thing Macklin had ever loved.

CHAPTER SEVEN

JOHANNA TUCKED THE fresh blouse into the clean skirt and secured the belt around her waist. She brushed her hair and carefully recoiled it, pulling a few tendrils of curls about her face. Scrutinizing herself in the mirror, she decided she looked coolly conventional, yet informal enough to suit her position in this house. With nerves firmly under control, she marched down to the kitchen ready to do battle with Burr when he came in for the evening meal.

The kitchen was spotlessly clean and shining. The trestle table had been scrubbed vigorously with a stiff brush, dried, and oiled. The seasoned old wood gleamed after being polished with a soft cloth. Lighting one of the freshly washed lamps, Johanna set it in the middle of the table and set plates and cutlery for five, thinking it better to set a place for Mr. Macklin although Ben didn't believe he would come to the table.

There was an abundance of food on the ranch. Codger and a young Mexican lad brought flour, cornmeal, sugar, rice, dried beans, dried fruits, and numerous seasonings up from the cookhouse. He showed her the smokehouse, which was filled with slabs of bacon, sides of beef, venison, and even a portion of bear meat that he swore was good eating if cooked long enough. There was a chickenhouse, so fresh eggs were available as well.

Codger proudly showed her a cave in the rocks behind the house and near the spring where milk and vegetables were stored.

Johanna was astonished at how well organized the ranch was outside the house. It seemed to her that the ranch house was like a desolate island in a sea of plenty.

Evening came early. When the sun passed over the crest of the mountain, its long shadows engulfed the valley, cooling it. The cookstove made the kitchen pleasantly warm, and the shining chimneys on the lamps helped give the room a rosy glow.

Ben sat in the chair by the hearth and watched Johanna. She moved from stove to workbench, her color intensified by the heat from the stove.

"We'll have to set a time for supper, Ben. I work better if I have a schedule to go by." Not wanting to admit to herself that she dreaded hearing the thud of Burr's boots on the stone floor, she chattered on. "Tomorrow I think I'll start cleaning the room across the hall." She looked up. Burr and Bucko had come quietly into the room. She glanced at them and quickly took in everything about them.

It appeared that Bucko had come unwillingly, from the pouting expression on his face. He was, however, dressed in a clean shirt and his hair had been combed. His small hand was engulfed in Burr's large one. Burr was wearing Indian moccasins, the reason she hadn't heard him come into the kitchen. He had also put on a clean shirt without the ever-present Western vest, and he had attempted to control the mop of curly hair, without much success, Johanna noted. His expression was unreadable; not friendly, but not surly. She decided his look could only be described as determined.

"Supper is almost ready, Mr. Macklin," she said formally. "And I would like to know if this is a convenient time for the meal. If it is, I'll have your meal ready at this time each evening." He did not answer her immediately, but instead let his eyes travel the room, taking in every change she had made. When he'd finished he met her cool gaze.

"If it isn't, I'll let you know." His voice was barely cordial.

"Thank you," she said in a voice equal to his own, then

glanced down at Bucko. "I hear you met my sister today, Bucko. Did you know she's quite good at making a slingshot?" She spoke in Spanish.

"Speak English," Burr said harshly. "Bucko must learn English."

"Yes, of course," she said, refusing to let his manner intimidate her. She took the pan of biscuits from the oven. "Come, Ben, the biscuits are done. You and Bucko sit down, Mr. Macklin," she said, delighted to see a flush of anger come into his face at being invited to sit at his own table. After she placed the food on the table, Johanna whipped off her apron and went to call old Mack.

When she did not find him on the porch, she knocked on the door of his room, but there was no answer.

"Supper is ready, Mr. Macklin," she called out.

There was no reply. Johanna went back to the kitchen.

Burr was seated at the head of the table, Bucko on one side and Ben on the other. Johanna couldn't help but wonder what would happen if old Mack came to the table. She sat down beside Bucko. Ben was waiting for her, but Burr had placed food on Bucko's plate and his own and had started to eat. It was difficult for Johanna to keep from smiling at the childish act of defiance. It was plain her cool reserve had got under the skin of the confident Burr. She smiled at Ben; his eyes twinkled. There wasn't much he missed.

After his first attempt to start a conversation failed, Ben sat quietly, eating and observing. Johanna could tell he was enjoying the meal. He had faultless manners, and she was surprised to discover that Burr's manners were good also. Probably the result of Ben's teaching, she thought. Judging from the quantity of food that disappeared, Burr was also enjoying the meal, or else he hadn't eaten for several days.

Johanna poured coffee for herself and the men and brought milk for Bucko before she set down a large platter of bear claws. Bucko looked disbelievingly at the warm, sugar-coated cakes before his eyes found hers. She winked at him, and she was almost sure she saw a flicker of friendliness before he lowered his eyes. As she rounded the table to take her seat she felt Burr's eyes on her, but paid no attention to him.

"Later I'm going to go down to Mr. Redford's, Bucko. Would you want to walk with me and show me the way?"

The boy, reaching for a bear claw, halted when he heard her words. He looked at Burr, as if hoping he would answer for him. Burr reached over and placed a cake on his plate.

"If you want to go, Bucko, say so," he said. "If you don't want to go it will be all right."

Johanna couldn't believe the gentle, patient voice had come from the man who had only a few hours ago been so boorish. She looked at him and saw a softening in his face that changed his countenance completely. Evidently Ben and Bucko saw nothing unusual in this direct manner of speaking, because Ben continued eating and Bucko turned big serious eyes in her direction and said he'd like to go.

"I'm glad," Johanna said with mock relief. "I'll need someone to carry my guitar."

To her surprise the boy's face lit up, and her heart lurched. He's lonely, she thought, and realized there was one Macklin at least, who was human and reachable.

The meal was more pleasant than Johanna had anticipated, yet she was glad when it was over. It irritated her that Burr's presence made her nervous. Each time he looked at her the bold, masculine magnetism he emitted aroused a sense of excitement in her. It was unthinkable to imagine being married to such a man.

"Burr, come talk to me while Bucko stuffs himself with cakes," Ben said.

When he stood up Burr's large frame seemed to fill the room, causing Johanna to hold her breath until he moved away. He sat opposite Ben and brought out the makings for a cigarette. Bucko sat at the table, eating slowly but steadily.

While preparing a tray for Mr. Macklin, Johanna listened to the conversation at the hearth.

"Have you decided what you're going to do about the men who followed the train in?"

"For the time being, nothing. Luis is keeping an eye on them, and if they move from the spot where they're camped, or if it looks like they plan to stay, I'll act. Meanwhile, we have plenty to do getting the stragglers down out of the hills and breaking the string of horses Luis brought in. And there's the windmill to put up."

"Did Luis find anything in town to add to his string?"

When Burr answered, Johanna caught her breath, for the change in his face was miraculous. The stern lines relaxed and his lips spread in a smile that showed even white teeth. He was undeniably handsome, and no doubt he was aware of it, she told herself. She attributed her own racing pulse to nervousness, not willing to admit she was attracted to him.

"He found a fine-boned little mare he wants to put to the stallion he got from the Apache. He thinks he'll get a colt with the speed of lightning."

"Well," Ben said, "that boy knows horses, and I'll bet he'll get just what he thinks he'll get."

The men talked of the two Mexicans Luis had killed and the chance he had taken against two armed men as well as the speed with which he could draw and shoot.

"He's practiced for years. I thought the day might come when he would use that speed here on the ranch." Ben knocked the bowl of his pipe sharply against the stone hearth.

"It'll never come to that now, Ben. Luis will have his horse ranch and Bucko will have his chance, too. I'll see to it. Nothing and nobody is going to prevent it."

Johanna thought he said the last for her benefit, and a brief flash of anger swept over her. She kept her head turned so he couldn't see the flush that flooded her face.

The tray was ready. She put more food on the plate than she thought the old man could eat, but she wanted it to be ample. Covering the tray with a clean cloth, she felt a sudden rush of uncertainty and looked helplessly at Ben. She really couldn't bear another encounter with that frightful old man.

He reached for his tobacco can to refill his pipe and spoke.

"All I can tell you, lass, is take the bull by the horns. Rap on the door. Mack won't answer, but open it and go in. You'll find him propped up in bed. Just place the food on the table and leave. He may swear at you, but he'll not strike you."

"No, I'm sure he won't," she said lightly and picked up the tray. Not for the world would she let that overbearing dolt by the hearth know that Mack could cause her a moment of concern. She walked calmly through the door, but paused in the hall to prepare herself for the old man's onslaught. He did not answer her knock, as Ben had predicted. She hesitated only a second, afraid her courage would leave, then opened the door. The room was in semidarkness, but she could see the bed at the end of the room. The offensive smell of sweat, unwashed body, and a spittoon that badly needed to be emptied assailed her. She could hear the sound of heavy breathing but wasn't sure whether the old man was asleep.

"Mr. Macklin?" she called softly.

The bed creaked as he shifted his weight. As she walked toward Macklin her foot struck an object on the floor, and she barely managed to keep her balance and the tray upright. Moving aside a lamp, she placed the tray on the table near the bed.

"Shall I light a lamp for you, Mr. Macklin?" she asked.

There was no answer. Feeling along the table, her fingers found a box of sulfur matches, and she lit one. She lifted the chimney from the lamp and applied the flame. The old man was propped up in bed watching her. His sunken blue eyes cold, his mouth open to gulp air.

"I've brought your supper."

"I ain't blind," he growled.

Johanna smiled. "Is there anything else I can get for you?"

The lips snapped shut and the look on his face was one of distaste. Johanna didn't know why she should be reminded of a puma ready to spring. Perhaps it was the growl, or it might have been the glow in his eyes that followed her every move. Resisting the temptation to rush from the room, she walked slowly to the door, where the sound of his voice halted her.

"About what I asked you," he said caustically, "are you still of the same mind?"

Thinking she had better get this settled once and for all, she said calmly, "Mr. Macklin, I never even considered your proposal. What you suggest is absolutely impossible."

With surprising agility the old man swung up to sit on the side of the bed.

"You goddam slut!" he bellowed. "You goddam whorin' slut! What more are you a-wantin'? Me to go down on my knees and beg? That goddam Cash! I been a waitin' six months for you to get here. Waitin' six months for a goddam bitch to stand there and tell me my valley ain't good enough for her." His face was almost purple with rage, and Johanna stood as if in a stupor. She had never seen a person lose complete control.

"You'll wed the bastard, or I'll sell the whole goddam valley out from under him," he roared. "I'll not have a goddam bastard have my valley, not a goddam bastard that robbed me of my foot. He'll wed you, I say! Once he gets you on your back he'll know what to do. I seen to that!"

Johanna went through the door and closed it behind her. She could still hear his voice coming through the closed door.

"You goddam bitch!"

She stood in the quiet of the hall, her hands pressed tightly over her ears. Burr came through the kitchen door. With the light behind him she couldn't see his expression, but she thought he had a smirk on his face. Her features clearly showed the strain of the encounter with the old man.

As he passed her he said softly, "If you're going to get the honey you must expect to get stung by the bee."

"You . . . you shut up!" she hissed at him, and the soft chuckle that followed infuriated her.

"Damn him!" she muttered as she entered the kitchen.

Ben sat puffing on his pipe. Johanna knew he and Burr had heard every word old Mack had said to her, but she decided she wasn't going to mention it. In all her life Johanna had never been subjected to the kind of abuse she had received since she'd come to the valley. She could never even have imagined such behavior, nor did she know how to deal with it. Dear, dear Ben! Maybe his calm assurance would help her to survive in this house of evil. She had arranged her thoughts and regained her composure by the time he spoke.

"You'll never get used to such talk, lass, but don't let it touch you," he told her gently.

"I won't, Ben. Their problems have nothing to do with me." She smiled down at Bucko. "I'll run up and get my shawl and the instruments and we'll go." At the door she said, "Ben, will you come with us?"

"No, girl, but I think I may come down later. It's only a short walk, and I could use the exercise—and besides, I can't wait to hear the music."

Bucko was waiting at the foot of the stairs when Johanna came down. She handed him the violin case, because it was the lighter of the two instruments and less bulky. They went out and across the front of the house.

From the rooms at the end of the porch a path of light shone out onto the stone patio. Johanna glanced into the room as they walked past. Burr was sitting in a chair, his long legs stretched out before him, and on his lap, her dark head snuggled close to his, was a young Mexican girl. They looked up. The girl's arm curled possessively about Burr, her fingers fondling his hair. Stung by an unexplained anger, Johanna quickened her steps.

The night was dark. Bucko led her down the smooth, well-worn path that started at the back of the bunkhouse.

"Can you read, Bucko?" Johanna asked.

"Sí. Burr teach me . . . and Ben."

"Good. Would you like to learn to play my guitar?"

Although they were walking slowly, he stumbled. His affirmative answer came in a clear strong voice, and with more emphasis than she had heard him speak before.

"I'll teach you then," she said cheerfully. "We'll start next week."

As they approached the Mexican quarters they saw a large fire in the center of the semicircle of adobe houses. People lounged around the fire laughing and talking, and the children ran about, shouting to each other. The scene was so completely removed from the soberness of the ranch house that Johanna felt a pang of homesickness for the happy home she had had before her parents were killed. The children, seeing Bucko with the strange light-haired woman, stared, awestruck. Bucko lifted his head proudly and clutched the handle of the violin case.

Jacy came out of the circle of light to meet them. Johanna noticed at once the lightness of her step and the eagerness in her voice.

"Johanna, we've been waiting for you. Come, I want you to meet Rosita."

Jacy pulled her toward the fire. She seemed happy. Actually happy! Johanna was delighted, and a large part of the heaviness she had carried for so long lifted from her heart.

A small, plump woman with shiny black hair and large expressive eyes came toward them. She smiled her welcome, her bright eyes moving from Johanna's striking blond hair to Jacy's dark coloring.

Jacy laughed. "I told you she had hair like a silver cloud."

"*Sí*, Jaceta. You were right."

"Good evening," Johanna said. "Thank you for allowing Jacy to spend the day with you."

"Ah . . . her *español*, it is good like yours, Jaceta."

Rosita's friendly, lighthearted disposition had affected Jacy, and Johanna could hardly take her eyes from her sister's smiling face. *It's worth it all . . . it's worth it all*. The words kept flashing through her mind.

"Are ya a-makin' out, Johanner?" Mooney appeared beside her.

"Just barely, Mooney," she said and laughed. Then seriously, "I'm glad you prepared me, or I'd have been struck dumb."

"I figured ya was in for a jolt."

Bucko stood shyly by her side, and Johanna gently took his hand. A bench had been cleared for her, and as she sat down she pulled the boy down beside her. Jacy took her violin from the case and plucked the strings to be sure they were in tune.

"Let's play some Spanish music first, Johanna."

"You lead off, as Papa used to do, and I'll follow." Immediately Johanna wished she hadn't mentioned Papa, but a quick look at Jacy reassured her that she hadn't upset her sister.

Jacy struck up a lively Spanish tune, and Johanna played the accompaniment. Exhilarated, her fingers flew over the strings of the guitar. Bucko, sitting beside her, watched intently, his eyes bright and the corners of his mouth turned up. Johanna was surprised by his interest in the music and how the different tempos affected his expression.

After several numbers the audience began to clap their hands and sing. Soon they were calling out: *"Bueno, bueno!"*

Johanna watched her sister carefully for signs of fatigue, but Jacy was totally carried away by the vibrant music she played and the utter joy and freedom of the moment. To the delight of everyone she swung into a fiery, rousing piece, and a shout went up: "Isabella, Isabella, come dance for us."

A girl stepped out of the darkness and raised her arms up over her head. It was the girl who had been reclining languorously on Burr's lap. With animal grace she poised on tiptoes, then pivoted and twirled. Around and around the circle she went pirouetting and posturing, her movements inviting the attention of every man. Hands clapped in unison, keeping perfect time with the throbbing beat of the music. The girl's feet were bare, and as she stamped out the rhythm of the music she whirled before each group, arms raised, boldly provocative. She halted briefly before Johanna, her flashing black eyes sending forth a challenge to the woman she thought her rival. Then with an insolent flicker of her lashes she dismissed her. Johanna's intuition told her this girl resented her and her action was a warning that she didn't intend to be cast aside. Her suspicion was confirmed a moment later when the girl's searching eyes settled on the face of the man standing out of the circle of light.

Isabella, her dark hair whipping around her, whirled and swayed her body sensuously as she danced toward Burr, displaying every seductive curve of her body before his smiling gaze. Her dark eyes beckoned seductively. She wriggled her hips in wild abandon, and her full skirt billowed and flounced with every move. Her dance became wilder and more intense. The tempo rose and the clapping was so fast that Isabella's whirling skirts showed flashes of bare thigh.

Johanna felt embarrassment, tinged with pity, for the girl. Obviously she had been intimate with Burr or she wouldn't have been in his room. No doubt he found her an amusing plaything, and Johanna conjectured that he more than likely used her in the same way he had used and discarded Bucko's mother.

As she glanced his way she caught him watching her with a glint of mockery in his eyes that said her thoughts were plainly written on her face. Angry with herself and with him, she gave all her attention over to the guitar.

Waves of laughter and applause followed the end of the dance. Jacy swung into the less feverish "Greensleeves," and when Johanna looked up again neither the dancer nor Burr was there.

Jacy finally put down her violin and sat down. She had been playing for an hour, and although she was tired her eyes were bright and she was still smiling.

"It's almost the way it used to be, isn't it, Johanna?"

Before Johanna could answer, a young voice drawled, "Sing us one of them songs of yourn, ma'am."

"Sing us a ballad, Johanner," Mooney called.

"All right. I'll sing first in English, then in Spanish."

Her fingers stroked the strings of the guitar, and then she sang, her voice clear and sweet. The song was a story about a small boy who wanted to ride on the train, but didn't have money to pay his fare. Her audience listened attentively, and she sang the chorus.

> "Oh, please, Mr. Conductor,
>   don't put me off of the train,
> The best friend I have in this world,
>   is waiting for me in pain. . . ."

Her next song was about a young cowboy killed during a stampede and of his sweetheart who waited for him in vain. The tragic lyric was popular with young men who spent many lonely hours on the prairie. She sang the touching war ballads "Lorena" and "Just Before the Battle, Mother," and the best-known of all the songs to come out of the war between the states, "Dixie."

Her eyes roamed over the faces before her. Luis was there, standing quietly beside Ben, his face in the shadows. Codger, Paco, and Carlos; all were there. The only person who hadn't put in an appearance was the old man who had discovered the valley, fought for it, developed it, and become bitter because of it.

Johanna finished singing and handed her guitar to Bucko. She was tired, the weariness of her flesh equal to the weariness of her spirit.

"Señorita?" Luis spoke from behind her. She turned and saw him standing beside Burr. Suddenly she was angry that Burr was here when she thought he had gone. Ignoring him, she smiled up at Luis.

"Your sister say I must ask your permission to walk with her."

There was no hesitancy in his voice, nor did he seem reluctant to speak in Burr's presence. He was an extraordinarily handsome man whose face showed not only strength, but character. Had it not been for his deep-blue eyes, she thought it almost impossible he could have been sired by old Mack. Looking at the half brothers, standing together, she could see that their features were somewhat similar, yet the chiseled lips that in Luis curved easily to a smile in Burr became an almost malevolent sneer that engendered a lack of trust. Both men were tall, but Burr was taller and more heavily built.

Johanna's eyes found Jacy, standing slightly to the right and behind Luis, her eyes anxious.

"Jacy?" she questioned before speaking to Luis. "It is the custom to ask permission and I thank you for the courtesy, but Jacy is a grown woman and the decision is hers."

Luis turned toward Jacy and held out his hand for her violin case. She smiled up into his face, and they walked off into the darkness together. A sharp feeling of apprehension struck Johanna as she watched them.

Burr studied Johanna for a long time. She could do nothing but stand there helplessly, no longer knowing what to say, feeling hot, uncomfortable, and unsure of herself. She cursed him under her breath. Reading her thoughts, he smiled, his eyes telling her she could hide nothing from him.

"Galls you, don't it, to see your sister enjoys my brother's company," he taunted softly.

Johanna had to fight the impulse to slap his face, to mar that handsome countenance with her nails. She struggled with the primitive desire to hurt. The murderous impulse increased as the blue eyes, with more than a hint of malicious amusement in their depths, looked into hers.

"I'll thank you to keep your observations to yourself!" she said frigidly. She was surprised and pleased that the voice that came from her tight throat was so calm. She braced herself for another mocking jibe, but when he spoke it was to Bucko.

"How about a piggy-back ride, cowboy?" He lifted the boy to his shoulder and walked away.

Anger flared anew in Johanna at his rudeness before she dismissed him as an overbearing, ignorant, completely self-serving oaf.

"You two really strike sparks off each other," Ben said.

"Yes, we do," Johanna said.

They walked down the path, Johanna adjusting her stride to his slower pace. The shimmering glow of the moon illuminated the landscape, and the night sounds took over. Somewhere an owl hooted his mournful song and the crickets sounded loud in the darkness. The faint murmur of voices came from behind them as families separated to go to their homes.

"Ben," Johanna said when she was sure they were out of hearing of others, "tell me about Luis. Is he a gunman?"

"Are you bothered, Johanna, that Luis wants to court your sister?"

Now the suspicion that she had been pushing to the back of her mind was out in the open. She laughed nervously, unwilling to give voice to her thoughts.

"I doubt that he's courting her, Ben," she said lightly. "I'm just curious to know what kind of man he is."

"Luis isn't a killer, Johanna," Ben said after a while. "He's killed, as most of the men in the valley have at one time or the other, but never without just cause. I consider Luis a good man. Not a perfect one, but a good one.''

"With Mr. Macklin's dislike for Mexicans, Ben, it hardly seemed likely that he would have . . . would have . . .'' She fumbled for the words to phrase her question.

"I understand what you're saying. Mack took his pleasure and didn't consider it any more than his due. It was the same with any woman,'' he said sadly.

"And his son is following in his footsteps,'' Johanna said bitterly.

Ben looked at her sharply, then said slowly, "You mean Burr?''

"It's obvious.''

"Don't be so quick to judge Burr. He bought Bucko from the Apaches; gave six ponies for him. I don't know how he managed it, because the Indians almost never give up a child, even a malformed one. The boy was nothing but a bag of bones when Burr brought him here about four years ago. They told him the boy was six summers at the time. He was so weak he couldn't walk and so cowered he cringed every time he heard a human voice. That's probably the only reason they let him go. They're very intolerant of the old and the weak.''

Johanna walked along in silence, then said dubiously, "I find it hard to believe Bucko is ten years old. I've had ten-year-old boys in my class that were as tall as I am.''

"When I first saw him he was like a babe in arms. Burr's brought him a long way.''

"You talk as if Burr's done him a favor,'' Johanna said contemptuously.

Ben didn't answer for a long while, and Johanna's anger and disgust for Macklin's older son flared anew.

"He could have left him there,'' he said quietly.

"Indeed!''

CHAPTER EIGHT

L UIS RODE HIS tired horse down the dusty street and paused before the shambling two-story hotel, its sign dangling askew.

He sat his horse and his eyes took in every detail around him. The Mexicans in their loose, light breeches and full shirts, their straw sombreros straight on their dark heads, paid no attention to him. Three gringos in dusty trail clothes who leaned against the unpainted buildings eyed him, but Luis dismissed their look as one of curiosity. Chickens squawked and scampered from the road as a freight wagon went past with several dogs trailing it, barking and trying to catch the rolling wheels with their snapping teeth. Down the street a door opened and a man, with a well-placed boot at his back, went sprawling in the dust.

Still cautious, but satisfied the street scene was as it appeared to be, Luis walked his horse to the rail and dismounted. The gringos turned to watch him, more than casual interest on their faces.

"Ain't that the Mex they's a-talking about up at Las Cruces?"

"By God if it ain't!"

"What about him?" the third man asked, picking his teeth with a long, thin-bladed knife. "He don't look like nothin' but a Mex to me."

"Shut up!" the man standing next to him hissed.

"God, yeah!" the other cowboy said. "He's a fightin' son of a bitch! Fought in the Battle of Glorieta in '62 and the general, he said that iffen he'da had six more like him the Yanks woulda never drove 'em out."

"They say he's faster than greased lightning with those guns."

"Gunfighter?"

"Wal, I don't know as he's that. Feller didn't say he was hired or nothing like that, jist said he ain't touchy, but ya better not push him."

"Seemed kinda spooked when he come in, kinda like someone was a-trailin' him."

"Probably jist natural spooky. Them fellers allus got some fool a-wantin' to try 'em."

Luis walked up the worn steps to the porch of the hotel, paused and looked around, then went through the open door into the dusty lobby. Beyond the desk a grossly fat man dozed. He wore a dirty shirt open to reveal a hairy chest, and greasy wisps of hair straggled across a nearly bald pate.

Starting, he peered through watery eyes, then struggled to his feet.

"Room?" And looking toward the street, "I can put your horse up, too." The man thumbed his triple chins and the watery eyes became evasive. "Air you staying long?"

Luis signed the register.

The fat man looked at his name, then squinted up at him. "Be here long?" Luis didn't answer him, but the hotelman kept prodding. "Come a long ways?"

"Where's the stable?" Luis asked coolly, ignoring the questions.

"I'll get a boy—"

"I care for my own horse." Luis left the lobby, the heels of his boots sounding loud on the bare plank floors.

Later in his room he lighted a lamp on the scarred bureau and tossed his hat onto the sagging bed. He removed his gunbelt, then peeled off his shirt. The cracked mirror above the bureau showed his naked chest, with its long red wound. He uncorked a bottle, had a swallow, then poured whiskey into his palm and applied it to the knife cut where a little dried blood showed the wound had opened. He next spilled water from a cracked pitcher into a crockery bowl and washed. The mirror showed his lean, tired face, eyes bloodshot from days of dusty travel. He decided he was more tired than hungry. After checking the door, he stretched out on the bed, got up to blow out the lamp, then lay down again, hands folded across his stomach.

It was morning when he came instantly awake and sprang to his feet. The floorboards in the hall had creaked. Quickly he put on his shirt, buckled on his guns, and went to the window. The street was quiet. The hotel was quiet. The creak came again, followed by shuffling sounds. Luis edged to the side of the door. He had meant to camp out tonight and give his tracker the opportunity to catch up, but now that he was here there was no need to delay the inevitable.

His door opened slowly and a rifle barrel appeared. In one quick motion, Luis kicked the door open, gripped the barrel, and jerked hard. With a startled oath the person holding the weapon was pulled over the threshold. The rifle fell to the floor as the man clawed for his six-gun. He didn't stand a chance. Luis fired and heard the bullet plop as it struck the man. Quickly he twisted through the doorway and into the hall, where he flattened himself against the wall. He didn't expect to find an accomplice, but it was best to make sure. A pale light came from the dirty window at the end of the hall. As Luis made his way along the corridor, doors to the other rooms opened to reveal the cautious though strangely unaffected faces of other lodgers. They watched calmly as the tall man with the silver-handled gun scanned the stairs, then, satisfied, turned back toward his room. They could see the man sprawled on his back, his arms and legs flung wide, dead, and they had no intention of tangling with his killer. Luis shoved his gun back into the holster and stepped over the dead man. He picked up his hat and saddlebags and left the hotel.

Wariness tightened his nerves as he stepped out onto the boardwalk, the heels of his boots sounding loud in the morning stillness. He looked both ways along the walk, then moved toward the cantina at the end of the street.

The cantina was empty except for a Mexican woman working over a stove and two customers bent over plates of food. He ordered tortillas and eggs and took a seat at a table with his back to the wall.

"*Gracias, señora,*" he said when the woman set the food in front of him. Her plump face wrinkled into a smile. Only a few polite strangers came into the cantina.

Luis ate hungrily. The woman, keeping an eye on the plate of the handsome stranger, brought him an additional egg wrapped in a hot tortilla and filled the tin cup with strong coffee.

The morning wore on. He sat quietly looking out the door and down the busy street. No one approached him, but he was eyed by everyone who came in, and he suspected his presence was the reason for the smile on the face of the plump señora as she served the customers and collected their pesos. Luis was used to sitting with his back to the wall or looking over his shoulder. That he had fought well in the Battle of Glorieta, not as a member of the Confederate Army but as a volunteer, had earned him a reputation as a fighter. More times than he cared to admit, he was forced to prove his skill by facing some reckless fool hoping to earn a reputation. That wasn't the case, however, with the man he had killed this morning.

Sudden impulse had caused him to ride out of the valley and head for El Paso. His thoughts, of late, had been completely taken up with the small, dark-haired sister of the old man's housekeeper. This protective longing he felt for her was a new feeling, and he needed time to think, to try to understand, to find out if it was just a woman he needed, or this particular woman.

The second night out he met two drifters. They seemed to be friendly enough and he was glad for their company. The first night he realized there was a suspicious intimacy between the two men. He was accustomed to sleeping with one eye open and was surprised to see one of the men creep over to the bedroll of the other. He watched long enough to become sick with disgust, then dismissed it as being their affair. The next night he was awakened by a hand caressing his hair. He came awake instantly. The man reached down to touch his face and then his body. Luis pushed him away, but the man persisted. Nauseated, Luis drew back his hand and slapped the man across the face. He sat back and whimpered for a minute or two, then swiftly drew a knife and slashed Luis across the chest. The reflex was instant. Luis pulled his gun and shot him.

The other man sprang to his feet and stared with horror at the dead man, then dropped to his knees and cradled his head in his arms and sobbed. Luis gathered up his gear, saddled his horse, and mounted. The man looked up, his dirty face streaked with tears.

"I'll kill you. I swear I'll kill you!"

He had tried.

The children playing in the dusty street were a ragged but happy lot. Their shrieks of laughter drifted into the cantina, and the fat señora smiled indulgently and shook her head. Childhood memories came flooding back to Luis, forcing him to remember his mother, lovely and gentle Juanita Gazares, and his own tortured beginning.

Summer of 1844 . . .
Evening was drawing in. For one wildly desperate moment Juanita Gazares clung to the hope that the señor wouldn't come. The weird shape of the trees against the evening sky, the endless shadowy folds of the tree-covered hillside, and the soft sound of the clear creek water as it traveled over the stones on its way to the river; it was all too peaceful. Her people now would be drifting along the dusty road toward the quarters, enjoying the pleasure of doing nothing after a hard day's work. Even the half-naked niños were playing in the road or were being carried on strong shoulders. If she allowed the señor the use of her body they would have cornmeal for tortillas and pinto beans to boil in their pots. If she didn't submit to him it was certain they would go hungry. Her uncle believed it and said as much, and her aunt was of the same mind; and so her degradation had come about.

Juanita leaned her dark head back against the tree trunk and closed her eyes briefly. He was later than usual and she thanked the Virgin Mother for it, for it gave her time to recover her senses; time to control the screaming inside her, the revulsion she felt for what he did to her body. She heard a sound and her eyes flew open. It was only a ground squirrel scampering among the rocks.

She closed her eyes again. It was futile to believe the señor would not be angry when he discovered the wee *niño* growing inside her slender body. Had he not sworn not to give life to a "Mex bastard"? He had taken the only precaution known to him to see this didn't occur.

Always he played on her body for as long as possible before allowing his seed to spurt on the ground between her parted thighs. The times when he had been unable to remove his swollen, throbbing member in time, he had forced her to squat in the flowing stream and wash herself. He would know soon about the *niño*, perhaps today, for her waist had thickened and her small breasts were swollen. In a sudden flurry of panic she prayed for the strength to climb the steep cliff and throw herself down onto the rocks below. But she knew that she wouldn't do it, even if she had the strength. It would be a cardinal sin and her soul would burn in everlasting hell if she destroyed herself and the tiny *niño*.

Her eyes caught the sound of a horse's hooves striking the stones that bordered the stream. Any vague hope she had nurtured that he wouldn't come was dashed, and her heart thudded against her ribs. Her eyes, now void of expression, were turned in the direction from which he would come.

Mack Macklin, mounted on a dun gelding, left the ranch buildings and walked his horse past the stone house with only an uninterested glance. Calloway and the milk-pale bitch were sitting on the porch in the hide-covered chairs. His lips curled with scorn. Calloway could have her. A lot of pleasure the skinny slut would give him, he thought, and a caustic smile hovered about his wide-lipped mouth.

He turned the horse toward the stream, urged it to cross, then followed the stream down to where it widened and the grass and bushes grew thick and lush. He felt an excitement in the pit of his stomach and a hot ache in his loins. It was always the same when he was on his way to meet Juanita. He didn't understand it, but when he thought of her his passion flared. The Mexican disgusted him, but her body drew him like a magnet.

He remembered the first time he had seen her and was so aroused that his buckskin breeches became uncomfortable. He had been sitting on his horse watching a family of Mexicans come into the valley to work his irrigation ditches. She was plodding along on a little burro, sitting erect like a queen. He continued to stare at her for a long time, then she turned and looked at him. Her eyes were as black as night and as full of concealment. They rested on his face, then moved away. He felt hot and cursed her under his breath.

"Goddam mestiza wench!"

He couldn't forget her. "A nice little piece of hot baggage like that with no stud bull in the barn!" he told himself wryly. This would take some thinking about.

It had been amazingly easy. A few hints to the uncle, a few extra days of hard work for him, and Juanita waited for him by the spring. What started out as a way to relieve himself developed into uncontrolled lust; he craved her, he hungered for her. At times he was so angry with himself for wanting her that his temper flared and he struck her. She accepted his blows without a whimper. She never cringed or cowered, nor did she allow him access to her personal thoughts. This also infuriated him. During these angry periods he would force his thoughts to dwell on another time and another place, and he would use her roughly and ruthlessly, then push her from him and ride away.

He rode into the clearing, and his pulse quickened. There she stood waiting for him, as she had done every evening for the past few months. Her thick, coal-black, waist-length hair hung free, just as he liked it. She wore the thin off-shoulder blouse and the full skirt, also just as he liked. He dismounted and threw the reins over a bush and came toward her.

"Did you think I wasn't coming?" he asked in the voice he

used only in speaking to her. It wasn't the harsh voice he used when talking to the Mexicans, but it wasn't soft. It was restrained, as though trying to be gentle.

"No, señor, I knew you would come." Her voice had music in it, he thought, and any man who ever heard it would not forget it.

He lifted her full skirt and ran his rough hands up and over her soft hips. He had never felt anything as smooth as her flesh. Taking his hands from beneath her skirt, he pushed aside the soft blouse and wrapping his arms about her legs just under her hips, then lifted her up until his face nuzzled against her soft breast. He rubbed his face with its stubble against the smooth flesh, neither knowing nor caring about the pain he inflicted. He took one of the nipples between his lips and pulled on it hungrily, then grinned up at her.

"You're some little hot pepper, Juanita," he said huskily. Then, holding her with one arm, he pushed one of her legs up into his crotch and held it there between his thighs.

"Feel it," he said. "I'm fair about to bust."

He set her on her feet, and she walked away from him and lay down. His hands, clumsy with haste, worked with his buttons, then pushed his buckskins down beneath his hips. He fell on her and without any preliminaries entered her and commenced to thrust furiously. She felt his jerking spasms, and he uttered soft animal sounds as his fluid gushed into her. He stayed inside her, embedded in her, his breath coming in gasps. Finally he lifted his head and whispered hoarsely in her ear.

"Jesus Christ, I done it again! Lay still—can't be no worse if I do it some more."

Juanita clenched her teeth and turned her face away so she wouldn't smell his breath. *Madre de Dios,* she prayed, help me. Help me!

Mack worked feverishly to satisfy himself. Placing his hands beneath her hips, he held her to him while thrusting into her slender body. When it was over he rose immediately and pulled up his clothing and strapped on his gunbelt. Juanita covered herself with her full skirt, then got up and walked to the stream. Mack reached out and tugged at her hair.

"Leave your clothes, Juanita." His eyes narrowed, and his face had a set expression.

With her back to him she unfastened her skirt and let it drop, she then pulled the blouse over her head and walked quickly into the water until it was mid-thigh. She squatted down and let the cool water flow around her, washing the thick semen from her thighs. He knows! He knows, she thought, and her heart beat wildly. *Dulce Madre de Dios*, let him kill me quickly. Please let it be quickly!

"Stand up and turn around!" It was the harshest tone he had ever used with her.

She got up slowly and turned to face him. She stood tall as she could, her head held proudly, her eyes looking straight into his. He inspected her, thoroughly and silently, for a while, then his breath came out in a long, low whistle.

"I thought as much! I thought there was something different about them titties. You goddam whorin' bitch, you're gonna whelp! I told you I ain't gonna have no goddam Mex bastard. Come out of that water!" he roared.

Juanita walked slowly out of the water. The air hitting her wet skin felt coolly pleasant, though she was almost numb with fear. She stood on the bank, the long hair her only covering. Finally one of his big hands came out and he slapped her. She went down on her knees, but got back to her feet and raised her head.

"It ain't mine! You been with them!" The words burst from his lips and he took a handful of her hair and pulled her up close to him. "Ain't you? You been with them goddam Mexicans!" he gritted. "You bitch! You *hijo de puta!*"

"No, señor." Her voice was so calm and steady that he was convinced she was lying.

Still holding her by the hair with one hand, he drew back the other and struck her with the back of it on one side of the face and with the palm on the other. Blood spurted from her nose and covered his hand; still he continued to hit her. Finally he pushed her from him, and she fell heavily on the stones by the stream.

"You're lying, you goddam whorin' bitch. If I ever see your face again, I'll kill you. Do you hear? I'll kill you!"

He got on his horse and kicked it cruelly, and he was gone.

Juanita sat up slowly, her black eyes filled with pain and terror. Her face was bruised all over and blood oozed from a hundred scratches on her knees, thighs and hips. Slowly and painfully she crawled to the edge of the water and bathed her face. Tears she had not allowed to come in his presence now rolled down her cheeks, mingling with the blood on her face. She washed her body while the tears washed a small part of the misery from her soul. She dressed herself, then got painfully down on her knees.

"Our Father," she prayed silently, "and our Holy Mother, who has compassion for sinners and those of us who are weak. Why have you put upon me, thy lowly one, the burden of the wee *niño? Madre mía*, why? Help me to face my uncle. Help me to face my friends, who will know I gave my body outside thy holy sanction. Oh, *Madrecita mía*, have pity. Have pity upon me!"

Juanita rose and draped her rebozo over her head and wrapped it about her face and shoulders. With resignation she went up the dirt track to her uncle's home.

Luis rode out of El Paso, headed north, then veered across the badlands toward the mountains. He was anxious to get home to Macklin Valley and to the lovely sad-eyed young woman who constantly occupied his thoughts.

CHAPTER NINE

JACY WAITED AT the door of their room while Johanna felt her way to the table and lit the candle.

"We should make a curtain for the window, Jacy."

"Luis has been gone two weeks, Johanna," Jacy said, unable to hear anything but her own thoughts. "I thought he liked me!"

A pang of fear struck Johanna's heart as she went to the wall peg and hung up her shawl. She had suspected Jacy's depression had something to do with Luis's absence. Her statement confirmed it.

"Don't jump to conclusions, Jacy. Walking you back to the house didn't mean he was courting you."

Jacy moved to sit on the edge of the bed. "It was the way he looked at me that made me think he liked me. And he talked about himself, as if he wanted me to know about him." Sudden tears filled her eyes. "Do you think . . . he could want *me?*" She stumbled over the words as if afraid to utter them.

"Jacy!" Johanna was almost angry. "You've got a lot to offer a man. Why . . . you're educated! Papa taught you book learning and Mama taught you how to make a home for a man. You're sweet and you're pretty, but most of all you have integrity. I won't listen to you doubting yourself. We are just as good as we think we are, and don't you forget it."

Engrossed in her own thoughts, Jacy continued as if she hadn't heard. "He told me about his horses and the hacienda. He wants to breed a lighter, faster strain of horses. And Johanna, he never mentioned . . . what happened to me." There was kind of a desperate note in her voice when she added, "You do like him, don't you?"

She's already fallen in love with him, Johanna thought. She's afraid I'll disapprove. Oh, God! What kind of man would pay obvious court to her, then go away without a word? Is he only playing with her? Of the two brothers he seemed the kinder, the more understanding, and he had seen Jacy when she was mute. He wouldn't, he couldn't be so cruel to her, to give her hope merely to amuse himself. One more emotional upheaval in her life and she would be pushed beyond her endurance.

"Of course I like him," she said, perhaps too emphatically.

"No, you don't," Jacy replied stubbornly and looked as if she was about to cry. "Is it because he's a . . . bastard?"

"Jacy! You know better than that. Papa didn't bring us up to be snobs. He always said the best people can be found in the most unusual places. Luis can't be blamed for something his father did."

"I wish he would come back," Jacy said wistfully.

"Ben expects him back soon. But Jacy, please don't read too much into the attention he gave you. Let's just wait and see what happens. This is a good place for us right now. We'll stay until after the baby comes, then we'll decide what to do."

Resigned, Jacy got up and took off her dress.

After a while the moon, on its journey across the night sky, shone through the small window. Jacy lay awake, but motionless, lest she disturb Johanna. Stable, practical Johanna could always be depended upon to put things in their proper light. It had been wildly impulsive of her to think Luis was interested in her. The evening they spent together seemed now no more than a dream. He was a handsome man and gentle, but more than that he was open, direct. He had watched her all evening and hadn't looked away when their eyes met. Luis wasn't one of those men who wanted to talk about himself. She could see him now, tilting his head toward her and listening intently to what she was saying as though her words were important to him. I was almost sure he liked me, she thought despairingly as tears rolled down her face.

Morning came suddenly. Jacy awakened to see daylight streaming into the room. She could hear activity down by the corrals and went to the window to peer out. Men were driving in a herd of horses, and her eyes searched for Luis's slim figure. Disappointed not to see him, she forced herself away from the window and dressed.

Jacy always dreaded leaving the room. The house had an eerie, cold feeling about it that disturbed her. It was as though a heavy curtain of invisible mist cloaked her and moved with her about the house. She longed to leave it, to run down the path to Rosita, but she couldn't leave Johanna to cope with the backbreaking work of getting the house in order by herself.

The sound of angry voices came from the front of the house as Jacy started down the stairs. Johanna came out of the kitchen.

"Jacy, go out to the back porch. I'll bring your breakfast."

Johanna followed her to the bench at the end of the porch, her lips pressed tightly together. Jacy knew the sign. Johanna was angry.

"That old man is the most impossible creature I have ever met," she sputtered angrily. "He is rude, demanding, and . . . unreasonable. He's been cursing and shouting all morning. It just isn't in him to ask for anything. He demands, and regardless of what you're doing he expects you to jump when he shouts."

"This place makes me uneasy, Johanna. I can't explain it, but I know this house has had unhappy times. It's so dark and gloomy and sad. Sometimes I'm afraid."

"There's nothing here to be afraid of, Jacy. Nothing at all." Johanna's manner softened. "Red invited you to come and stay with him and Rosita. Would you rather go there?"

"No. I'll not leave you here alone."

Johanna hugged her. "I'd miss you, love." In a lighter tone she said, "There's something you can do for me. I promised Bucko I'd teach him to play my guitar, but I can't seem to find the time."

"I can do that. I haven't taught for such a long time, and I need something to take my mind off . . . other things."

Jacy drank her coffee while sitting on the bench. Burr came around the end of the house, his steps a bit hesitant when he saw her sitting there. In one of his big hands he was holding Johanna's straw hat, its pink satin rose crushed and dirty.

"This thing was blowing down by the corral and scaring hell out of the horses," he said gruffly, holding up the hat for her inspection.

Jacy giggled. She liked the big, gruff man even if Johanna didn't. He and Luis had real affection for each other. It was obvious when you saw them together.

Burr pushed the hat down on a peg that stuck out high over the door. The peg came through the crown of the hat and the faded pink rose tilted down at an odd angle. He stepped back and cocked his head to one side, his eyes mischievous.

"I'll bet you it looks better there than it did on her head," he said confidentially.

Jacy's eyes danced. "She'll be fit to be tied when she sees it there!"

He lifted sun-bleached eyebrows and looked up at the hat again. "Yup," he agreed, "she will."

Johanna came through the door carrying a cup of coffee and a plate with several buttered biscuits. Burr stepped aside to let her pass, nodded to Jacy behind her back, and disappeared inside the house.

Johanna handed the plate to Jacy. "I can see that he has an entirely different effect on you than he has on me," she said curtly.

"I like him," Jacy said, biting into a biscuit.

"Well, I don't!"

Johanna went back into the house, and Jacy's puzzled eyes followed her.

From where she sat on the porch Jacy could distinguish the harsh angry words coming from the front of the house. It seemed the argument was about the windmill and where Burr was building it. After a while he came out of the house, showing no signs at all that he had been involved in a violent argument. He glanced up at the hat above the door.

"Guess she didn't see it."

Jacy's eyes twinkled up at him. "She liked that hat."

"She can still wear it, if she likes it so much." He started to walk away.

"Señor," Jacy called, "if you see Bucko will you tell him to come to see me here? I'm going to teach him to play chords on the guitar."

Burr paused and turned back. "Whose idea is this?"

"Johanna's," Jacy said hesitantly, "but she is too busy, and she didn't want to disappoint him, so she asked me to do it. Don't you approve, señor?"

He squatted on his heels beside her. "Yes, I approve. I approve of anything that will help Bucko. Ben and I have been teaching him to read, and he can write some. I don't suppose you'd take on that chore?"

"Johanna is a much better teacher than I am, but I'd like to try."

"Perhaps I'd better ask Luis first," he said, teasing, his smile turning to soft, deep laughter when the crimson tide flooded her face.

"Señor!" she gasped.

Burr got to his feet. "Call me Burr. And Jacy, speak English to Bucko."

"Sí . . . Burr," she said as he began to walk away.

Briefly he turned, smiled again, and said, "I'll round up your pupil and send him up."

Bucko was an interested if not talented pupil. Jacy showed him how to pluck the strings, but his small fingers pinched and pulled. She soon discovered Bucko liked the sound that came from the strings. Any sound, regardless of tone. Finally she gave up and allowed him to play with the instrument. Physically, Bucko was the size of a seven-year-old child, and although he was unusually bright he was emotionally immature.

"Bucko," Jacy said suddenly.

The wide blue eyes that looked up at her were so like Burr's that she was startled. Now was the time to ask him about his mother, but the words wouldn't come. The thin little body, that horrible clubfoot, and the sad look on his face touched her heart. She decided she couldn't do it; couldn't awaken memories better forgotten.

"Would you like me to teach you to write?"

"*Sí.* Burr teach me to read," he said in his halting English.

"You can read? Well, in that case we can play a game where you read a little and write a little. We can start tomorrow. Would you like that?"

"*Sí, señorita!*"

It was the mention of the game that caught his interest. It was a trick her papa had used. How wise he was, Jacy mused. I wonder how he would have handled old Mr. Macklin?

They sat on a big flat rock, the sun warm on their backs, and Jacy showed Bucko how to lace his fingers together to form a church, to lift his thumbs to form a steeple, and to fold back his hands to show the people.

She was explaining the purpose of the steeple when she saw Luis. She looked up and he was there.

"*Buenos días,* Jaceta. *Buenos días,* Bucko."

Jacy's heart beat a mad tattoo against her ribs. She got to her feet, but she was standing alarmingly close to the head-tossing stallion, so she sat down again.

"Good morning," she said in a light breathless voice.

Luis moved the restless horse back a few steps and looked down at her, almost as if he knew the reason for her momentary confusion. She expected him to say something, but instead he simply sat there as still as his restless mount would allow and looked at her steadily.

He wanted to tell her that he had thought of her every minute during the long ride back from El Paso, that she was nothing like any woman he had ever known. She was warm and gentle and lovely. He couldn't say any of those things to her yet. He would have to move cautiously, treat her like a skittish mare that had been mistreated.

Jacy found words at last. "You've been away."

His eyes gleamed, and suddenly he smiled. Jacy was unable to tear her eyes from his face.

"*Sí*," he said softly.

Bucko carefully laid down the guitar. "*Puedo cabalgar Rey?*"

"Speak English, Bucko," Luis said gently.

"Ride on King, Luis?"

"*Sí*," Luis said and looked at Jacy. "I came for your teacher, hombre. I want to take her to my hacienda. But first you may have a ride on King."

He spoke a soft word to the horse, who ceased his restless movements and stood perfectly still. Bucko didn't hesitate but limped forward, and Luis bent from the saddle to grasp him and lift him up to sit in front of him. The usually quiet boy was laughing, almost shrieking, in his excitement. He grabbed great handfuls of King's mane, and Luis withdrew his supporting arms and allowed him to hang on by himself. The big horse, as though aware of his responsibility, walked slowly and evenly along the trail. In a moment they were out of sight and Jacy allowed herself to relax.

Luis's words echoed in her mind. He had come for her! She fervently wished her wildly throbbing heart would behave so she could think. After a quick glance down at her wrinkled skirt, she looked away, not wanting to see her protruding abdomen. She smoothed her hair and reached around to feel if her hair ribbon was in place. She closed her eyes tightly, and a quiver ran through her slender body. Even with her eyes tightly closed she could still picture his face, which was like a sculpture she had seen in one of her papa's books. She could hear him talking to Bucko before they came into view.

"I have not forgotten, vaquero, about the pony, but you must grow some so you will not fall as you go racing like the wind." He stopped the horse beside Jacy and dismounted, but allowed Bucko to sit alone atop the big horse. He looked so small on the powerful animal that Jacy became anxious. Luis saw her concern and reassured her that the horse would not run wild. His voice was deep and quiet, speaking his own fluid tongue. Jacy felt her heart race wildly again.

He lifted Bucko from the saddle and set him on his feet.

"Hombre," he said seriously. "I have an important job for you. I need a man I can trust to take a message."

"I can do it, Luis. I can take message. I am a man to . . . to . . ." He stumbled over the English word.

"To trust," Luis finished for him. "I know that, Bucko."

Bucko nodded his head gravely.

"Go and tell Señorita Jaceta's sister that she is going with me to my hacienda, that she will be safe with me and I will return with her before the sun goes down. Do you understand?"

"Sí, Luis," he said proudly and turned to leave.

"Bucko," Jacy called, "will you take the guitar to Johanna?"

Luis picked up the instrument and handed it to the boy. "Careful, vaquero, and do not fall on it," he cautioned.

When they were alone, Jacy found herself tongue-tied. Her mind went blank and she could think of nothing to say. Her eyes sought his face and found him staring at her. Her face colored and she looked away.

"I like to look at you, Jaceta."

The softness in his voice brought her eyes back to him briefly before a swift new wave of color filled her cheeks.

"Do you mind, *querida,* for me to look at you?"

Her heart gave a lurch. He couldn't have said what she thought he said: *querida*—beloved. She looked anyplace but at him and shook her head.

"You will come with me?"

"*Sí*," she finally managed to say, then, "Is it far?"

"Not for King. Will you ride with me?"

She shook her head. "Can't we walk?"

"It is too far for you, Jaceta." He looked down at her, a speculative glint in his eyes. "Do you not ride?"

"Not . . . very well," she said, not wanting to admit to a fear of riding since she had returned to consciousness on the back of her abductor's horse.

"I will teach you," he said gently.

She shook her head. "Oh, no, not . . . now," she said hastily. "I can't . . . I can't. Not like . . . this."

He swung easily into the saddle, and Jacy felt a flash of fear that he would ride away.

"Do not be foolish, my little Jaceta," he scolded gently. "Later I will teach you. Now you will ride with me on King. Come," he invited softly. The horse tossed his head, blew and pawed the earth. Luis spoke sternly and he stood motionless again. His hand was extended and he smiled, a challenging smile that was reflected in the bright gleam of his eyes. "I would not let you be hurt, *mi pichón*," he assured her. "You need have no fears up here in front of me. Give me your hand. Come, I will not let you fall. I promise you."

Jacy's mind responded to the persuasion of his quiet, seductive voice, and obediently she reached out and put her hand in his. She let out a small cry of surprise as she was pulled swiftly up in front of him. A strong arm encircled her while the horse shifted restlessly in protest at the extra weight. Another sharp word from Luis and the horse stood still again. Then he adjusted her position so she was sitting across his lap.

The nearness of him was something she hadn't anticipated. She could feel every nerve in her body respond to his lean hardness. She pressed close to his broad chest, and his powerful arms not only held her safely in front of him, but controlled their lively mount as well.

"You like it up here, *pequeña?*" His voice was deep and soft, close to her ear. She nodded a little uncertainly, for she had to cope not only with the unaccustomed sensation of being on horseback again but with the effect his tender words and the physical intimacy of the way in which he held her.

"I don't know," she stammered, then looked down to see how far she was from the ground and immediately shut her eyes tightly.

He laughed at her timidity. *"Tímida,"* he teased as he put his heels to the flanks of their mount. The animal responded willingly, and before she realized it she wrapped her arms about Luis and buried her face against the warm, sensual comfort of his chest.

"Querida mía!" His voice vibrated with tender emotion. "I will let nothing hurt you."

Jacy dared not look up. Her face was pressed against his shirt, and she kept it there, not wanting him to see the tears that had filled her eyes when he had called her his beloved. She was aware of the smooth easy stride of the horse as he carried them easily across the open ground, and of the wind that stirred her hair. Finally she raised her head, and her eyes, bright with excitement, met his. He laughed, a soft thrilling sound that came musically to her ears. Her fear was gone now in the sheer exhilaration of the ride. She tightened her arms around Luis, hugging him, her face nestled against his strong body.

There was a comfortable silence between them as they shared their feelings each for the other. And for Jacy there was something more, a kind of miracle in this moment. As she reached up and laid her palm against his face, he turned his lips into it, his eyes holding hers.

"Does it make you happy to be with me, Jaceta?" he asked, his voice barely above a whisper.

"*Sí,* Luis," she murmured. "Very happy."

He continued to gaze down at her and ran his fingers lightly over her mouth and down her cheek; his hand cupped the back of her head and he held her firmly against him.

"Mi bella querida!" he said, then repeated it in English: "My beautiful beloved."

Jacy squeezed her eyes tightly shut as tears welled. Her heart swelled and she struggled to keep the sobs from breaking loose.

"Querida mía, you weep," he said anxiously.

Her eyes still closed, she shook her head. Luís lifted her chin, then wiped the tears from her cheeks with his finger tips.

"Why?" he asked hoarsely. "Why weep, my little Jaceta?"

Unable to answer and knowing she owed him an explanation, she took his hand and placed it on her abdomen. Jacy was vaguely aware the horse had stopped. Luis lifted her chin again, gently but firmly, and she could feel his warm breath on her wet cheeks.

"Look at me," he urged.

Jacy opened her eyes, but tears blinded her. She tried to wipe her wet cheeks, but he moved her hand away and held it in his.

"Weep, if you must, my Jaceta, for you have been truly sinned against."

She turned her wet face into his shirt, and her voice when it came reflected the misery in her soul.

"I . . . I'm . . . soiled!"

His arms tightened about her, the flood of emotion she had kept in check for so long broke. She cried as though her heart would break. Luis held her tightly against him and stroked her hair until she was quiet.

"Dulce, dulce," he crooned against her hair. "You are immaculate!" His hand tilted her head against his arm and his eyes devoured her face. "Believe me, *amante*, you are as unblemished as the babe unborn."

Heavy lashes lifted from tormented eyes only inches from his, and the look she saw in them brought a great swell of joy within her. She was too confused to hide her secret feelings, and her eyes glowed with love.

"You could . . . love me?" The thought now came out before she realized what she had said.

"Can and do, *amada!*" His eyes laughed at her, and she cherished a joy she had never expected would be hers. If at this moment he had asked for it, she would have given him her soul. "I knew when I first saw you that you were for me," he said lovingly.

Jacy took a deep breath. What had to be asked must be asked now. "The . . . babe?" she asked haltingly.

Luis lowered his head, and his warm lips caressed her forehead. "The *niño* will have *madre* and *padre*." He moved his hand down and gently stroked the mound that was the unborn babe. "I came to life much as this one, *amante*, but this one shall have a papa to guide it, to teach it and to love it."

Jacy felt the tears coming to her eyes again and looked away.

She was grateful, filled with love for the man who had accepted her as she was, yet unable to let him see how much his words meant to her . . . unable to let him see how much emotion she felt.

A feeling of faintness seemed to sweep over her, and she wanted to cling to him, to give him love, and, still, to shield and protect him. She clasped her arms about his waist, and her lips gently brushed his chest.

With his lips in her hair, he said softly, "Rest now, *querida*. We will be home soon."

Luis's house was built from the earth, like the houses Mexicans had been building for hundreds of years. Massive beams held the structure together and protruded from the sun-browned adobe walls. A stone patio extended across the front of the house, which was set on a rise with its back to a steep cliff. Water flowed through a crevice in the dark, red rock into the irrigation system that Luis had developed. He'd channeled the water so that it flowed past the house and formed a pool inside his fenced pasture. Near the house, where the stream curved, willows offered shade from the hot afternoon sun. The horses were corralled down a slight incline and to the right of the house. There was a bunkhouse and the unmistakable outlines of a smokehouse, and inside the network of pole corrals were outbuildings of various sizes. An enormous number of horses milled about in a stockadelike structure, and several vaqueros were working with them.

Luis turned the horse toward the willow trees and pulled him to a stop. He placed his hands under Jacy's arm and gently lowered her to the ground. He dismounted quickly, for she was hanging on to the saddle, her numbed legs having refused to support her.

"Are you all right?" he asked anxiously.

Jacy's heart was so filled with joy that her laugh came bubbling up from deep within her. "I'm so all right, Luis, I'm afraid I'm going to die!" The happiness she felt was reflected in her face, and he bent to kiss her. His kiss was gentle, reverent, as though she was something infinitely precious. Her arms closed tightly around him as their lips touched and clung. Her shyness was gone, and her uninhibited desire to show him her love set him trembling.

"Luis," she breathed huskily.

"Your smile fills me with the warmth of the sun, *querida*." The soft caressing words were whispered in her ear, and he led her to a seat under the tree. "I'll take King to the corral."

Watching him go, Jacy's heart swelled with pride and love. She'd found her heaven at last. This peaceful hacienda, away from the ghost in the stone ranch house, was heaven. It was home. It was Luis.

CHAPTER TEN

WILLARD RISEWICK SAT atop the slick Arabian stallion and looked down at the distant stone house. The two men he had hired to guide him to the valley sat their horses a few yards away and talked in low tones. Willard neither knew nor cared what they talked about; their opinions were no concern of his. He was a man who had fought with the Union forces during the war and won a battlefield commission and two decorations. A shrewd man, he took no unnecessary risks, and he possessed as well an amazing knowledge of both military tactics and men. He had returned from the war with the reputation of being the best rifle and pistol shot in the command and an excellent swordsman as well. An ambitious but honorable man, he had undertaken this mission with all the zeal he would devote to a major campaign.

He had followed the train of freight wagons from Fort Davis, in sight of the wagons, close enough to be seen but not close enough for contact. Risewick knew he and his men were being watched by the Macklin people. He had planned it that way. He took out his glass to get a better look. A drab place, he mused, remembering the rich and colorful plantations he had seen in the South during the war. He studied the country below, and, as he suspected, saw the rider hightailing it to the ranch to report on their progress. Boldness was the only policy now, so swinging his mount around, he went over the rim and started down into the valley. The other men followed.

They went down through the forest. The trail was difficult to follow, but there simply appeared no other way to go except straight ahead. The trees around them were mostly Rocky Mountain nut pine and mesquite. Occasionally, when they rode out onto some knoll, over the tops of the trees they could see the peaks and ridges of the timberline, and above that the white streaks of snow on bare rock.

Risewick set an easy pace. He calculated how far they had to go and how long it would be before they reached their destination. He took a cigar from an inside pocket and bit off the end. It was then he saw the Indians. They came like ghosts out of the shadowed trees, riding single-file. There were four of them, and for an instant each Indian was starkly outlined against the sky as he reached the edge of the wash. In that brief moment a hoof struck stone and alert dark eyes swung in their direction.

The Indians wheeled and raced back into the shadows even as Willard's rifle leaped in his hands. He spurred his horse and raced for cover behind a boulder. He jumped from the saddle as his men joined him.

"Hold your fire," he ordered sharply. Cautiously he studied the terrain before him. He gave it a quick glance, then scanned it methodically with his glass. He studied each rock, tree, and shrub with particular care, making allowances for the light and length of the shadows.

He waited, his rifle ready, but there was no further movement or sound.

There was a stir beside him and one of his men moved up.

"Dirty, stinkin' Apaches," he whispered. "I ort to a knowed it was too easy. What we gonna do?"

"Nothing," Willard said calmly. "Nothing, until we see what they're going to do."

Squatting in the shade of the boulder, Willard took stock of their situation. There was a chance the Apaches might retreat down the valley, but there was a greater chance they would make a fight of it. It was doubtful that he and his men would last ten minutes against an all-out attack. He had never fought Indians, and he was beginning to doubt the sticking quality of his companions. The very silence worried him, because the Apaches knew exactly where they were. Even now they could be circling to attack from the rear.

He shifted his rifle in his hands and started to speak, then broke off sharply as a faint whisper of a sound reached him. It was a sound he knew from his military days.

"Stay down, señores," a heavily accented voice said. "When you see Apaches, be afraid; and when you see no Apaches, be twice as afraid."

"Who the hell are you?" one of the men growled.

"Luis Gazares. These men have come to trade with me, but they will take your hair if they can."

"Goddam," one of the men swore. "Ain't nothin' worser than a goddam Indian-lovin' Mex."

"That's enough!" Risewick said sharply. Then, "Señor Gazares, we would appreciate your advice."

"*Sí*. I will circle around and talk with them. Wait until we move out, then make for the stone ranch. That was your intent, was it not, señor?"

"It was. And *gracias*. Will I see you to thank you properly?"

"It is likely. *Adiós*."

Risewick settled down to wait. He was a patient man. He had learned to be patient through experience. He sat still now, but alert, waiting to pick up any movement. When the sound came, he motioned to the men, mounted his horse, and rode out toward the ranch.

Willard received a cool greeting from the old man sitting on the porch of the ranch house. He offered his hand. Mack took it and grunted a greeting.

"It's a pleasure to meet you, Mr. Macklin. I've heard many stories about you. I think you are fast becoming a legend in the Southwest. My respect for you grows, sir, now that I see with my own eyes what you have accomplished here."

117

"Wal," Mack said when Risewick was seated, "you got somethin' on your mind, or you wouldn'ta followed the wagons, or stayed on in my valley."

Risewick hadn't expected to have to jump right into his reason for being here. The old man was blunt and direct, he'd have to give him that. Several thoughts whirled through his mind, ways to postpone the proposal, but he discarded all in favor of being equally direct. He opened his coat, took out his cigar case, then offered it to Mack, who refused.

"Girl!"

The bellow was so sudden that it startled Risewick. He turned his head and found Mack's eyes fastened on the door leading into the house. It opened, and Risewick got quickly to his feet. A tall, slim woman came confidently through the door. She walked and moved as if she were in the drawing room of a town house. Seeing her in this setting was even more of a shock than hearing the old man bellow.

"Bring whiskey."

The woman came toward Risewick. "I'm Johanna Doan, Mr. Macklin's housekeeper." She smiled and held out her hand.

"Willard Risewick, ma'am." He took her hand and found her handclasp strong.

She went inside without even looking at the old man, and Risewick sat down.

"You're fortunate to have such a lovely housekeeper, Mr. Macklin."

"The girl ain't no concern of yours. What brought you to my valley?" The old man's voice was tinged with impatience.

"I'm here to make you an offer for your holdings," Risewick said briskly.

"They ain't for sale. Leastways, I ain't decided yet." Mack's eyes narrowed and he stared at Risewick, but Risewick had the distinct impression the old man's mind was busy with other thoughts.

"It is my understanding, Mr. Macklin, that you have no family. I thought rather than have your holdings go into litigation until an

118

heir can be found, you would perhaps prefer to sell now and know that your life's work will be continued.''

Mack was silent, and Risewick wasn't sure the old man was listening to him.

"It's understandable, sir," he continued, "that you would wish to occupy the ranch house. Our offer need not include the house and buildings.''

The old man still said nothing, and it was impossible to tell from his expression what he was thinking. The only visible emotion was in the big hands that gripped the arms of the chair. Risewick decided to say no more until Macklin spoke.

Johanna came out with a whiskey bottle and two glasses. Willard got to his feet again.

"Ain't no need for you to go a jumping up and down like a jack-in-the-box. The girl's my hired help and before that a saloon gal.'' Mack growled out the words, then gazed sharply at Johanna, expecting to see in her face the offense he'd meant her to feel. Johanna smiled pleasantly.

"Mr. Macklin is quite right, Mr. Risewick. Please keep your seat.'' She sat the tray down and turned to go. "He's right also about my former employment. I was a singer in the Wild Horse Saloon in Fort Davis. A very lively place. If you happen to be going back through there you might wish to spend an evening. If you do, give my regards to Mr. Basswood, the bartender.''

A glimmer of admiration flicked in Risewick's eyes, and he returned her smile. There was definitely animosity between Macklin and the girl. The old man had wanted to embarrass her, but she had turned the tables on him.

"What do you want with my valley?'' Mack poured himself a liberal drink and shoved the bottle toward his guest.

Aware of his rudeness, but ignoring it, Risewick uncorked the bottle and poured himself a generous amount of the whiskey.

"The company I represent will bring in settlers to farm the land.''

Mack looked at him with disbelief, then his hard face crumbled as he broke into a loud laugh. The sound came harshly from his throat, but it was genuine, and had Risewick but known, it had been the first time in years that the old man had laughed. It stopped as fast as it started.

"Plow up my land?" he asked.

"That's the plan."

Mack leaned back in his chair. The half-smile on his face reminded Risewick of a lynx he had once seen exhibited in a cage. Folding his hands over his ample stomach, Mack looked down over the valley, then back to Risewick.

"I'll give it thought. Might be we'll deal."

There was a moment of silence while each absorbed the statement and its ramifications. Risewick's mind pieced together all the scraps of information he had gathered about the man, worried that his opinion of Mack would be shaped by the uneasy feeling of dislike Mack engendered in him. He never allowed himself to be influenced by personal feelings when taking a man's measure. He knew he must be dispassionate; he must examine the situation coolly before handing in his report.

"May I impose upon your hospitality for myself and my men? A few days is all we will need. I'm sure we can come to an agreement, one way or the other."

Mack had already retreated into himself but lifted his hand casually. "Tell the girl to find you a place to sleep."

Control almost shattered, Johanna went back into the house after delivering the whiskey to the porch. The smile she had pasted on her face vanished the moment she stepped into the hall. For the first time in her life she felt hatred, hatred for that cruel, vindictive old man. She was feeling the effects of the effort it had taken to appear calm in the face of the deliberate affront. Glad beyond measure that Jacy was away from the house, she pushed herself away from the wall and walked slowly back to the kitchen.

Jacy was spending a lot of time at the hacienda with Luis. It wasn't proper for a young lady to go alone to a man's house. Such behavior could ruin a young woman's reputation. Oh, God, what was she thinking? Jacy's reputation! She had no doubt she would be safe with Luis, and she was away from the house where the old man couldn't hurt her.

As supper hour approached Johanna grew apprehensive. Surely old Mack would come to the table if they had a guest. Would he make a scene with Burr? Would Burr control his temper? Ben had taken charge of Risewick as soon as he left the porch. They had been closeted in his room for hours, and Johanna fervently hoped he had told Willard Risewick about the bitterness between the old man and his sons. She wished she could set the food on the table and escape to her room, but she knew it wasn't possible. It's their affair, she told herself. Why should it matter to her if they went at each other hook and tong? It had nothing to do with her. Yet her fear of a scene remained as she prepared the meal.

Burr and Bucko were the first to come to the kitchen for the evening meal. She smiled at Bucko and nodded coolly to Burr. He ignored her until he had built up the fire in the hearth. When it was crackling pleasantly he sat down in the fireside chair and rolled a cigarette. Johanna had her back to him when he spoke.

"Luis and Jacy are down at Red's. When they come back, Luis wishes to speak to you."

His calm voice plucked at her already taut nerves, and only a momentary burst of common sense prevented her from snapping at him.

"He knows where to find me," she said calmly, though she wondered why Luis needed to talk to her.

"He wants to talk to you . . . outside the house." Burr spoke slowly and firmly.

"I'll be here," she said without letting him see her concern.

"You're the most mule-headed woman I've ever met!"

"And you're the most asinine man I've ever met!" The words were out before she could stop them. Never would she have believed that a brief encounter with a man could cause the turbulence she felt the moment she came in contact with Burr. Her pride had taken a beating at the hands of Macklin and his son, and she wasn't sure she was equipped to handle so much as one more abusive word. She put her hand to her head, her lips forming another retort, but before it came out, Ben and Willard Risewick came into the room.

"Evening, Johanna," Ben said evenly, his eyes flickering at Burr, then back to her flushed cheeks.

"Ma'am," Risewick greeted her formally.

Ben had a soothing effect on her, and she moved to dish out the food.

Burr got to his feet and extended his hand. "Burr Macklin."

The two men shook hands, and Burr urged Bucko forward, his hand on the boy's back. "Bucko Macklin," he said, and Johanna could swear she heard pride in his voice.

"Hello, young man." Risewick's eyes went from the boy to Burr, and the question about the boy's parentage, though on his lips, was not given voice. Still, the thought was apparent in his face and not lost on Burr.

The last of the dishes were on the table when Johanna heard the thump of Mack's walking sticks in the hall outside. She glanced at the table to be sure there was a place setting for him, then brought the hot biscuits from the oven.

"Evening, Mack," Ben said, as if he regularly came to the kitchen to eat.

Old Mack ignored the greeting and eased himself down in the chair at the end of the table, the one Burr had occupied. He had shaved for the occasion and put on a clean shirt.

Burr motioned for Risewick to be seated on the old man's right, and Ben sat across the table from him. Burr took the chair at the other end of the table, and Bucko sat beside him. The place left for Johanna was on Burr's right.

She wasn't at all sure she would be able to eat. Her stomach was unusually tense and her hands felt as though they were weighted. She looked often at Ben's calm face. He chatted easily with the guest while Old Mack sat at the head of the table watching and listening, his eyes unusually bright, his face flushed. Burr was civil when spoken too, and Johanna began to hope the meal would go on without conflict. Bucko picked at the food on his plate. He looked frightened. Perhaps he sensed the tension between Burr and Mack, knowing that whenever the two were together in the past tempers had flared.

Burr leaned over and spoke to him. Bucko nodded, and Burr handed him a pie from the plate on the table. The child got up as quickly as his lame foot would allow and without looking at anyone limped out of the room.

"Humpt!" Old Mack said scornfully.

"What brings you to the valley, Mr. Risewick?" Burr asked, and Johanna knew instinctively that the explosion would come.

"I've come to make an offer for this land," Risewick said smoothly. "I represent a company that will bring settlers out here." Risewick glanced at the old man. "I'm happy to say Mr. Macklin is considering my offer."

Johanna's eyes were unwilling to go to Burr's face, afraid of what she would see there. She did look at Old Mack, and what she saw on his face brought a chill down her spine. His steely eyes were on Burr, and his mouth had a demonic twist.

Burr showed no surprise at the announcement. "Risewick," he said, firmly but calmly, "Mack may accept your offer and take your money, but this valley belongs to me and my brother, Luis. He has no right to sell it to you."

"Mr. Calloway told me about you and your brother. I've no wish to become involved in a family conflict, sir." Risewick looked straight at the big blond man as he spoke. "But if we buy the land we will bring a large enough force with us to hold what is ours."

Burr's voice had an edge to it. "I suggest you find other land and save yourself some trouble. I'll not only fight you with men and weapons, I'll go to the courts."

"You just try!" Old Mack leaned back in the chair, his sunken eyes cold and a strange sort of smile on his face. "What good would it do you?" he jeered. "You ain't my legitimate heir. I never married your ma, didn't need to. Saved her from a scalpin' and I plowed her. 'Twas no more than my right, and more'n she deserved, common as she was." He looked pleased with himself, his eyes going from the fury on Burr's face to the horror on Johanna's and the shock on Willard Risewick's. He failed to see

Ben's face; it was chalk-white and the hand that gripped his eating knife trembled violently.

Burr's mug came down on the table with a bang. He got to his feet, his eyes dark with anger, his voice more deadly because he spoke softly.

"I don't know how I've kept from killing you, but I swear to God, if you mention my mother again, I'll kill you if I hang for it!"

"You ain't got the guts, you bastard. And if you did you still wouldn't get my valley. I done told you the only way you're gonna get it. Grandsons! Legitimate grandsons! If I could bed this gal here, I'd do it myself, but if you don't, by God, I'll sell to Risewick and hope he brings back an army that'll blow you the hell out of here."

There was silence. A bitter aching silence.

Johanna seethed with anger, not because of the reference the old man made to her, but because of the fiendish delight he was taking in humiliating his son. Burr had been rude to her, and had even made her angry enough to strike him, yet now she felt an unexplainable protectiveness toward him. She'd never felt the kind of anger that she'd felt for Burr, and now for his father because of his callousness toward his son.

"I'll talk with you later, Risewick." Burr left the table, his meal still on his plate.

Old Mack grunted. "Damn cur thinks 'cause he's running things around here the land belongs to him. Wal, I'll show the bastard. Ain't no bastard ever gonna get this valley!" He reached down for the walking sticks and heaved himself up and out of the chair. "Goddam the son of a bitch," he cursed. "The bastards took off my foot while I was laid up with a fever, but I'll see both of them in hell before they get my land."

He was still cursing as he went out the door and down the hall. There was a long, uncomfortable silence, and when Ben spoke it seemed as though his voice came through a long tunnel.

"Please accept our apologies, Mr. Risewick. Mack takes some getting used to. I'll pour fresh coffee and we can enjoy these delicious pies Johanna made for us."

"I'll get the coffee, Ben." Johanna jumped to her feet, glad to have something to do for a few minutes so she could gather her wits.

"I'm mystified," Risewick said, "about Mr. Macklin's foot. Don't think I'm prying, but I can't help but wonder about the statement he made."

Ben took his time about answering. "It's true," he said sadly. "Burr and Luis came back to the valley after the war and found Mack in the line shack where Luis and his mother lived until she died. He was raving with fever. They removed his crushed foot and saved his life."

"A strange man," Risewick said thoughtfully. "A very strange man."

"He is that," Ben agreed.

"Do you know where he came from originally, Mr. Calloway?"

Ben smiled before he answered. "I know nothing about his background, Mr. Risewick, though Mack gave me the impression he was from back East someplace. He never mentioned a family or any specific town. It was as if he'd never had a life before he came here."

Johanna rose from the table and collected the empty plates. Her mind was flooded with impressions. The depraved old man enjoyed hurting Burr and Ben. She was sure of that. It must be that he was demented, that his mind had gone bad. No man in his right mind could do these terrible things to his own child. He was evil! The word kept pounding in her head. Evil . . . evil . . . evil. Evil was all through this house; she could see it now, and feel it. The house was filled with brooding memories; memories of young Anna. And of a small boy, lonely after his mother's death, neglected and hated by his natural father. Jacy had felt the presence of the ghost in the house, and it was her reason for not wanting to stay here. Wearily Johanna raised her hands to her head, and her fingers massaged her aching temples. She was glad Jacy had not witnessed the scene that had taken place at the table tonight.

CHAPTER ELEVEN

WITH SO MUCH on her mind, Johanna was almost finished with the cleanup before she remembered that Luis wanted to talk with her. She was disgusted with herself. This house, with all its conflicts, had so absorbed and muddled her mind that she had confused her priorities. Jacy was her first concern. Jacy, and her welfare. She was convinced now that she and her sister should not remain here. The episode this evening had brought that realization clearly into focus.

Looking up from the pan of sudsy water, she saw Burr lounging in the doorway, and she made a decision.

"Mr. Macklin," she said firmly, "I wish to leave. Mr. Redford offered to escort me and Jacy back to town if the . . . position was not suitable." She looked straight into his eyes, determination clearly visible. "It is not suitable and I want to leave as soon as possible."

He stared at her, then moved his eyes slowly over her body.

"You know," he said, "you'd make a right pert woman if you'd get some flesh over your bones. We like our women strong and healthy out here."

"Like your horses," she retorted sharply.

"Exactly." He sauntered into the room and sat down.

She turned her back to him and continued to work. "I'm not

interested in your opinion of me. All I want from you is your cooperation in arranging our departure.''

"It's not likely you and your sister will be leaving . . . Johanna. I'm sure you'll realize that shortly.''

She breathed deeply in an attempt to calm her nerves. She could feel his eyes on her but refused to turn around.

"If you don't wish to help us, I'll speak to Luis.''

Suddenly he was out of the chair and there behind her. She couldn't speak, couldn't raise her head, in fact, couldn't do anything. If he touched her she knew she would fly into a thousand pieces.

"Johanna," he said, "I've decided to wed you. If Mack sells the land there'll be a fight, and I saw enough blood during the war to last a lifetime. I'm no prize, being a bastard, but you're no prize either, being the headstrong shrew that you are. We should fit well together.''

Johanna barely managed to check the urge to hit him with the pan she was washing. Her next impulse was to weep. She chose to do neither, and he turned around and went out the door. Shaking her head, she took her hands from the water and held the sides of her head as if to squeeze him and what he had said from her mind. On no account must she let him suspect that he held such a powerful sway over her emotions. She also knew that marrying him was out of the question. They would go to El Paso, and if she couldn't get a teaching job she would take another singing job in a saloon.

Damn, damn, damn him! she thought. I wish we had never come to this godforsaken place!

Burr was waiting for her on the back porch. A tremor shook her when she saw him, and she blinked nervously. His hand came out of the semidarkness and his fingers closed around her wrist, where she allowed it to stay rather than uncurtain the wild panic she felt at his touch. When she neither spoke nor moved, he slid his hand up her arm and gripped it with warm fingers. His touch evoked turmoil within her. She longed to jump away from him, but her limbs were stiff and unresponsive.

"Don't do anything to spoil my brother's happiness."

In the stillness that enclosed them the statement moved sluggishly through her mind even as she battled the violent storm that pounded inside her, threatening to accelerate beyond control. She had to do something; she tried to pull free of him, and with all the coolness she could command said, "Don't . . . don't touch me!"

Instead of loosening his grip he moved forward to imprison her other arm and pull her against him. Like an avenging monster, he loomed over her, so close she could feel his heart beat. Almost panic-stricken, she managed to control herself sufficiently to meet his eyes and with deliberate sweetness she said, "Release me, please. Luis and Jacy are waiting for me, and I suspect Isabella is waiting for you."

After a tense second, his rigid frame relaxed and the anger her words had provoked gave way to laughter.

"You certainly are a shrew, Johanna, but then I never did like a tame horse." He moved his face closer to hers. "Do you expect me to be flattered because you're jealous of little Isabella?"

"If you don't mind," she said, carefully blending a touch of sarcasm with her words to give them credibility, "Luis and Jacy are waiting for me."

"Us." He emphasized the words. "Luis and Jacy are waiting for us."

The trail he took inclined upward toward the cliff and the spring. Johanna caught her bottom lip in an agitated nip as she stumbled along beside him, his hand so firm on her arm that it seemed almost part of her. The evening was warm and alive with the soft music of cicadas and crickets. The moon, dim behind a wayward cloud, shed a pale light on the hard-packed earth. To her right a bluff of sheer rock rose darkly into the night; to her left and ahead, screening the spring, was a tangle of willow and juniper. The cloud passed, and in the now bright moonlight she could see Jacy and Luis so close that their shadows fused.

The intimacy of the image made Johanna's heart plunge, and Burr's words came back to stab at her, their implication sending a quiver through her body. A thin spear of moonlight slanting through the trees beamed on her sister's glowing face. Even while Johanna watched, Jacy tilted her face upward as Luis whispered to her. She turned away.

"Johanna, Johanna!" Jacy would have run to her, but Luis kept a firm hold on her hand and pulled her back against him.

"Hush, hush," he scolded gently. "The telling shall come from me."

"Jaceta," Burr said using the Spanish name with a teasing note in his voice. "I've brought your waspish sister to you."

"I haven't seen you all day, Jacy." Johanna finally found her voice and with it a new desire to be free of the hand clamped to her arm. She tried to move away without being obvious, but the grip tightened, and to her annoyance he drew her closer to him.

"Jaceta has been with me, señorita," Luis said. "We have been spending much time together and know we wish to spend all our lifetime with each other. You are the family of my beloved, and I ask your blessing."

Johanna caught her breath sharply. Her mouth suddenly went dry. Luis's words had wiped away all her plans for leaving the valley. Her head whirled giddily. Event piled upon event until she was surrounded by a welter of confusing possibilities. For the first time in her life she stammered.

"Ja—Jacy?" she said hoarsely. "Are you . . . sure? You don't really know him."

"I know I love him, Johanna," Jacy said confidently. "I loved him even before we reached the valley, and I think loving him saved my sanity, Jo. Please say it's all right!"

"I want what's best for you, Jacy," Johanna said, a tremor in her voice. "It isn't for me to say what's right for you, but think carefully before you decide to spend the rest of your life here."

"I've decided, Johanna. Be happy for me," Jacy pleaded.

"Of course I'm happy for you, darling." Burr had released Johanna's arm at some time during the conversation, though she couldn't have said when. Free to move now, Johanna put her arms around Jacy, and their tears mingled as they held each other close.

"Señorita," Luis said when they parted, "I know of your

concern for your sister. She and the tiny *niño* will be my concern. I will care for the babe as if it were my own. Indeed, it is already dear to me, for without it Jaceta might never have come to the valley.''

"Thank you for telling me that, Luis. I've cared for Jacy for so long it's going to be difficult to let go and allow someone else to do it.'' Johanna spoke evenly, trying to keep the anguish she felt from her voice.

"Our home will be yours,'' Luis said sincerely and drew Jacy back into his embrace as if reluctant to have her away from him.

"That's kind of you, Luis, but I have my work with Mr. Macklin, and I'll not leave the valley until my six months are complete. After that, I have a number of teaching jobs I can choose among. You and Jacy are not to worry about my future.''

"Johanna,'' Jacy cried, "you'll not leave?''

"Hell no, she won't leave!'' Burr's voice boomed in the quiet night. He reached out and took her two arms in his big hands and almost hauled her off her feet as he pulled her back against his broad chest. "She's gonna marry me, Jaceta!''

"Johanna?''

The question in Jacy's voice coupled with Burr's presumptuous announcement inflamed Johanna. "I'm not marrying Burr Macklin, Jacy. I haven't completely lost my mind!''

To add to her irritation, Burr laughed, then intimately nudged her face.

"Yes, she will,'' he said confidently. "I've made up my mind to it. She's willful, balky, pig-headed, but she'll do nicely once I get her broke in.''

Johanna allowed his words to wash over her, knowing full well he was trying to provoke her. Only when the soft sound of Jacy's giggle reached her ears did she feel hurt. Instead of being indignant with him for his insulting words, her sister had laughed with him . . . and at her. Tears sprang to her eyes and she lowered her lids. She didn't want anyone to see how upset she was. Luis's sharp eyes saw the trembling lips, though, and he turned the attention to himself and Jacy.

"Jaceta and I wish to marry as soon as possible, Burr. I am

thinking of sending Paco and Carlos over the mountain to bring the padre. I would take Jaceta to him, but the trip might do her harm at this time."

"Send them," Burr said. "Good idea to bring the padre here—he'll have much to do. You can wed Jaceta and I'll wed her waspy sister—if I have to hog-tie her to do it." He laughed.

"I hesitate to speak of this, señorita," Luis said to Johanna, "but I must. In the week or more it will take for the padre to come I wish my *novia* stay with Red and Rosita. I have spoken with them and asked them to do me the honor of caring for her until I can take her to my hacienda."

Johanna felt the vacant feeling in the pit of her stomach expand. She was losing everything so fast! She looked from Jacy to Luis and finally said with a slight quiver in her voice, "She can stay with me at night and go to Rosita during the day."

"If Jaceta wishes," Luis said and ran his hand over the top of her head and down over her hair, which hung loose to her waist.

He really loves her, Johanna thought. He looks at her as though she was the most precious thing in the world. I'm glad for her, but oh, God, how I'll miss her!

She shook herself mentally. Jacy's future was secure. This is what she had hoped for, what she had prayed for. It had just come so suddenly, and so soon, that she wasn't prepared for it.

"Thank you," she whispered, and she didn't know why she said it.

"We'll go on back," Burr said, and pulled her around. "You coming, Luis, or are you-all gonna spark for a while?"

"I'll bring Jaceta shortly, señorita," Luis called softly.

Walking beside Burr, Johanna was hardly aware of him. The grip on her arm had loosened, and now his hand merely guided her. Her thoughts were full of the events of the last half hour and their implications. She was trapped. Trapped in this valley as surely as if her foot were caught in a snare. She couldn't leave Jacy now. Perhaps later, but not now. Meanwhile she had old Mack and this younger addition of him to contend with.

She stopped, shivering. Burr watched her but said nothing. She started to move on and his hand stopped her.

"Luis loves her," he said impatiently. "When Luis loves, it's with all his heart, and it's the same when he hates!" He took her by the shoulders and shook her, not roughly, but not gently. "What more do you want for her? Luis is the best man I know." His voice was sincere and had almost the same tone he used when talking to Bucko.

Thinking of Bucko, a wave of anger stormed through her. She twisted out of his grasp and faced him like a spitting cat.

"You've got a nerve! Telling Jacy I'm going to marry you. Do you think I'd sentence myself to a life of hell with you? I'd rather die!"

"You'd rather die than wed a bastard! Go on, say it. Say what you mean." He yanked her up close to him and glared down into her face. "You'd rather die? How about your sister? Do you want that on your conscience? You wed me or that old devil will sell to Risewick and this valley will flow with blood. Do you understand?"

Involuntarily she recoiled from his cold, reasoned planning. Wildly, she said, "Conscience! You Macklins don't know the meaning of the word! What about Bucko? Do you have Bucko on your conscience? How many more children in this valley have blue eyes? And you think I'd marry you? I want more out of life than to be a brood mare to satisfy a cruel, demanding, selfish . . ." She couldn't bring herself to say the words that came to her lips.

Burr's hands slid up and around her soft throat, and for a brief second his strong fingers squeezed. His eyes were hooded as he peered down into her face.

She swallowed dryly, feeling the frantic clamor of her heart even as some devil prodded her to say recklessly, "And Isabella! What do you plan to do with her? Cast her out . . . after she produces another bastard?" She took a ragged breath. "You're the lowest kind of a man . . . the kind I despise . . . the kind I . . ." His fingers tightened and she choked back her words.

"So that's what you think, eh?" For a long moment he looked down into the fragile white face. One slender hand came up and tried to pull his hands away from her throat. Realizing the futility of the gesture, she let it drop to her side. She stood quietly, her head tilted up, his big hands supporting it. "Don't think," he said cruelly, "that your opinion of me matters in the least. At this moment, all I'm concerned with is what I want!"

Abruptly his arms were around her and she felt another rush of panic as they tightened their hold, until she was crushed against him so hard she could feel every tense muscle in his hard body throbbing. His mouth was hard and angry, and she made only a small murmur before his lips cut off both breath and sound. Moon and sky were blotted out by his dark, angry face as he swooped upon her trembling mouth and besieged it with all the fire and passion he had inherited from his lusty forebears. His kisses were a brand of shame she suffered numbly, too shocked to protest. Later, she tried to turn her mouth away, but he would not be thwarted and held her prisoner by threading his lean fingers through the pale-gold hair that tumbled down her back. He kissed her deeply, again and again. Violently and ruthlessly he plundered her mouth until she sagged against him, unable to stand.

His hand slipped down to her buttocks, holding her there, his hard muscular thighs forcing intimate pressure upon her. Frantically she resisted, a sob in her throat, but her movement only inflamed him more, and his lips pressed her mouth open, crushing her into helpless surrender. She tried desperately to stop herself from making obvious the inevitability of her own response, but when his hand found its way inside her shirt and began to caress her warm, rounded body, she gave a long moan of surrender, her own hands helplessly seeking the warmth of his chest beneath her fingertips.

Burr was shaking. She could feel the tremor in the body pressed to hers. His mouth moved down her throat, the heat of the kiss searing her skin.

"Burr," she whispered shakily, her voice betraying her emotion. She knew suddenly that if he took her, hating him as she did, she could not resist him.

Delicately, but with deep passion, she brushed her lips along his cheek, quivering with the temptation to find his mouth with her own. Burr raised his head, and she looked up at him. Her heart stood still and crimson colored her face as she saw the mocking blue eyes observing her and realized he knew the feelings that flooded her. For a moment she was unable to move or speak, trembling with humiliation and pain.

Johanna could hear him chuckling as he walked away. She gritted her teeth in rage and darted into the darkened house.

Jacy watched Johanna and Burr move out of the shadows and down the path toward the house, their blond heads shining in the moonlight. The joy she had felt before Johanna came was dimmed just a little. The look on her sister's face belied the words that she spoke. Johanna was worried about her staying in the valley with a man she had known but a short time. She turned in Luis's arms and pressed her cheek against his chest. Time didn't mean anything when you were sure of love. Papa had always said there was someone special for everyone and only the very fortunate were able to find each other. It had been that way with her parents, and it was that way with her and Luis. If only Johanna . . .

"Luis," she whispered in a small, husky voice. "It would be wonderful if Johanna married Burr."

Luis took his time in replying, first kissing her eyes, the tip of her nose, the corner of her mouth.

"Only if they are in love, *querida,*" he said against her ear. "I would wish my brother to know what I know, that he is loved by the woman he loves."

"Do you think he could love my sister? Oh, Luis, he looks so much like that old man! Could it be that he's . . . like him in other ways?"

"Hush, *querida,* hush! Do not speak of it, do not think it. My brother must live with the fact that he was made in the old man's image, but only on the outside. On the inside he is a man much like me."

"He said he'd made up his mind to marry her. It was as if she had no say in the matter. Johanna won't marry him unless she loves him. He's so harsh, Luis. Not gentle, like you. Oh, I'm glad it's me you want!" She lifted her arms and wound them closely about his neck, and he bent his head to kiss her throat and the softness of her neck and shoulders.

"Do not worry, *mi bella novia*," he told her. "What is meant to be will be. I waited for you, looked for you, my heart cried for you, and . . . you came. It will be the same with your sister and my brother, but perhaps not with each other. Come, you are tired."

"Not yet, Luis!" She closed her eyes and slid her arms around him as she had done when they rode the black stallion together. "Luis, Luis!" She buried her face against him, then looked up at him, bright-eyed and feeling so light-headed she wondered if this could really be happening. Her wide eyes scanned the beloved face and cherished every feature. She laughed, tipping her head back until her dark hair fell past her hips.

"I love you, love you, and I'm so happy!" she said in a breathless, husky voice. "And to think I was wanting to die. Oh, Luis, don't let me wake up and find it all a dream!"

He put his fingers over her lips. "If this is a dream, *amante*, I wish that neither of us wake up."

Long after Jacy was asleep, Johanna lay awake, unable to control the turmoil that filled her head. Her plans to leave the valley had vanished the moment she saw her sister's glowing face. That was what Burr had meant when he said she would know shortly that it was impossible for them to leave.

She put her fingers to her bruised lips. What was the matter with her? It had been so pleasant leaning against him, having his arms hold her close, his mustache soft against her face, his lips hard, yet caressing. She had liked it, even knowing the sort of man he was!

Papa, Papa, she cried silently. You always said the Lord never puts more burdens on people than they are able to bear. I know what I've got to do. I've got to swallow my pride and marry him, and I had almost rather die than do it.

CHAPTER TWELVE

JOHANNA WAS AWAKE and dressed the next morning just as dawn streaked the sky. She hurried down the steps, crossed the hall, and plunged into the empty, chilled kitchen. She stoked up the cookstove and put the coffee pot on to boil, then kindled a small fire in the hearth and huddled down in front of it. The small twigs caught and blazed, then spread to the larger pieces of wood. She sat back and watched the shadows play on the walls. She was listless and had no desire to stir from where she sat. Closing her eyes, she gave herself up to the dreamless state between repose and wakefulness.

One second she was asleep and the next she was awake. She opened her eyes and saw the tall blond man standing beside the fireplace. His intense eyes fastened on her face. In the flickering firelight and in her confused state she saw old Mack, and she cowered in the chair. As her vision cleared she saw Burr, his head tilted toward her, his brows drawn together in a frown.

"I've no intentions of attacking you," he said, sneering.

Johanna looked up at him, dark circles emphasizing the blueness of her eyes.

"I thought you were . . . old Mack," she said, her voice barely above a whisper.

The look he gave her was one of suppressed frustration. "No!" he said sharply. "Anything but that!"

He was gone almost before the words left his lips. Johanna continued to sit by the fire, and it was as if she had only dreamed he was there.

Ben came in for breakfast and told Johanna that Burr had instructed Mooney to escort Jacy and Bucko down to Red's and that he or Luis would return with them.

"The Apaches are coming into the valley for their seasonal camp. It's nothing to be alarmed about, Johanna," Ben told her reassuringly. "Luis and Burr are especially watchful at this time. They keep a wagonload of supplies ready, and the Indians know they're here. It's an arrangement that's worked very well for the past few years."

"Ben," Johanna said nervously, "Jacy is going to marry Luis."

Ben puffed on his pipe for a few minutes. "Burr told me this morning." He paused, and Johanna didn't say anything, so he said, "This bothers you, doesn't it, Johanna?"

She looked steadily at him. "No. I'm happy for her. Luis loves her and she loves him. It's just . . . just that she will be making her home here and the situation is so unsettled." She walked to the end of the room and with her back to him said, "I guess you may as well know, Ben, I've decided to marry Burr." She said it bitterly, as though the words were nasty and she wished to hurry them out of her mouth. Then she turned to gauge his reaction.

Ben looked at his pipe before she could see the hurt look in his eyes.

"Don't do it, Johanna. Don't wed him if you don't wish to."

"I don't wish to, Ben, but I'm going to do it."

The conversation ended abruptly when Risewick came in. He talked with Ben while Johanna prepared breakfast.

It was the middle of the afternoon when Johanna went silently down the stone porch and passed the window of Ben's room.

"Don't do this, Burr," she heard him say.

"Don't interfere, Ben."

"You're going about this the wrong way. Given time . . ."

"There's no time," Burr said curtly.

Johanna quickened her steps, not wanting to listen to the conversation, yet wanting to. She wasn't sure what they were talking about, but guessed their marriage was the subject. She was sure Ben had great influence over Burr, but she was also sure that if Burr made up his mind to do something it would be hard to change it.

She had an hour or so before she would start the evening meal, so she walked down toward the cook shack, then past it toward the corrals. There wasn't anyone about as she strolled along the path, kicking up the dust with her feet. It was like Indian summer, warm, with a smoke haze across the valley. The rise and fall of a quail's cry came from the willows on the creek below. Time seemed to stand still in the answering silence, suspended forever in the warm, bright afternoon.

She didn't hear the horseman coming up behind her. She looked up and he was there. Nodding, she expected him to pass on, but he slowed his horse and kept in step with her. He was one of the men who had ridden in with Willard Risewick. He grinned down at her, his teeth showing yellow when he parted his lips.

"Yer meetin' someone, girlie, or just awaitin' fer someone ta come along?"

Johanna didn't answer, but walked a little faster, sure that he would ride on.

"Ah, come on. I know what ya are. Little Mex gal tol' me. High-class whore, air ya? Well, now, ain't my money good as any? I'll treat ya right. No rough stuff. 'Twill be jist like ya like it."

His words shocked her, and she glanced up at him, a look he interpreted to be flirtatious. He moved the horse closer and reached out a hand. Johanna jumped back, frightened now, and looked wildly about, then turned quickly and started back toward the house, walking as fast as she could. The man wheeled his horse and came up beside her.

"You get away from me!" Panic made her voice shrill.

"That little old building over there'll do jist fine. 'Twon't take long, as horney as I be."

With his horse he started crowding her. She tried to break and run, but he used the horse as though he were dogging a steer, laughing at her attempt to get away. He was between her and the path to the house, edging her closer and closer to the small stone building. Johanna ran back and forth and struggled to keep from screaming. Trapped between the building and this lust-driven beast, she whirled and bolted behind the horse. Then she saw someone running down the path.

Burr's long legs ate up the distance, and the man, enjoying his game, didn't realize he was there until Burr grabbed the horse's bridle and jerked it to a halt. The startled hatchet-faced cowboy looked down into the angry face with surprise.

"Get off that horse, you son of a bitch. I'm going to kick you to death!" The savagery of his tone reached the man, who was clearly scared out of his wits. He got off the horse, slowly, on the other side, and started backing away. Burr walked after him.

"She's only a whore, mister, and I didn't think—"

Burr's huge fist sprang up and hit him squarely on the mouth. He was knocked flat on his back, his arms and legs sprawling in the dust. Shaking his head, he rolled over onto his knees and got to his feet, spitting teeth and blood. He started to say something more, and Burr hit him again, lifting him off the ground, driving his broken nose back into his face. Blood spurted.

"Go to the house, Johanna!" Burr commanded, and she went, not looking back.

Her legs were so weak they could hardly carry her. Badly shaken from the experience, she went straight to her room. Wetting a cloth, she bathed her flushed cheeks. A whore! That's what they thought of her. No . . . a "Mex girl," he'd said. Isabella had told him! But why? Why would Isabella say such a thing? But of course—Isabella was jealous, afraid she was going to take Burr away from her. The spiteful cat!

Johanna was mad. She took off the drab work dress, washed herself, then dressed again in a white blouse with a puckered drawstring at the neck. The soft gray skirt fitted perfectly, and she buttoned it tightly around her slim waist. She felt better. She was dressed as though going to her classes again. The clothes draped neatly about her body and, controlling her movements, also clothed her emotions. She twisted her hair in a firm chignon, allowing only two tiny curls to escape and hover in front of her ears. Her lips were soft, her face smooth, and her heart determined. She left the room to find Mack Macklin and tell him her decision.

Willard Risewick spent the day helping to erect the windmill. He became so interested in the enterprise that he picked up a hammer and worked along with the men. When Burr had to leave to supervise another crew, Risewick took charge of the operation. Luis translated his instructions to the Mexicans. It was enjoyable work, and Risewick got to know and admire Luis, who seemed to hold no animosity toward him for trying to buy the valley. When time allowed they talked horses and made plans for Risewick to visit the hacienda.

Later in the afternoon Risewick went back to his room and spent several hours writing the report he would take back to Rafael Macklin, Old Mack's half brother. The people he met in Macklin Valley would be a complete surprise to his employer, as they had been to him, a man who in his line of work met many people under odder than normal circumstances. The five people in his thoughts all had forceful personalities, each in a different way.

Risewick's most pleasant surprise had come in meeting Ben Calloway. The man's stature might be small, but he was the strongest of them. A man of means whose family headed a shipbuilding empire, he could have left the valley anytime he wished. But he had set his mind on a course and had not deviated. Risewick chuckled. Ben Calloway would have his revenge. By using his wits he would win against the big-muscled Macklin.

He was deep in thought when Burr came unannounced into the room. Risewick knew immediately that the man was boiling.

"I just beat hell out of one of your men," he announced. "You might want to go down and take a look at him. He's in no shape to ride or I'd have forked him on a horse and run him out of here."

Risewick got up slowly, a puzzled frown on his face. "What did he do?"

"He bothered Johanna, that's what he did!" The words seemed to make him all the more angry. "I should have killed the son of a bitch!"

"Bothered . . . Miss Johanna?" Risewick's shock was genuine. "I'm sorry, Macklin. I'm very sorry. I'd have thrashed him myself. I may still do it." He picked up the notebook and put it in his inside pocket. "I'll go down and see about him."

"You do that," Burr said, "and while you're at it, tell him if he so much as shows his face outside that bunkhouse before you're ready to leave this valley, I'll gut him."

Burr stomped out of the room and went to the kitchen. He paused in the doorway and looked into the room. There was no one there, so he went in and poured water in the granite washbasin to soak his bleeding knuckles. He emptied the bloody water in the big tub that had been set at the end of the washstand to receive the waste water and refilled the basin. He washed his face and dried it on the neatly folded towel that hung nearby. He could not remember there ever being a folded towel near the washstand. He looked about the room; it was spotlessly clean. The table was set and a clean cloth covered the dishes and necessaries that were placed in the center of the table. The stove was clean and the coffee pot set on the back of it. The lamp chimney glistened and the copper teakettle shone. Candles were placed conveniently on the mantel, and a small rug, dug up from heaven only knew where, was in front of the chair Ben usually sat in.

A poignant longing struck Burr. He'd never missed these homey things because he hadn't realized they even existed.

"Goddam," he said softly. "Goddam."

He left the room, his boot heels ringing on the stone floor. He was out the door and onto the porch before he saw Johanna sitting in one of the bulky chairs talking to Mack.

"The girl's come around," Mack said. "She'll marry you."

Burr looked from one to the other. Old Mack sat gloating. Johanna was calm and distant, her face composed, every hair on her beautiful head in place, and her skirt folded demurely over her ankles. Her calm reserve and cool appraisal sparked a dash of resentment in him. His pride was hurt too that she had chosen to tell the old man her decision before talking to him.

"Well, now, isn't that nice," he said flatly. "Maybe I've changed my mind."

He stayed long enough to see the color come up and flood Johanna's face. He grinned a satisfied grin before he turned and walked away.

"Come back here," Old Mack shouted. "Come back here, you bastard!"

Burr's steps never faltered, and he disappeared around the corner of the house.

"He'll wed you, never fear. He'll wed you, if he knows what's good for him." The old man glared at the place where Burr had disappeared and muttered, "Stubborn son of a bitch, always a-buckin', always a-buckin'. Must be my blood in him. That lily-livered thing that whelped him didn't have no guts atall."

"I've said I would marry him and I will," Johanna said firmly, "but I don't want to hear any more about the past or anyone in it. Is that understood?"

Old Mack looked at her and frowned. "You know, missy, it's a good thing for you that I ain't fast on my feet no more or I'da boxed your ears more times than you got toes."

Johanna leaned forward and looked him straight in the eye. "You'd have boxed them only once, Mr. Macklin. The next time you tried I'd have laid your skull open with anything I could get my hands on."

The old man sat back, and a sly smile played at the corners of his mouth. "If I'da met a woman like you thirty years ago, missy, we'da stocked this valley with sons that would a set the West afire.''

Johanna got to her feet. "I can think of nothing," she said icily, "that would be more revolting than having to submit to you and give birth to your child." With that she turned and left him.

"You'll do, missy," he called after her. "You'll do."

Johanna went through the house and out onto the back porch. She stood by the support post and shivered at the thought of being touched by that lecherous old man. "Please, God," she prayed, "let me get accustomed to these people and this house."

Her troubled eyes turned back toward the darkened doorway, and she barely choked off a profanity that sprang to her lips. High above the door, on a peg, hung her straw hat, the faded pink rose swaying gently in the afternoon breeze. Flushing with humiliation and pent-up fury, she saw the hat as a symbol of her treatment since she had come to the valley. She had no doubt as to who was responsible for putting it there and decided she would leave it as a reminder and a guard against any soft feelings she might have about the man she had promised to marry.

A door opened at the far end of the house, and she whirled, thinking the recipient of her contempt was coming to enjoy her discomfort. It was Isabella . . . Isabella coming out of Burr's room, her arms loaded with his clothing.

"Isabella . . . come back here!" Burr's voice reached Johanna where she stood at the end of the porch. "You've not got nothing better to do than be with me, have you, sweet thing?"

The words stabbed Johanna like a knife, and she marveled that she could stand there so calmly while the Mexican girl's eyes flashed a clear message of victory. After Isabella turned back into the room Johanna seemed to sag, then pride came to her rescue. She went to the kitchen to prepare the evening meal.

Burr was first to come to the kitchen that evening. Johanna wasn't aware he was there until she turned and almost collided with him.

"Must you sneak about so quietly?" she said crossly.

"Sneak?" he said. "Can't a man walk into his own kitchen without being accused of sneaking?"

About to retort, Johanna caught the glint in his eyes, and refused to allow him the pleasure of riling her. She clamped her mouth shut.

Burr stood near the table, where he constructed a cigarette, then moved to the cookstove to poke a twig into the flame until it caught fire. All the time he watched her.

His attitude puzzled her. He veered from angry derision to defense of her honor by physical force to curiosity. Now was the time to thank him for coming to her rescue, but she didn't know how to broach the subject. Finally she decided the direct method was best.

"Thank you for what you did for me this afternoon, Mr. Macklin."

He didn't say anything for a long while, and after a time she wished she hadn't bothered to thank him. His very presence was making that shameful weakness creep over her again. She was determined not to give in to it, and she had turned on him, a spitting remark on her lips, when he spoke.

"Don't you think you should call me Burr now that we're going to wed?"

"I haven't given it any thought, Mr. Macklin," she answered.

"I've never met a woman who could make me so angry!" The soft words barely reached her ears. She ignored them, and he continued, "Usually it's safe for you to be out and around the buildings. It puzzles me why Risewick's man did the stupid thing he did."

Johanna looked directly into his face.

"Someone told the man I was that sort of woman."

"Who would do a thing like that?"

"Ask him," she said abruptly.

Burr grinned. "He won't be talking for a while."

In spite of herself Johanna let a fleeting smile pass over her lips.

Ben and Risewick came in, and she cut off her reply.

"I hear congratulations are in order," Risewick said.

144

"Yes," Burr said and took the hand Willard extended. "I'm a lucky man."

Johanna pressed her lips tightly together and looked at him sharply. He was grinning and accepting the good wishes as if . . . as if . . . She bit back a scathing remark and turned back to the stove, but not before she saw the mockery in his eyes.

Willard Risewick was waiting for her on the porch after dinner.

"Ma'am, I asked Ben if I might have a word alone with you. I wish to apologize for what happened this afternoon. If Burr hadn't given the man a good thrashing, I would have done so myself. The only excuse he could give was that he thought his attentions would be welcome. However, he should have known that his information was false. I've seen men hung for doing what he did to you today."

"It was frightening, and I'd rather forget it," Johanna murmured.

"Certainly, ma'am. May I walk with you?"

Johanna saw Burr's light head as they neared the clearing in front of the bunkhouse. He was sitting on a bench beside Luis and Jacy. Next to Jacy, sitting as close as possible, was Bucko. Johanna smiled. Children always loved Jacy; she drew them to her as a pitcher of honey drew flies.

Jacy came to her the moment she saw her, and Risewick moved away to join Ben.

"Johanna!" She was bubbling with excitement. "Burr told us! Now we'll be living here together! I can't believe how things have turned out for us. You are happy, aren't you, Johanna?"

"Jacy, Jacy, calm down. Of course I'm happy, darling. You know me well enough to know I do what I want to do. Now, tell me, how is Rosita? I don't get to see her nearly enough."

"She's all right. I'm just so happy, Jo. I never thought it possible to be this happy. Sometimes I wonder if I'm alive!"

"You're alive, all right," Johanna said, laughing.

Burr came up behind her and put his hand on her shoulder. She turned and glanced up in surprise and started to pull away, but he held her fast.

"*Buenas noches, señorita.*" Luis loomed up out of the darkness to stand beside Jacy.

"Evening, Luis." Johanna forced a smile, but she knew she couldn't maintain the pretense. Her frantic eyes found Bucko, and she whirled around to go to him and brought the heel of her shoe down on Burr's instep. She was pleased to feel the bone beneath the soft leather of his moccasins. She took a few steps . . . then felt a sharp pain. He had pinched her! Pinched her, viciously, on the bottom!

"Don't try that again," he murmured in her ear, "unless you want Jacy to know how we really feel about each other."

"Stay away from me and keep your hands to yourself," she hissed.

With a firm grip on her arm, he maneuvered her around and headed her toward the house. This man, Johanna fumed, is impossible. He's insufferably arrogant.

And yet at the same time there was something about him that fascinated her. She felt an attraction toward him that she resented and rebelled against, and that brought out a childish side of her she hadn't known existed.

They reached the porch, and he pushed her up against the wall, one hand on either side of her. She wanted to look at him but couldn't. The coil of hair on the back of her neck caught in the rough stones. She put her hands on his chest to push him away, but he didn't move. She could feel his breath stirring her hair, and he moved still closer until her breast slightly touched his chest. Still he said nothing. He smelled smoky, tangy, and of freshly washed clothes, which brought Isabella to mind.

"Will you please move back and give me room?" she said crossly.

He didn't move and finally he said, "You're like a little fox I once had. I built a nice little cage for him, thinking I could tame him and have him for a pet. He'd stand in the middle of the cage, too proud to try and jump out because he knew he couldn't make it. But one day I let the barrier down and he was gone; quicker than a flash, he was gone. He was all gold and silver and warm, like you. But smart and sly, and quick . . . like me."

"Just what are you trying to say?"

He drew in a deep breath. She could feel his face against her hair. Her heart flip-flopped, but she stood perfectly still. After a moment he moved away and she felt the tension go out of her.

"Do you want your sister to know why you're marrying me? Ben and Luis know. Luis would rather Jacy didn't know, but it's up to you. I don't give a damn one way or the other."

"You don't care for anyone, do you?" Her anger made her reckless.

"Yes, I care for Ben and for Luis and Bucko."

"And I care for my sister, and not for anything do I want her to know that I've made this sacrifice for her."

Johanna knew immediately she had used the wrong word. He was furious. He grabbed her and pulled her to him, lifting her off the ground so that their faces were level.

"Sacrifice!" he spat at her. "Do you think I want to marry a prissy old-maid schoolmarm, turned saloon singer, turned housekeeper? You want to know what you are? You're a damn bitch, that's what you are, and God only knows why I'm willing to marry you!" He set her on her feet with a jolt.

She rubbed her arms. "Then talk to your father. Make him understand we don't want each other." She put all the scorn she could manage into her voice.

"Don't call him . . . that!" he said hoarsely. "Ben's the only father I've had. I wouldn't ask that old man to piss on me if I was on fire!"

Johanna was shocked by the intensity of his anger. She turned away from him, miserably conscious of his eyes on her.

She moved farther away, and he let her go. "I don't want Jacy to know," she said in a muffled voice.

He agreed, calm now, and came to stand behind her. It was as though the harsh words between them had never been. Burr pulled her back against him and folded his arms about her waist. She stiffened, and he laughed softly.

Johanna suddenly found it pleasant to lean against him. She was confused and too weak to cope with all the anger inside her. And this other thing . . . this awful physical attraction she felt for him. She stood still and allowed him to nuzzle her. His face was smooth and his mustache pleasantly soft. She could feel his heart pounding against her back and the ripple of muscles in the powerful arms that enclosed her.

"That didn't hurt too much, did it?" he said.

Johanna tried to step out of his embrace, but he refused to let her go. She could feel the blush come up to flood her face. He laughed at her effort to stand away from him and nipped the lobe of her ear. Furious, Johanna dug her elbow into his ribs.

"Stop!" She strained away from him, but he loosened his grip just enough for him to turn her around. Before she could catch her breath, his lips met hers. His arms possessed an incredible strength as he bound her still closer to his hard sinewy body until she felt she must be crushed to death. Slowly, lingeringly, he kissed her mouth before releasing it. She felt again the sharp stab of pleasure and a weakness in her limbs. Then he laughed, a low savage laugh.

Passion's blinding, deafening spell faded away, and anger like bile came up in her throat. She slapped him, taking both him and herself by surprise. He loosened his hold and she scrambled back, but his arms snaked out to wrap her again in his strong embrace. Then, to her consternation, she was quickly pulled through the doorway and into his room. Effortlessly he scooped her up into his arms and kicked the door shut. Ignoring her protest, he carried her across the moonlit room until he reached the bed. He was close, suffocatingly close, and his arms imprisoned her like a vise. Anger radiated from his body like heat, and she opened her mouth to scream.

"Scream," he hissed. "Scream and bring your sister running!" He dropped her on the bed and fell on top of her, his body stretched out and pressing down against hers. He held her wrists, his weight pinning her down, his lips only inches from hers as he spoke in a harsh whisper. "I could strangle you. I could twist your little head right off your stupid neck."

The fury of his attack left Johanna speechless and frightened. She knew he was capable of violence, and she could tell he was genuinely angry. Jacy's soft laughter and Luis's voice came from beyond the porch, and she tightened her lips and silently struggled against the powerful body holding her.

"I'm going to teach you something, you little hellion. You're going to learn not to bait the bear. I won't rape you. I won't have to. I'll make it so good for you that you'll want to rape me. You don't believe it? Well, I'll show you. . . ."

She tried to struggle and twisted her head from side to side, but there was no escaping the lips that came smashing down. He stretched her arms over her head and pinned them down with one powerful hand while the other moved down, slowly, to the bodice of her dress. The strong, firm fingers slipped inside and moved caressingly over her soft flesh, halted as they reached the nipple, and slowly and expertly squeezed.

His mouth moved cruelly on hers, and he grasped her lower lip between his teeth as she struggled helplessly. His hand moved downward to shove her skirt upward to her waist. He quickly disposed of her drawers and with one swift movement, exposed her, making her nakedness accessible to his roaming fingers.

Using his knee he forced her legs apart and began to stroke with skilled fingertips between the thighs she fought to keep tightly together. He knew just where to touch, just where to caress so that she felt as though a thousand needles of fire were coursing through her.

My God, my God, Johanna thought. Her brain pounded with a million thoughts, and somewhere inside her a warning was screaming to be heard. Johanna could not listen, would not listen, not now, when spasms of unfamiliar joy obliterated all else. She wanted him, wanted him in a way she had never wanted anything. She could feel her muscles tightening, her insides straining, reaching out, longing for fulfillment of the strange, delicious hunger this man had aroused in her. His caresses continued. She felt hot and cold all at once. She wanted him to stop, and she wanted him to go on. She moaned softly and opened her legs.

She could feel his pulsating hardness against her thigh . . . this was what she wanted. She threw back her head and strained upward against him, but he waited until he had brought her nearly to the brink of madness with his lips and his fingers. When he came into her the combined force of their passions created a fierce, explosive, all-encompassing world. The hardness plunged inward and upward and began to move within her.

"No . . . no, I can't . . ." The feverish sound came from her own lips even as her lips sought his. She felt a sharp twinge of pain and whispered, "Please . . . please . . . please."

A giant wave of white-hot pleasure surged over her, and she sank down into a well of shooting stars, fighting to keep her screams of pleasure silent. It was heaven . . . it was hell . . . it was fire, lightning, the pounding of a thousand drums. It was everything, and surely she would never be the same again. She lay gasping, spent, bewildered by the explosion that had rocked her senses.

Rolling away, Burr sat up and looked down at her. He was smiling. She could see him smiling in the dim light, a smirking, knowing smile, and that brought her back to reality. She yanked her dress down and sat up. Turning her back to him, she adjusted her bodice. She raged inwardly. She had behaved like a wanton, a whore, a trollop, and she was sick with humiliation and disappointment. Scrambling to her feet, she fought to keep back the tears until she could be alone. She felt revulsion, disgust, hatred, for herself and for him.

He stood beside her and caught her arm.

She whirled on him in a fury. "I hate you," she sobbed. "I despise you. You sicken me!"

"I would have sworn you loved me a few minutes ago," he said, chuckling. "You may hate me, but you willingly gave me what I wanted. You wanted it, too. I could've done a better job if I'd had more time, and not been hampered with those clothes you're wearing. Bet you thought you'd be taken the first time by a gentleman on a feather bed. Instead you were taken by a bastard on a straw tick. You know, you're not bad. Given a little time and practice you could get to be as good as Isabella."

Johanna didn't care who saw her. She ran out the door, across the porch, and into the door leading to the stairway. Tears of humiliation almost blinded her, but she made it to her room, undressed in the dark, and crawled into bed.

Burr watched her go, a peculiar feeling moving through him. It was true that he did pride himself on giving pleasure to the woman that pleasured him, but there was something about this one that goaded him, made him tease her, torture her. Why did he go out of his way to make her hate him? Never had he touched lips so sweet, or flesh so soft, and never had he had to endure such agony in his loins as he held back his desires in order to fulfill hers. Why had he been so determined to give her pleasure? Why hadn't he gone ahead and emptied himself into her? He scowled to himself. I wonder what she thinks now? he thought. Ladies are taught to act as though they don't like coupling.

He admitted he didn't know much about ladies, but he knew Johanna was one . . . and she had liked it! Why should he care how she felt? He cared nothing for her. Only fools fall in love. A smart man should use a woman to pleasure him and still keep his heart free. That's what he was going to do with this one.

Burr stretched out on the bed and felt a strange envy when he heard Jacy's soft laugh come out of the darkness. For a moment he speculated on how it would be if Johanna responded to him out of love and not just in response to his passion. How would it be if she whispered words of love in his ear, and there was a softening of her eyes when they looked up into his? He suddenly felt the desire to know love, but seconds later he discarded the idea. Too much had happened to him to allow the delicate nurturing of a real love such as Ben had had for his mother and Luis had for Jacy. Besides, was that what he wanted, tied heart and soul to a woman for the rest of his life? He turned restlessly in his bed and wondered about the strange, twisting feeling that churned inside him.

CHAPTER THIRTEEN

L UIS RODE UP out of the wash and halted the stallion so the sorrel mare he was leading could scramble up the incline. He looked behind him to see if they had left a swirl of dust hanging in the air, then moved on toward the mountains. He trusted his intuition. Gray Cloud and his braves were near, and the Indian would kill him if he could, for the Arabian.

Since his last meeting with Gray Cloud Luis had had an uneasy feeling about the Apache. There was something eating at him. Luis had been trading with Gray Cloud for several years. It had started when the Indian had tried to steal his horse. Instead of killing Gray Cloud, Luis had whipped him and thereby gained his respect. An Indian would deal with a fighting man, whereas he'd kill without compunction a man who wouldn't or couldn't defend himself. It was unfortunate, though, that Burr had been present during the fight. Although he hadn't met Gray Cloud since, as far as Luis knew, the Indian hated Burr for having witnessed his defeat.

Luis had left his ranch at daybreak with the Arabian he had bought from Willard Risewick and the mare that was to be his gift to Jaceta. Of all his horses, he prized these two most. He intended to stable them in the stout barn behind the stone house. The rest of the remuda would be driven up by the vaqueros and put inside the pole corral. There they would be less temptation to the Apaches.

Squinting his eyes under the pulled-down hatbrim, he studied the terrain to make sure that no one was about before moving on. It had been a long time since he had been this cautious. His life suddenly had become precious to him. Perhaps it was because a small, bright-eyed girl had come into his life. When he thought about her it was like breathing clean, fresh air. Sometimes the most important things in a man's life came at the most unexpected time. He hadn't believed himself capable of feeling this all-consuming love for another person. Now no hour of the day passed that he didn't think of her.

He moved out of the shadows and onto a rise that overlooked the stone ranch house. He stopped and studied the terrain again. It was hard to focus his eyes in the bright sunlight, but he took his time, measuring the vastness, the great shoulders of red rock, the splashes of green and the splotches of brown that were the ranch buildings.

He turned his eyes toward the southwest. Something stirred among the tall grasses, then ceased moving. He waited. Again it moved, too cautious to be an animal, he thought. He squatted in the shadow of a rock and waited.

He watched the grass carefully until he was certain there was no more than one person moving about. He had also been able to observe the direction in which the intruder was headed. So that the horses could be protected he tied them under a slab of rock hidden from view by a cluster of scrub oak. He then ducked into a narrow space between the boulders and slowly made his way down the narrow, intricately weaving watercourse. He was reasonably sure the man in the grass was an Indian. Only an Indian could move so as to stir the grass so slightly. He was also sure he and the Indian would reach the spring behind the house at the same time.

Luis stopped and removed his hat, peered down the trail ahead, and wiped the sweat from his brow with the sleeve of his shirt. Before he continued his descent, Luis pulled his shirt out of his pants to cover the glinting silver handles of his pistols. He'd not be fool enough to give the Indian a perfect target in the bright sunlight. He moved on around a jog in the trail. At the spring he saw a flash of color, then heard a woman's angry voice. Burr and Johanna . . . he could see Johanna's blond hair.

Slowly, methodically, Luis searched the area for the Indian. He spotted him, then with infinite care inched to where he could look out onto the place where the man would approach. Maybe the Indian was just curious about the two white people by the spring. He would wait. Luis didn't want to kill him if he didn't have to.

The Apache came into view. It wasn't Gray Cloud but one of the braves who rode with him. Luis wondered if he had been sent to spy. The Indian ran in a crouch until he reached a clump of coarse gray shrubs, then knelt down. Luis moved quickly until he was no more than forty feet behind him. He pulled a long, thin knife from his boot, his eyes never leaving the back of the kneeling warrior. The words Johanna and Burr hurled at each other were the only sounds to be heard, though Luis could not have said what they were saying, so intent was he on the Indian.

Several minutes passed before the Indian moved. Slowly he reached into the quiver on his back and removed an arrow. Luis waited until the arrow was in place and the Indian rose to shoot the deadly missile. He let out his breath easily, stood, and hurled the knife. The body fell forward, but Luis could not tell whether he had killed the man. Cautiously he maneuvered himself toward the form, which now lay face down in the brush. In minutes he stood over the dead body of an Indian he recognized as one of those who had come to trade with Gray Cloud. No doubt, Luis decided, the young warrior wanted to be known for something other than stealing horses. To have killed Sky Eyes would have earned him much praise. Luis pulled his knife from the corpse, wiped it carefully, and returned it to his boot.

When Willard Risewick left the valley, some of the tension was gone from the ranch house. Although old Mack continued to take his meals in the kitchen, there was no longer a reason to bait Burr into loosing his temper. The old man sat sullen and quiet.

The days passed slowly for Johanna. She cooked and cleaned during the day and spent her evenings sewing Jacy's wedding dress. Glad as she was for Jacy's happiness, Johanna was tormented by thoughts of her own future.

Isabella flitted in and out of the house with a proprietary air, her long skirts swishing around bare ankles. Burr made no attempt to keep her visits to his room secret. In fact, it seemed to Johanna that he flaunted his young Spanish mistress at every opportunity. It was both hurtful and humiliating for Johanna. Though she tried to ignore both of them, she could not ignore the feelings inside her. It was as though the wound opened afresh each time she saw them together. She began to see Burr's smiles as cruel and insensitive, his glances as insolent. No venom-tipped arrow could have pierced her heart more deeply. Johanna dared not show this inner turmoil, and so her face remained placid, even as Burr's penetrating gaze searched it for some sign of emotion.

The subject of Bucko and his mother was constantly at the back of Johanna's mind. It was one subject Ben refused to discuss. He urged her to talk to Burr about the boy, but that was the last thing she intended to do. Anger and bitter shame began to churn within her each time she saw him. And each night, lying in her bed, filled with disgust and self-loathing, she would stare into the blackness of the room and hate him with a hatred which was part despair and part an unnamable something that caused her heart to beat faster. She knew that she would never forget, never forgive the man who had taken the one thing that she could have freely given only once.

One morning on her way to the spring she heard the sound of horse's hooves behind her. Glancing over her shoulder, she saw Burr mounted on his big bay, his hat pulled down over his eyes, and slumped in the saddle as if he was very tired. Thinking he might want to pass her, she stepped aside, but he pulled the horse up beside her. She saw a thousand white lines around his eyes and his face was covered with stubble. The hair that showed beneath his hat was wet with sweat and curled into tight ringlets. He looked as though he'd been working for days. Burr dismounted and reached for the wooden bucket she was carrying while he handed her the horse's reins. She walked beside him leading the horse.

"Do you ride?" The question startled her. She had expected anything but polite conversation.

"Yes, some. I don't ride well, but Papa taught me to ride astride. He thought it rather silly for a woman to perch on top of a horse when she had legs to help her hold on."

After a pause, he said, "Don't come here alone anymore until I tell you different. I'll see to it that water is brought up to the house."

They walked on to the spring, and Burr filled the bucket with the cool water, then tilted it up and drank deeply. He offered to hold it for her to drink, but she shook her head and cupped her hands and drank from them. Burr took off his hat and wet his neckcloth. He wiped the dust and sweat from his face and neck. Lately his mood had been quiet; he would not even rise to the old man's bait. Perhaps he was as sorry as she that they were being forced to marry. She decided to speak of it.

"Burr." She said his name quickly, and his head turned sharply toward her. "This is an awkward situation we are in. I'm sure you're not any happier about it than I am. I've been wondering if . . . if there is something we could do."

"No!" He put his hands on his hips and gazed down at her, his eyes narrowed, his brows drawn together. His scorn was obvious, and she felt impelled to speak rapidly before she lost her nerve.

"Why should we give up our future happiness so an old man can achieve his ambition? From what I've heard about him, he's never done a decent thing for anyone in his life." She gazed up at him pleadingly. Sweat glistened on her upper lip and her throat felt constricted. The look in his eyes made her apprehensive, yet she knew what he was going to say before he said it.

"When the padre comes we'll be married under the sanction of the church, Johanna. It's arranged and nothing is going to be changed. If you leave me after Mack is gone I'll come for you wherever you go. I don't easily give up what's mine." His voice was cold and determined, and she knew he meant what he said. Still, part of her rebelled.

"I'll not be yours!" she sputtered. "I'll not . . . I'll not be your wife! Why do you insist on marrying me? You've got Isabella. If you force me to marry you I'll not have that . . . that . . . your . . . that girl in my house, and I'll not . . . I'll not . . ."

"Sleep with me," he finished for her. His hand flashed out and closed around her wrist, and he jerked her to him. "Do you think I'm the kind of man who lets a woman tell him what to do? And as for sharing my bed, you didn't mind the other night. You didn't need much persuading at all, Johanna. You *will* sleep with me," he added with quiet assurance. "As for Isabella, she is no concern of yours." At his words her body went cold. She strove to pull back, but his grip was too strong, too painful.

She stood glaring at him, her eyes like bits of blue glass. Something in her face almost made him hesitate, and it brought to mind again the little fox he had captured and had wanted so badly to like him and to stay with him. He could see the rise and fall of her breasts, even though the shirt she wore was loose, and the thought of them, the sweet softness he felt when he held her, brought a surge of passion. His eyes searched hers, and he wondered at their beauty.

Johanna seemed to lose her own will as they stood with eyes locked, the powerful sway of his emotions filling her and drawing her to him. He was less frightening now, but she trembled all the same when she felt his hand at the small of her back drawing her closer. Abruptly he folded her into his arms, his face so close she felt the tickle of his mustache on her cheek.

"No," she whispered.

"Why not?" he asked against her lips before his mouth came down on hers in a hard, angry kiss that took the breath from her. His arms pinned the length of her against his body, and he kissed her hungrily, savagely, his tongue prying apart her tightly compressed lips. She thought she would swoon; a strange, feverish weakness enveloped her.

His hand went slowly up her back to the knot of silky hair,

loosening it from its neat coil. It tumbled down her back, and his mouth broke from hers and made a burning path across her cheek to her earlobe, then hungry lips unerringly sought hers again, taking possession of them, stifling words of protest she tried to utter when his warm fingers crept up under her loose shirt and closed about her warm bare breast. She struggled then, but he was holding her so tightly she felt her desire to struggle replaced by something else—something that started with her tingling lips, then flowed swiftly through her, spreading a burning flush over her whole body. She was drained of thought and will. He must have sensed her sudden surrender, for his fingers bit into her shoulders and he moved her away from him.

He grinned down at her wickedly, and said lightly, "Not now, sweet thing. I don't have the time."

His voice came from somewhere far away, but it was his words, the endearment he used when calling Isabella, that brought her to her senses. She pushed away and stood free of him, trembling.

"You're hateful!" she gasped. She sank to her knees, fumbling for the hairpins he so carelessly discarded when he loosened her hair. She found them and knelt there, twisting her hair into a rope and coiling it hastily into a knot on top of her head. "I hate you! I hate you! Oh, God, how I hate you!" she whispered softly.

He pulled her back onto her feet and turned her toward him, even as she struggled to be free.

"I hate you! Keep your hands off me!"

"I don't give a damn if you hate me. Love or hate, it's all the same when you're in bed with a woman."

She was jolted by the insult but pulled together the shreds of her pride and dignity and said calmly, "I'll never agree to that part of the marriage."

"You think not." He laughed. "I could have had you right here in the dirt if I had wanted too."

"You make it easy to hate you!"

"I'm used to hate," he said harshly. "I'm not used to a woman who wraps her arms about my neck, moves her soft breasts against me, opens her mouth and her legs to me, then tells me she despises me.''

Shame and anger seared through her. How could he be so vile as to remind her of her shameful behavior? For days now she had been torn between two desires. One was to reach out and touch him, feel, once again, the firmness of his skin beneath her fingertips, surrender to the ecstasy of lying close to him; the other was the desire to run, to put as much distance between them as possible before she became completely captivated by his animal magnetism.

''Oh!'' She took a step backward, and the color drained from her face. ''Is there nothing too low for you to say?''

''Is there a code of behavior for bastards, teacher?'' He said the last word scathingly, as if it were something to be ashamed of.

''That's what bothers you, doesn't it?'' she shouted. ''You can't live with the fact you're a bastard. Well . . . you are one! You'll always be one, and marrying a thousand times will not change that fact. You use that as an excuse for everything! An excuse for begetting bastards of your own, for forcing me to marry you. You use the fact you're a bastard to be churlish, brutish, and uncouth! I may marry you to keep my sister safe and happy, but I'll always hate and detest you if I . . . if I live to be a hundred in this godforsaken place!''

At this moment Luis stepped out onto the path in front of them, seeming not to have heard Johanna's words.

''*Buenos días.*''

Johanna collected herself sufficiently to acknowledge his greeting, picked up the half-empty bucket, and walked toward the house.

Luis watched her go.

Burr turned his back and picked up his hat, slapping it against his leg before slamming it down on his head. The bitch was completely oblivious to the raw emotions that were tearing up his insides. Of course, he couldn't really blame anyone but himself for the position in which he now found himself. He *was* forcing her to marry him. With a sneer of self-disgust tinged by self-pity—for he was, after all, doing it for Luis and Bucko—he turned to Luis and said gruffly, "What are you doing here on foot?"

Luis knelt down and drank long from the spring. He had seen the confusion on his brother's face and allowed him time to compose his usually unreadable features.

"Apache, brother Burr. An Apache who wanted that white hair to dangle from his belt. He is back in the bush. We can bury him now."

The weeks of hard work had taken a toll on Johanna's strength. She ate little, and soon her brown dress hung loosely and gave evidence of the weight she'd lost. Often her eyes welled with tears as she thought of the past, of the happy times spent with her parents.

Suppertime was the time she dreaded most. The old man came to the kitchen now. Sometimes he came early and watched her prepare the food. He seldom spoke, but his presence and the aura of animosity that surrounded him unnerved her.

That night she lifted her eyes from her plate and found old Mack's eyes focused on her face. He picked up a leather bag and tossed it down to her. The bag landed with a thump beside her plate, and the distinct clink of silver could be heard.

"Your pay," he growled.

Johanna lifted the bag. It was so heavy it slipped from her fingers.

"But . . ." she said hesitantly. "There's more than thirty-two dollars here."

"I hope to hell there is! More than two hundred."

"Why?" she asked.

"Ain't it enough?" he sneered.

"It's more than enough, and you know it. Why?" Her voice rose shrilly.

Old Mack's face lit up, and his faded eyes came alive. "Why? You mean you're going to wed this bastard 'cause you want him?"

"That's none of your business," Johanna hissed. "You promised not to sell the valley if I married him. That's the pay I'm getting, or are you trying to crawfish out?''

"I don't crawfish!" he roared.

"No," she shouted back, "you're too low to crawfish!"

The old man leaned back in his chair and gazed with open admiration at her angry face. The look got through to her, and she realized she had been led into the argument for the old man's pleasure. Appalled at her own lack of control, she forced herself to speak calmly.

"At the end of the month I'll take thirty-two dollars, and that is all," she said firmly and would have said more, but she looked down at Bucko's face. The little boy trembled with terror. She reached out and gathered him to her. "Darling, I'm sorry. It's all right. It's all right," she whispered.

"Humpt!" Mack snorted. "Ain't you got to her yet?" he said to Burr. "Ain't you man enough to get her on her back? Been me, I'da got between her legs before she got her hat off."

Burr pounded his fist on the table and the crockery jumped. "Damn your rotten soul!" he shouted. "Shut your foul mouth!"

The old man gave a nasty laugh. "So you ain't, and it's nettling you. Wouldn't think a big man like you'd need help with a scrawny thing like her."

Johanna got up from the table and pulled Bucko up with her. Her face was flaming, and she didn't dare look at anyone. With Bucko's hand tucked in hers she rounded the table and grabbed the piece of sugared pie crust she had been saving for him. They had reached the hall and started up the steps when Burr's voice came again.

"You goddam filthy old son of a bitch. Don't you have any decency at all? You keep your foul thoughts to yourself, or by God, as old as you are, crippled as you are, I'll break every bone in your rotten body!"

Johanna led Bucko to the chair by the window and lifted him up onto her lap. He snuggled close, and she held him tenderly. She pushed his dark hair back from his forehead, wet with sweat, and realized the effort he had made to climb the steep stairs.

"You don't have to be afraid of old Mack, darling," she said.

"It's best to face the fact that he's old and sometimes says cruel things." Johanna's voice was soft, and she spoke in Spanish. "Mack is a sad old man. He has no one to love him, so he says mean things, trying to act as if he doesn't care. But he must care, and for that reason we should feel sorry for him. You have many people who love you, Bucko. I love you and Jacy and Luis love you. You know Burr loves you."

"Burr gave ponies for me." His voice was muffled and drowsy in the soft folds of her dress.

"He must have wanted you very much to give ponies," Johanna told him.

"I wish Old Mack die!"

"No, we don't wish that. We wish he would be nicer, but if he isn't we'll have to try harder to close our ears when he says bad things."

The room was dark. Bucko's head sagged in sleep, and Johanna gently rested it against her. Her eyes were accustomed to the darkness, and she studied the child's face. It was delicately formed, and she couldn't see a feature she would attribute to Burr. The blue eyes with their fringe of dark lashes were closed. The slight frame had none of the big-boned, rugged construction of Burr's body. Such a little boy, she thought, carrying the burden of living in this house of dissension and with that terrible misshapen foot. She looked down at his foot in its loose-fitting moccasin; it was thick and heavy—too heavy for his thin leg to carry. He should have a special boot. If she made the pattern the harness maker could construct one for him, she decided.

It was much later that she heard the creak of footsteps on the stairs. She had been holding the boy so long that her arms were numb, but the child and the comforting quiet had soothed her mind. Somehow she felt her life would have more meaning with this small human being to love and to teach. He would fill the spot in her life that Jacy had held these months.

There was a rap on the door. Johanna rested her head against the back of the chair and ignored it. If it was her sister, she would come in; anyone else could go away. Ben would understand. The rap came again, insistent this time. After a pause the door opened.

"Who is it?" she asked sharply.

Burr came quietly into the room, his footstep muffled by the moccasins he wore. He set a candle on the table beside the chair.

Without looking at him, she said, "Why haven't you had a boot made for this child's foot?"

There was silence, then the creak of the rope springs as he lowered himself onto the side of the bed.

"I didn't know it would help," he said simply.

"It needs support from soft leather that can be laced tightly." Her words were short and abrupt.

"Have you seen such a boot? Can you show me how to make it?"

"I'll make a pattern."

They sat in silence.

"You like Bucko?" Burr asked quietly.

The question was so ridiculous that she turned her head sharply to look at him. He was sitting on the bed, his arms resting on his thighs, his big hands clenched between his knees. He was staring at the floor.

"You must have a great opinion of me," she said sarcastically. "Why wouldn't I like a child whose parents were not of his choosing and who lives in this vile house? His mental anguish must be tremendous each time that old man sneers at his limp. This child and Ben are the only things in this house I do like."

Burr lifted his head, and Johanna saw a forlorn expression on his face, but her own heart was so hardened against him she refused to acknowledge it.

"Bucko has as much right here as I do," he said slowly.

"You confirm only what I thought. It's his due, you said. You don't really think it's his due—you wish to flaunt him before the old man. It's your pride that keeps him here and not what's due the child."

Burr drew in a ragged breath. "Your tongue's got a sting like a scorpion!"

"I'll need it if I'm going to survive in this house."

"It doesn't always have to be this way."

She didn't answer. The child in her arms stirred, and Burr got to his feet and lifted him from Johanna's lap. He held Bucko upright in his arms and eased the sleeping, dark head to his shoulder. On his way to the door he paused, then turned slowly and looked down at Johanna.

"It doesn't always have to be this way," he said again. When she didn't answer he said angrily, "What do you want me to do?"

"I want this valley to be safe for Jacy without my having to marry you. That's what I want."

"No!" His voice bellowed above hers.

"I'll not live in a house where my husband's whore comes and goes when she pleases." Her voice was shrill.

"If Isabella bothers you so much I'll tell her to stay away," he said, infuriated that she'd brought up the subject. "But don't you mistreat her. She's not had the easy life you've had. Do you understand?" She backed away from his fury. "Don't cringe from me!" he ordered.

She stood immobile, and he went on in a voice more deadly because his tone suddenly became quiet. "The padre is here. Paco brought him in tonight. I'm going to wed you, and I don't want to hear any more about it. Understand?"

He turned on his heel and strode out the door, then turned back. There was something more he had to tell her, something she had a right to know.

"The Apaches are pouring into the lower valley. From the looks of things it will be the largest encampment that's ever been here. I'm going with Luis to bring in his horses, and we'll drive the remuda up in the morning. I want you women and Bucko to stay in the house and I'll send a man up to stay while I'm away."

That said, he turned to leave and once again changed his mind. He wasn't sure he'd quite convinced her of the danger they faced. In an attempt to exert his will he added, "I expect my orders to be obeyed."

*   *   *

Later that night Johanna woke from an uneasy sleep. At first she didn't know what had awakened her; her muscles were tense and her skin prickled with fear. The wind tearing at the tin roof, so close to the bed tucked beneath the sloped ceiling, moaned like a woman in pain. The phrase "death wind" slipped into her mind.

Far away she heard the sound of horses' hooves on the packed earth. Soon the familiar sound of the squeaking gates and the soft, calm voices of the men reached her. A feeling of relief washed over her and she sank back into the soft bed and dropped into a deep sleep.

CHAPTER FOURTEEN

THE STURDY SQUAW reached out and viciously pinched the scrawny arm of her husband's third wife. Sha-we-ne showed no outward sign of the pain that traveled up her arm, but inwardly she cringed and prepared to accept the blows from the willow switch held by the shorter, round-faced woman. Her cruel eyes offered no mercy. Sha-we-ne was to be punished for taking so long to bring firewood to their husband's fire. It did not matter that she had had to range far to find the sticks. It only mattered that she had caused the delay and Black Buffalo's meat would not be the first to be cooking over the fire. It was a matter of pride with Moon Rising that the smell of her cookfire should fill the air before that of the other squaws.

Sha-we-ne was to be punished, and no appeal would move Moon Rising. Her name should have been Snake Rising, Sha-we-ne thought. If she should run, Moon Rising would only pursue her, and then her punishment would be greater. She might even call the younger and stronger second wife, Bright Morning, to administer the lash. Sha-we-ne shivered, for it seemed to her that since coming to this valley, the place of her disgrace, her spirit had left her and only the shell of Sha-we-ne remained.

The spicy smell from one of the cookpots hanging over a small fire to the left of their lodge spurred Moon Rising to action. She seized Sha-we-ne's hair, twisting it so that she was forced down-ward. She laughed when Sha-we-ne's tears came.

"Bitch dog," Moon Rising shouted, making sure the other squaws would hear and come out of their wickiups to watch her punish her slave. "You cannot even gather wood for my husband's fire. Take a stick in your mouth and crawl on your belly." The slashing switch punctuated her words.

Sha-we-ne let a scream escape her lips, more for Moon Rising's sake than for her own. If the squaw thought she was inflicting enough pain to cause her to cry out, she would soon stop. She cringed before her tormentor, allowing her dark, gray-streaked, straggly hair to fall on the ground so the other woman could tred upon it. She placed a small stick between her broken teeth and dropped flat on her belly to crawl painfully forward. Vaguely she heard the yipping of the other squaws, who had gathered to enjoy Moon Rising's mastery with the willow switch, but she did not care. After so many years of being prey to the viciousness of Black Buffalo and his other two wives she had become numbed to humiliation. But she did dread the physical pain.

Satisfied that she had proved her dominance, Moon Rising placed a well-aimed kick to Sha-we-ne's ribs and basked in the admiring glances of the other squaws.

"Get up, slut," she commanded. "The hour grows late and my husband is hungry."

Sha-we-ne's drooping head rose and she laboriously got to her feet and swayed slightly. Her lids lowered to hide the hatred burning there.

"I will do what you command, Moon Rising," she said in a subdued voice.

Whatever she commanded! Moon Rising haughtily looked at her circle of admirers, now breaking up to return to their own fires. It was a good feeling to have a slave. She would tell Black Buffalo how the mother of the lame one crawled on her belly with a stick in her mouth. He would be glad he had never lain between her legs. When she was younger and before the lame one had been traded she had caught him looking at the firm body of Sha-we-ne with lust. Always she reminded him of the disgrace of having his strong seed returned in the form of a weak, misformed son, so he used his third wife in various perverted ways, but never so that she could be called mother.

The range of the Apache was from the middle of Arizona through the New Mexico territory and south into Sonora and the Sierra Madre Mountains of Mexico. This land was theirs, and within this area they lived and raided. Among their warriors were names that worked magic. Mangas Colorado, Cochise, Nana, Victorio, Chato, and a dozen others, some yet alive and some dead. The name of Geronimo was fast becoming the most respected of all among the warriors and their chieftains. Not a Chiricahua by birth, he had married into the tribe, and his leadership had been recognized immediately. A short, thick-set man with a perpetual scowl, he had the unlikely name of Goyathlay, "one who yawns," but was generally called Geronimo.

In the Apache culture the men were all-powerful, the women subservient and responsible for all the work. A warrior went hunting or raiding, and saw to his weapons. His women saw to everything else and looked after his comforts, as well. There were taboos in the Apache society that prevented a man from looking on the face of his mother-in-law, or conversing with her. Geronimo took one of Sha-we-ne's sisters for his wife and had come often to the wickiup and talked with Sha-we-ne. She was sure he would have taken her for a wife if not for her . . . disgrace.

She had dreamed of him often when she was younger, and her mind was still susceptible to pleasant dreams. She saw herself lying on the soft skins of his bedding. Her legs would be wide open to accommodate him. Naked, his loins would be hot and throbbing, and he would stand over her, letting her admire his huge, swollen tool. She would cry out to him to come to her and enter her, and her hands would reach out for the object of her desire. He would plunge into her, and she would fling her legs wide so he could thrust himself deep within her. She would be like a mare and he a fierce stallion riding her. He would bite her face and breasts and suck at her nipples. He would scream loud with joy when he emptied his seed within her.

The dreams were very real to Sha-we-ne. Now that Geronimo was becoming so great and respected a warrior she dreamed that she was one of his wives and Moon Rising was her slave. She would carry a sharp stick, and when Moon Rising lagged behind or displeased her she would mutilate her in all manner of ways. Moon Rising would grovel and plead, but she would show her no mercy.

There was one dream Sha-we-ne dreamed that gave her more pleasure than any other, a dream that even now caused her heart to race and her eyes to blaze with emotion. She would have the pale-skinned man, the one with hair like the clouds and eyes like the sky over a red anthill. He would be naked and spread out. His huge arms and legs would be tied to stout stakes. He would bellow with rage and she would laugh as the ants crawled upon his hairy chest, walked across his belly, and slowly devoured him. She would stay and watch until the end, until not even a single muscle in his big body twitched. She would be sad that he had died so soon, that his punishment couldn't have lasted longer, the way hers had.

Sha-we-ne had been little more than fourteen summers when she first came to the notice of the white man who lived in the valley. All her life they had used this place on their way south to the mountains and again when they came north in the spring. Here they would rest, slaughter cattle to fill their bellies, and prepare whatever meat they had not eaten for the journey. She was wading in the stream with a group of girls when she saw him sitting on his horse looking at her. She had thrust out her small breasts and lifted her skirts higher, as she had seen the older girls do when they knew they were being watched by the young bucks.

This was a man. Bigger than any warrior in their encampment. His hair was like a cloud. The other girls giggled and ran away when the man held a shining object up for them to see. He motioned for her to come to him, and he held out the bit of blue

169

glass so she could see the sun shine through it. Slowly and cautiously she approached, and she could see that his eyes were of the same color. He silently held the glass out to her and let it drop in her hand. She ran then, hiding the object in her dress so her mother wouldn't see it and ask where it had come from. When she was alone she took out the piece of sky and looked at it. It was beautiful, and it was a thing no one had but her.

Each day she went back to the stream, and each day the man would come. If the other girls were there he would ride away, so she would try and slip unnoticed from the camp and go to the stream to fish. When he found her there alone he would give her another shining object. They would not always be blue like the sky, but sometimes green like a leaf, or red like the sunset. She didn't run away now, and one day he got off his horse and she gasped as he towered over her. He reached out a hand and rubbed it over her breast. She felt an excitement. The next day he rubbed her breast and she smiled. He lifted her buckskin dress to her waist and pressed his hand between her legs, his fingers working into the soft moist folds. She was startled at the pleasant feeling that coursed through her. She spread her legs and stood quite still, enjoying this thing the man was doing.

She went early the next day to the stream in eager anticipation of meeting the white man and having him do with his fingers what he had done before. This time he took her hand and led her away from the water and into a place surrounded by thick brush and took off her dress. He motioned for her to lie down, and she complied, opening her legs. He removed the big belt from around his waist and opened his clothing. Sha-we-ne saw his extended man thing rising out of thick hair. She wanted to laugh. She'd seen this many times when the young bucks didn't know she was about. Their breechcloth would stand straight out and they would try to push it down with their hands. This man didn't try to push it down. Instead he knelt down in front of her and put the tip of it to the place his hand had been the day before. It felt good to her, and she smiled. Suddenly he thrust forward and the thing went up inside her. She opened her mouth to scream, but he covered it with one of his big hands. The pain was like none she had ever felt, and she thought the thing was going up into her belly. She looked at him with fear-filled eyes, but he wasn't looking at her. His eyes were closed and his mouth was open and he was breathing heavily as he moved back and forth. He let the thing come almost out, then he would push it back. Sometimes it touched a place in her that felt good and she forgot the pain and tried to tilt her hips so she could feel it again. Soon he shuddered and she felt a flood of something warm inside her. The man got up at once, fastened his clothing, and got on his horse and rode away.

Sha-we-ne went back to the place beside the stream each day while they were in the valley. Sometimes the man came and sometimes he didn't. He didn't bring any more pretty things, but she didn't care; she had come to like what he did to her.

She never told anyone about her meetings with the pale-skinned man until they were deep into the mountains of Mexico. Her mother was furiously angry with her when she discovered her flow of blood had stopped, and she beat her until she told her about the white man she had let go inside her and showed the pretty things he had given her. She was never welcome in any of the other lodges after her mother chased her through the village and beat her with a stick. Her sisters were also ashamed of her, and only the intervention of their mother kept them from stoning her.

When the white man failed to come for her to make her his woman, Sha-we-ne knew her fate. She would never be first or second wife to a husband, and only if she was lucky enough to be taken for third wife would she have meat to eat. She clung to the hope her child would be a big, strong warrior who one day would walk through the village forcing everyone to stand aside so his mother could pass. This hope died when she gave birth. To add to her disgrace, her son was small and weak and one of his feet was the size of a ripe melon. The gods were angry, her mother said, because she had coupled with the paleskin, and this was her punishment. She hated the child. Let him die, she had shouted, but her mother would not and forced her to nurse and tend him.

After Sha-we-ne's mother died, her sisters no longer brought meat to the lodge, and when Black Buffalo offered to make her his third wife to be slave for his other two wives, they accepted for her, and she moved, with the lame one, to the lodge of Black Buffalo, where her position was lower than that of a cringing dog, despised and reviled. She learned to endure the sly pinches, the kicks, the spit clinging to her face and her hair jerked so hard her scalp bled. It was as if her mind and body belonged to someone else and the only thing about her that was alive was her hate. It was coiled deep inside, and she nourished it and it festered.

It became a matter of pride to keep the fruit of her hate alive. She fed the boy, but that was all. She never held him, talked to him, or taught him. In fact, she never looked at him unless it was unavoidable, and never since the day he was born did she look into his shy blue eyes. Sha-we-ne spent as much time away from her lame son as she could, sometimes hanging his basket on the branch of a tree and not going near him all day. She didn't know when the white man came and stared at the blue-eyed child. She was relieved when she returned from picking berries one day and found the child had been traded for four fine ponies. Thinking the paleskin a fool, she looked anxiously at Black Buffalo, hoping he would notice her for the wealth she had brought him, but he scowled and shoved her aside. That night he came to her and used her while she was lying on her face, and without the bear grease the pain was almost more than she could stand.

The seasons passed: winter, summer, winter, summer. Sha-we-ne lost count of how many. Wearily she tended the great fire in the middle of the circle of wickiups as well as the one in the lodge of Black Buffalo. She had more and more to do as Black Buffalo's family increased. There was firewood to gather, the contents in the cookpots to stir, children to tend, and the never-ending softening of pieces of hide which she did with her spittle and the grinding of her teeth. More and more moccasins had to be made and more and more garments pounded clean on the stones beside the streams.

The Apache warriors were masters. They sat cross-legged before their wigwams, boasting of their deeds and their power with the bow and arrow, each man seeking to make himself appear braver and stronger than the others. There was talk in the encampment of an uprising, of raids against the paleface settlers of their land. Knives were sharpened, short powerful bows were tested, and new flint-head arrows were made by the older men. The braves lucky enough to possess rifles flaunted them before their poorer brothers.

The chieftains and their chosen warriors sat around the big fire in the circle of wickiups. The discussions were about whether or not the white man called Sky Eyes would bring the wagon with supplies to the camp. He had come for five seasons, but this encampment was the largest ever to stay over in the valley, and some said the white man would be afraid to come among them. But it did not matter, they said; they would go take what they wanted and kill all the paleskins. They would kill and eat what cattle they wanted and drive off the rest.

Geronimo sat quietly and listened to the talk. Not yet powerful enough to stand up and command, he nevertheless knew his opinion was respected. His narrow black eyes rested often on the face of Gray Cloud. When the warrior spoke of the white man his eyes glittered with a ferocious hatred. Geronimo began to wonder about that hate and how many of the warriors would follow Gray Cloud into battle.

"We sit like women and talk," Gray Cloud said angrily. "Why do we not go and take what we want? Kill the white man and take his horses and his guns. We are many and there are no bluecoats to come help him."

"We will drive them from our land," one brave said, his voice rising with excitement.

A murmur of approval came from the braves surrounding Gray Cloud, and a war drum was produced as a dozen warriors sprang to their feet to begin the dance.

Geronimo thought it time to speak. He held up his hand, and the group fell silent.

"Hear me well," he said. "It is not yet time to make war on the white man. For many seasons we have come to this valley and had cattle to feed on and to kill and take with us on our journey. We are not using the land as Sky Eyes is using it, and he brings us blankets and tobacco. If we run off his cattle we will have none when we pass this way again. It would not be wise to kill Sky Eyes at this time. The bluecoats would come before we are ready.''

Gray Cloud was angry. The voice of Geronimo was becoming too powerful; too many heads turned to listen when he spoke. Gray Cloud didn't dare show his hatred for the chief's favorite chieftain, so he directed it toward the whites in the valley, and to Sky Eyes in particular, who had watched and enjoyed his humiliation when he had been beaten, having been caught stealing his brother's horse.

''Sky Eyes came in friendship because he is afraid. Can it be he is not the only one afraid?'' Gray Cloud had not meant for his words to be a challenge. He waited to see how Geronimo would receive them.

Geronimo got to his feet. The faces of the other Indians were impassive as they watched the two men.

''Before I retire to my lodge there is this thing I will say to you, Gray Cloud.'' Lifting a finger he pointed it at him. ''Words flow from your lips like the water in the stream. It is not words that make a man, but deeds. If you wish Sky Eyes dead, kill him. But do not take our braves to their deaths when it will serve no purpose but to weaken us for the war ahead.''

The chieftains nodded their heads in agreement, and Gray Cloud felt a rising tide of fury that they would listen to the words of this man who was not Chiricahua. It made him uneasy . . . it was almost as if they were conspiring to belittle him. A great hot anger toward the white man rose in him. He had not grown weak and soft. He was a man, and to prove it he would meet the white man from the house of stone and kill him.

Sha-we-ne was sick. There was fever in her body, her head was throbbing, and her tongue was thick. Her brain registered the news that Gray Cloud wished to kill the white man. Her thoughts whirled in hot confusion. She did not know at first why she was disturbed by what Gray Cloud had said, then, with a cry of

despair, she realized the white man would die quickly and honor-
ably in battle. He must not die before he knew of her hate, before
he suffered long agonizing moments of pain. Perhaps she could
appeal to Gray Cloud to capture him and let her torture him with
burning sticks. She closed her eyes and gave herself up to the
pleasure of devising ways of bringing pain to the white man.

She was going to die soon. She was in much pain and her body
refused to do her will. She could accept death, even accept what
torture Moon Rising and Bright Morning chose to inflict upon
her, if only she could see the white man once again before she
died. Looking up at the sky, she saw his face. He was bending
over her. It was strange that he was there. She put up a weak
hand, but encountered only air. Her swollen lips stretched into a
smile. The message was clear.

CHAPTER FIFTEEN

BURR SAT HUNCHED over the table in the cook shack; his stomach empty and grumbling, his big hands circling the mug of hot coffee while he waited for Codger to cook the refried beans and eggs.

"How many men would you say was in the camp, Luis?"

"Between three and four hundred, I'd guess."

Burr was tired. After the remuda was safely inside the corrals, he had spent the remainder of the night supervising the fortification of the ranch buildings. Luis had scouted the Indian camp.

"That's twice the number that usually come through. Do you think it means anything?"

"I think it means that a leader has emerged who can draw all the tribes together. They don't appear to be warlike, but the old men are busy making bows. There's excitement among the people. I think they plan to make war. Perhaps not now, but soon."

Burr rubbed his hand across his face. "I'll take the supplies down tomorrow. Don't think we ought to rush it. They might get the idea we're running scared."

"We will go together, as usual."

"I'll go alone," Burr said firmly. "One of us must stay here. Surely you understand that?"

"Then I will go." Luis's sharp eyes narrowed with determination.

"They expect me, Luis. Now be reasonable." Burr's voice softened and he grinned at his brother. "The padre wishes to leave in the morning. There's a sickness in a village in the mountains. I told him there wasn't too much danger of running into the Apaches if they circled the big butte and went up. So, brother, we'll have to be wed today." He rubbed the stubble on his cheeks. "Do you think I ought to shave?"

Luis's face relaxed, and he smiled.

"*Sí*," he said, "and wash off the cow smell, as well."

"Eat up," Burr said, taking the plates from Codger. "We'll go break the good news to the ladies."

From the moment Burr appeared in the kitchen door to announce the wedding ceremonies, time had ceased its meaning for Johanna. She went through the motions of preparing for her and Jacy's wedding without quite realizing what she was doing. Because of the need to be alert for an unexpected attack, the weddings would take place without festivities.

Jacy was beside herself with excitement. She and Luis wished to be married at his hacienda, but because of the distance from the fortified ranch buildings, they had accepted Red and Rosita's invitation to be married in their home. Burr asked Johanna for her preference, and when she shrugged indicating indifference, he arranged for their wedding to immediately follow his brother and Jacy's. With numbed heart and shaking hands, Johanna slipped the wedding dress over her sister's head.

"I wish Mama were here," Jacy said with a catch in her voice.

"Perhaps she is, Jacy." Johanna blinked the tears from her eyes.

"I hope she knows I'm happy," Jacy said wistfully.

"I'm sure she does, honey. Now . . . about your hair . . ."

"I'll let it hang loose, Johanna. Luis likes it that way." Jacy's eyes gleamed and her cheeks turned rosy red. "I'm glad its just been washed."

After brushing her sister's hair, Johanna placed the mantilla she'd made from four white handkerchiefs over her head, allowing one of the corners to fall over her forehead. She turned Jacy around so she could see herself in the small mirror.

"I really do look like a bride!" she said, her eyes sparkling. "Oh, Johanna, thank you!" She threw herself into her sister's arms. "We'll both wear it. I'll wear it while I say my vows, then you wear it."

Johanna dressed with a heavy heart and a shaky stomach. For her wedding she was going to wear a fresly washed white shirt and her gray skirt. She brushed her hair back severely from her brow, then twisted it into a rope that encircled her head—like a noose, she reflected wryly. A noose that would slowly tighten to cut off her independence and perhaps make her as bitter as old Mack himself. Her face was pinched and white, her eyes shadowed as she struggled to maintain composure. Above all, she did not want to spoil the most important day in Jacy's life.

At the sound of footsteps coming up the stairs, her nerves tightened. She felt weak, unable to face the ordeal of the ceremony. She clutched the iron bedpost, praying for strength. It was Jacy who finally answered Ben's knock. With old-world courtesy, he bowed.

"Lovely ladies, your future husbands have given me the honor of escorting you to your wedding."

Both gazed at him with amazement. He wore a dark suit, white shirt, and string tie. His black shoes were shined until one could almost see a reflection in them, and his hair, parted in the middle, was slicked down on each side. He limped into the room, his neck held stiffly away from his starched collar.

"Johanna," he said shyly, keeping his eyes averted from hers. "Will you give me the pleasure of seeing you wear Anna's brooch on your wedding day?"

The tears Johanna had managed to hold back all day suddenly appeared. She went to Ben and kissed his wrinkled cheek.

"Ben! I'll be proud to wear it!" She took the small cameo from him and pinned it to the neck of her shirt.

Beaming with satisfaction, he urged, "If you ladies are ready, we should be leaving."

They reached the bottom of the stairs and were waiting for Ben to take the last few painful steps out of the house when Johanna saw old Mack standing in the doorway of his room. For one heart-stopping moment she thought he meant to attend the ceremony, then she saw he was leaning against the wall without his sticks. The look on his face made her feel sick. It was the self-satisfied look of an animal that had made a kill. His face was flushed and his eyes overbright, and the slight slurring of his raspy voice was sufficient indication that he was not entirely sober.

"Ain't one to be bought, eh, missy?"

His words had a steadying effect on Johanna, and she said, "Only a fool turns down a bargain for a few principles, Mr. Macklin."

She drew erect and lifted her head, tempted for a moment to send Jacy and Ben on without her. But she wasn't going to let Macklin stand in the way of Jacy's happiness. She knew she was sacrificing her own happiness but that was her choice. Jacy had already suffered too much. With Ben's hand on her arm, Johanna turned toward the door.

Outside, Jacy asked anxiously, "What did he mean, Johanna?"

Johanna laughed lightly. "Who knows what he means, Jacy. I think he's slightly drunk. Does he drink much, Ben?"

"Hardly at all," Ben said thoughtfully. "But let's forget about him. This is your wedding day."

In front of the bunkhouse, every ranch hand who wasn't out on sentry duty was lined up waiting for them. They stood somberly in a half circle, their hands awkward with nothing to do. To them, the ceremony was sacred, and each and every one of them wished to witness it. These hard-looking men were shy to the point of boyishness, Johanna thought. Each wore his best, be it a colorful poncho or a flannel shirt. Boots were wiped clean of dust and spurs removed. Some showed small cuts on their faces where they had nicked themselves scraping away a week's beard. Without exception their lean faces, tanned as leather, wore expressions of solemnity.

"I didn't see Mooney," Johanna said, glancing back at the men who followed a discreet distance behind them. She almost giggled at the pained looks on their faces. Cowboys despised walking!

"Mooney is on watch up by the spring. Luis thought we should have a few extra patrols."

"And Bucko? Will he be there?"

"He went on ahead with Burr."

They walked on silently. Ahead Johanna could see groups of people standing in front of Red's small adobe house, staring intently in their direction. To her relief, Isabella was not among them. The garb of the men and women could hardly be called elegant. All had an air of practicality, of making do with what was available. They stood quietly and waited for the wedding party to reach them.

Jacy broke loose and hurried to Luis the moment she saw him standing beside the small balding padre. Her face was radiant, and her shining eyes saw no one but him. He was breathtakingly handsome in slim tan trousers with a wide colorful stripe running down the side. Over his soft full-sleeved white shirt was an elaborately embroidered vest, and around his waist was wound a colorful sash. His black boots matched the shine on his carefully brushed hair. It was clear that this was the most important occasion in his life. He took several long steps and greeted his beloved with outstretched arms. He feasted his eyes on her beaming face.

A sense of rightness swept over Johanna, and the great weight she had carried for so long lifted from her heart. How wonderful for Jacy and Luis! Two people who had been so cruelly wronged had found each other. She could hardly tear her eyes away from the couple, who had eyes for only each other.

"My reluctant bride," a voice said close to her ear.

"Burr, please," Ben said impatiently.

Johanna looked up and caught the gleam of mockery in Burr's eyes. In spite of his careless manner, a nerve in the corner of his narrowed eyes twitched and the fingers that adjusted the silk scarf about his throat trembled. Johanna smiled and gave herself up to the pleasure of knowing the big brute was nervous. He was not dressed as elegantly as Luis; however, he was a fine-looking man in his spit-polished boots, neat dark pants, and white shirt. The scarf at his neck matched the blue of his eyes, and in spite of herself she felt a thrill of pride in his handsome appearance.

Johanna's eyes searched the crowd for Bucko. Finally she saw him standing with his back against the side of the house. She left Ben and Burr, abruptly, and went to him.

"Bucko, I've been looking for you."

It was the same as on the first day she had met him. He stood silently with head bent.

"I would like very much for you to stand beside me today."

Dejectedly, he broke the small twig he was holding and threw it on the ground.

"You be Burr's woman."

Johanna blushed crimson. "Burr will still be yours, Bucko. It won't make any difference in the way Burr feels about you. You'll have me, too."

"Isabella say you make me go."

Johanna stood stone-still, almost speechless with anger. "She is wrong, Bucko. Isabella is disappointed because she won't be Burr's woman, and that's the reason she said this to you. It is not true. When I marry Burr you'll be my little boy. I could never send my own little boy away."

"You be my mama? Like . . . Roseta and Harley?"

"Of course. I thought you knew that." She grimaced slightly as she pictured Burr's reaction if he were to hear the discussion.

Bucko lifted his head, squared his small shoulders, and reached out to take her hand. "I will stand by you," he said proudly.

With equal pride she thanked him, and together they walked back to where Ben and Burr stood watching.

"I've invited Bucko to stand with us," she said evenly, aware of a sparkle of amusement in Burr's eyes. He shrugged with seeming indifference, then reached out and ruffled Bucko's hair.

"That suits me fine, cowboy."

As if in a dream, Johanna played her part, seeing nothing of the interior of Red's small house, or the people who crowded in to witness the ceremony. The service uniting Jacy and Luis was over before she realized, and Burr had taken her arm to urge her forward. Her hand in Bucko's, she dragged him along beside them. She was numb, ice-cold from head to foot, yet terribly conscious of the presence at her side uttering words with cool deliberation, deceiving every listener with promises. "With my body I thee worship . . . to love and to cherish . . . till death us do part." The soft voice of the padre droned on. "Do you, Burnett Englebretson Calloway, take this woman . . ."

Startled, Johanna looked up at her bridegroom to see a mocking grin on his face. Burr quickly turned away and gave the padre a firm reply. When it was time for Johanna to reply, her voice was a mere thread of sound. The brave facade she had managed to pull together almost crumbled.

Burr's steely hand clasped hers, the long brown fingers wiry and tough. Then his lips fleetingly touched hers and the ceremony was over. It hardly seemed possible she'd experienced it. Johanna embraced a tearful Jacy, and Luis kissed her on the cheek. He shook hands vigorously with his brother, who claimed the right to kiss his bride.

A cheer broke from the crowd when the two couples stepped out of the house, and Johanna blinked, dazzled by the brilliant sunshine that replaced the dimness they left behind. A horde of well-wishers descended upon them, showering them with flowers picked from their gardens. Jacy squealed as Luis lifted her from the ground and clutched her to his heart. The women were delighted by his action, and the men grinned at the color that transformed his new wife into a creature of shy enchantment. They turned their attention to Burr and Johanna.

It was difficult for Johanna to remain aloof in the festive atmosphere that surrounded them. She was soon relaxed and smiling, then laughter came as Burr was pelted with one outrageous remark after another. Her eyes met his, and Burr gave her hand a comforting squeeze, a gesture so warm and surprising that it released from deep within her a flood of pleasure.

"Kiss her, señor! Kiss her!"

Burr took her lips still parted in laughter and crushed her in an embrace so fierce and bone-crushing that it took her breath away. So overwhelming was the wonder of her own feeling that Johanna made no protest. Every nerve in her body was alive in a way she had never before known, and she knew, too, that never as long as she lived would she ever again feel quite this way. He released her lips, and she leaned against him, faintly sick with churning emotions. She gulped for air and, finally, sanity crept back to calm her mind and senses. She looked at him then, fully expecting his face to show the mockery she had come to know. But Burr was unmistakably serious. He put his hand out and lightly touched the brooch fastened at her throat. Someone called, and he turned to acknowledge the good-natured joshing. Johanna felt a twinge of disappointment that the moment was over.

The afternoon shadows lengthened quickly and the cool evening air swept down from the mountains. The wedding party broke up, the men going out to relieve the patrol and the women to their homes with the children. Burr's promise of a real celebration with a whole barbecued steer after the Apaches left the valley brought a buzz of excited voices all talking at once about kettles of frijoles, platters of tamales and vats of peppery chili. The excited men whooped on hearing the barrel of whiskey in the locked storehouse would be opened for the occasion.

Jacy and Luis were staying in the Mexican quarters until they could go to their own home. Luis, of course, wouldn't come to the stone house and Jacy wouldn't leave him, so Johanna offered to pack her sister's belongings, provided Burr brought them down after he dispatched the men to guard duty. He and Luis stepped aside and talked in low tones.

"Burr and I will be away for a few hours, *mi corazón,*" Luis told Jacy gently. "You are to stay with Rosita and I will come for you."

Jacy started to protest, then stopped. *"Sí, mi marido,"* she said, love and gladness shining in her eyes. "I will obey my husband."

Burr looked at Johanna with raised eyebrows. "Words I hope to hear very soon," he said mockingly.

An impudent smile came to Johanna's lips without her being aware of it. "It's foolish to hope for the impossible," she said.

Luis kissed Jacy tenderly and murmured to her.

Burr came to kiss Johanna, but she turned her head sharply. He chuckled.

"I'll be back. Your waspish temper won't keep me away from you." She seethed with resentment at his words and made no effort to hide her feelings.

Burr ignored her sullenness. "I'll not be back for supper. Leave something on the table. I've got to keep my strength up now that I'll have regular . . . night duties." He flicked her cheek lightly with his fingertips and walked away.

Ben had been quiet during and after the weddings. He stood by watching with a solemn expression.

"Ben," Johanna asked with a puzzled look on her face, "why did the padre add Calloway to Burr's name?" Ben, as usual, took his time answering.

"I wanted to tell you, lass, but Burr said he would do it. I adopted Burr and Luis when they were lads. Their legal name is Calloway."

"Why didn't someone tell me?" she asked. "Why so secret? If Jacy knew about it she didn't say anything."

"I doubt if Luis thought to say anything about it. He uses his mother's name, Gazares, except in legal matters. Burr and Luis have always kept those things that are important to them to themselves. They take special pains to keep Mack from knowing about their private lives and Burr enjoys rankling Mack by using his name. I'm sorry, Johanna, you weren't told before."

Johanna digested the news with a feeling that was beyond anger. The whole ghastly reality now hit her, and she felt hurt in a way that she had never hurt before. She had been duped by a man who had used her to keep control of his land. He didn't love her, but clearly intended to use her body for his own sexual gratification, and he also intended to continue his relationship with his mistress. The humiliation was almost more than she could bear. And yet, she asked herself, how else could she have handled the situation in which she had found herself?

CHAPTER SIXTEEN

"E'LL SEE IF the bastard is man enough to fill your belly."

Johanna pretended she hadn't heard Mack's remark and went about her work. The old man's hot, bright eyes followed every move she made until she was ready to scream. He had come early to the kitchen and settled himself in the chair by the fireplace to watch her prepare the evening meal. Whenever she glanced up he was staring intently at some part of her anatomy. Occasionally she could hear the hiss as a stream of tobacco juice hit the fire.

Ben came in, and Johanna breathed a sigh of relief.

"Burr thinks there's near four hundred Apaches in the lower valley, Mack." He paused and waited for a comment, but none came. Dear Ben. Johanna realized he was striving for a civilized conversation with old Mack for her sake. "It's been years since that many Apaches have gathered here. Burr left about fifty head of cattle down there. That should be enough for them." He turned to Johanna. "It's a matter of pride for the Indians to steal the cattle."

"Humpt!" old Mack snorted. "Where's the bastard gone to now?" His eyes fastened on Johanna's face. "He'd be a fool to waste hisself straddling one of them Apaches."

Johanna thought she had never hated anyone or anything as much as she hated this vile old man.

"Burr's on patrol. He'll be back soon." Johanna didn't know how Ben could be so patient.

"Be a goddam fool if he didn't." The smirk on his face made his meaning clear.

Johanna shrank from the vulgar remarks of the old man and the pitying looks Ben gave her each time her face burned. Time had failed to dull the embarrassment of old Mack's tactlessness and the shocking ways he used to focus attention on himself.

She found herself wishing she could hear the ring of Burr's boot heels on the stone floor of the hall. Her breath caught in her throat and her heartbeat quickened as a thought floated across her mind. What if something happened to him and he didn't come back! The realization of that possibility brought her up short, and she stood motionless facing the dancing fire. She was aware now of the truth that had escaped her mind for so long. Johanna Doan, the woman who was sensitive to beauty and softness, books and music, a thoughtful person brought up to care about people, had fallen in love with a crude, insufferable, arrogant, overbearing cattleman! The thought went around and around inside her. Stop it, she said to herself. She must stop this obsessive thinking— must concentrate on what needed to be done. There was nothing she could do about the situation in which she found herself, so best get on with the work. She picked up the copper teakettle and went to the wooden bucket, intent upon blotting out all thought, but Burr's face, his brilliant blue eyes, his animated features, looked up at her from the clear water in the bucket. She walked back into the kitchen.

The scraping of old Mack's chair on the stone floor sounded loud in the quiet room. She could just about see his features in the lamplight, but his sharp, piercing eyes seemed to see right through her. He hobbled out the door, and she could hear him muttering to himself as he went down the hall to his room.

"Come sit down, lass, and eat your supper."

Johanna busied herself putting a stick of firewood in the cookstove. "Thank you for keeping Bucko out of the kitchen tonight, Ben." She poured coffee for herself and Ben, and sat down at the table. "He's terribly afraid of Mr. Macklin."

"There's no reason why you have to suffer Mack's presence now, either, lass. You're no longer an employee here. Remember? If Mack continues to be so offensive, and I see no prospects of him changing, Burr will have to arrange for other living quarters for you and Bucko."

"Oh, Ben, do you think he would? The thought of spending the rest of my life in this house is enough to make me go . . . mad!" She hated the tears that sprang suddenly to her eyes and blinked them away before Ben could see them.

Ben patted her hand. "Bucko will stay down at the bunkhouse with Codger while the Apaches are camped here. Burr's afraid they might get it in their heads to steal him back. Codger'll keep an eye on him every minute."

Johanna searched Ben's face. "I wish I knew more about Bucko."

Ben continued to pat Johanna's hand. "Lass, I wish I knew more to tell you, but I don't. I don't know who fathered him, but it's a sure fact he's a Macklin one way or the other."

"If there was a chance that Bucko wasn't Burr's child you would think that he would have said so." A sad note crept into her voice and made Ben look at her sharply. She got up from the table and carried the dishes to the work bench.

"Let me help you tonight, lass."

"No, you've put in a long day and a busy one." She smiled at him fondly. "You're quite a handsome man, Mr. Calloway, when you get all dressed up."

"I'll never get dressed up for a bigger occasion, Johanna. Both my boys were married today . . . and to two lovely sisters." His eyes twinkled at her.

Johanna went to him and put her arms about him. "Ben, you're so much like my papa. And, Ben . . . I love you." She kissed his cheek and saw tears come into his eyes. "Oh, I've embarrassed you. I'm sorry."

"Not one bit," he said hastily. "Not one dadgummed bit,

lass! I just can't believe my luck, is all.'' His seamed face broke into a bright smile.

"Luck has nothing to do with it, Ben. You're a very nice man . . . and a tired one, so off with you. I'll clear up and leave some food on the table for Burr.'' She walked with him to the door and watched his slow progress down the hall. A small glow of light shone from the partly open door of old Mack's room, and she prayed he wouldn't decide to come back to the kitchen.

She was fixing bread, butter, and meat for Burr when she heard his voice outside the back door.

Johanna struggled to maintain her composure and managed to ask lightly when he appeared in the doorway, "Who were you talking to?"

"Mooney." His voice had a strange husky quality. "I told him to get some sleep. We scouted the camp and there's no sign they'll ride in on us. At least not tonight.''

"I'm glad.'' Her relief showed in her voice.

Burr took the kettle from the stove and poured hot water from it into the washbasin, then ladled in several dippers full of cold water from the bucket.

"You sound more afraid of the Indians than of me,'' he said just before he scooped water up with his two hands and splashed his face. He did this several times before wiping it dry with the neatly folded towel he took from the rack.

"At least I know their intentions,'' Johanna replied tartly.

"And you don't know mine?''

She turned her back on him and brought the plate of food to the table. She wanted to look at him, but didn't dare, afraid he might read in her face what she was feeling. Try as she would she could not control the turmoil within her. He sat at the table, and she poured his coffee. He caught her arm as she turned away.

"Sit down, Mrs. Calloway, and talk to me.'' His voice was soft, and evoked still further confusion within her.

She pulled her arm away. "In a minute.'' Her tone was sharper than she had intended.

Fumbling with the crockery on the workbench gave her a few

minutes to collect herself. She poured herself a cup of coffee and returned to sit at the other end of the table. He stood up and reached for the cup and set it down on the table next to him.

"I'm not going to pounce on you, if that's what you're afraid of. I'm too goddam tired." He glared at her with red-rimmed eyes.

Johanna moved down beside him. He did look tired. "Did you get any sleep last night?" she asked nervously.

He lifted his head, and his eyes searched her face. Johanna bridged the awful silence that followed by lifting the cup to her lips. She realized the reason for his surprised look. It was the first bit of personal conversation between them.

"No." His voice was steady. "Luis and I drove the horses up and spent the rest of the night moving wagons out to use as blockades in case of an attack."

She cleared her throat nervously. "Do you do this each time they camp in the valley?"

"We always drive the herds to the upper valley, leaving only enough for them to steal. It's horses they want, but we've got a good strong corral over next to the cliff, and they'd have to go past here to get to them." He talked quietly, then fell silent.

The silence dragged on while he ate. She searched her mind for something to say, but could not think of anything.

It wasn't until his plate was empty that he spoke again. "I meant to tell you about Ben's adopting me and giving me his name, but every time we talked the fur would fly and I'd forget about it."

Johanna got up to refill his cup. "It doesn't matter. I was just surprised, that's all." She could feel his eyes on her face as she poured the coffee.

"It was a long time ago and I don't think about it much."

"Why do you call yourself Macklin?"

"I guess it's because I'm not saddled with the name." He grinned devilishly. "And because it gripes the hell out of the old man."

"Well, I'd rather be Mrs. Calloway than Mrs. Macklin."

"Glad to hear it." His eyes lighted with amusement. "I

189

thought you might be disappointed not being Mrs. Macklin of Macklin Valley.''

"I didn't want to be Mrs. anything, you know." She could have bit her tongue the moment she said it.

His expression changed immediately. "I know," he replied sarcastically, and she could feel him withdraw.

He rolled a cigarette with not quite steady fingers. Clearly he wanted no further conversation.

Johanna cleared the table and put away the food, Burr's eyes following every movement. Finally when she had done everything she could find to do she turned and faced him, her nervousness intensifying. He was sitting quietly, his arm on the table and his long legs stretched out in front of him. He had removed his neckerchief and his shirt was open, revealing an expanse of brown chest lightly sprinkled with blond hair. Johanna froze as his eyes bored into hers, sending a message she was not too confused to interpret. She was silent, her mind searching frantically for a way to deal with the situation, her eyes locked with his. As in the past, she took refuge behind cool hauteur.

"Excuse me," she said and started to leave the kitchen.

His arms snaked out and she was hauled off her feet and onto his lap so suddenly that she was taken unawares. Before she had time to protest he covered her mouth with his own. He kissed her deeply, again and again, pressing her against his hard unrelenting chest. Violently and ruthlessly he plundered her mouth, until she was lost in a storm of passion, responding, forgetting her desire to struggle. He molded her to him, as if she was a missing part of him and kissed her mouth, her eyes, her cheeks with insatiable hunger. His lips traced a searing path over her. Her breath came in heated gasps, and a moan began deep within her and slowly rose to her throat, caught there as she felt his hand free her breast from the tight bodice of her dress.

"You smell like . . . woman," he muttered against her mouth.

A wave of sexual desire swept her. She wanted to yield, wanted to cast the last vestiges of restraint from her mind and body and let him carry her away again on the flood of his passion and give him kiss for kiss. But the thundering of his heart against hers, the quivering of his body, and the roughness of his demands set off a warning bell in her brain. She had given in to her body's demands that night in his room, and he had humiliated her. It wasn't going to happen again. Sex should be an act of love, she thought wildly. The coming together of a man and a woman should be something to cherish, to hold sacred, not merely a gratification of carnal desires.

She tore herself free, knowing she would never make it past him to the door, and ran to the hearth, where she rested her head against the broad mantel. She leaned there, her heart racing madly, her stomach churning. Her lips felt bruised and tortured. She was humiliated by her own desire. With shaking hands she restored order to her clothing.

She tensed as she heard his footsteps on the stone floor, and flinched when she heard his mocking voice. "What the hell's the matter with you?"

She clenched her fist but did not move from the hearth. He came closer but didn't touch her, and she closed her eyes tightly and prayed he would go away and leave her in peace; a vain hope. He pulled her around to face him.

"I said, what the hell's the matter with you? What did you expect?"

Goaded beyond endurance, she sobbed, "If you ever come at me again like that / . . I'll kill you!"

It was seconds before he took the import of her incredible words. "You'll what?"

"I'll kill you," she repeated.

There was a silence while he glared at her with disbelief. Finally he said again, "What did you expect?"

She looked up at him then, her tear-filled eyes locked with his. "I expected . . . tenderness!"

The puzzled look that crossed his face was genuine. "Tenderness?" he questioned, and his expression changed to one of exasperation. "Tenderness!" he said again and turned on his heel and started for the door, his broad back a blur through her tears.

In the seconds of silence that followed, Johanna heard a loud curse from old Mack's room. Burr paused, a questioning look on his face, and then came the sound of a shot and the impact of the bullet as it pierced the wall to strike the storage cabinet. In one swift movement Burr squelched the light.

"Stay down and back from the fire!" he commanded and bolted for the door.

Johanna stood frozen for a second, then fear for Burr lent wings to her feet and she raced after him. When she reached the hall she saw him fling open the door and disappear into Mack's room. On trembling legs she ran down the hall and peered in from the doorway. What she saw made her gasp with horror.

The lamp on the bureau was still burning, and in its faint glow she saw old Mack on the bed, the handle of a knife protruding from his chest. He was writhing in agony, his gnarled hands pulling at the handle. Burr stood, gun in hand, his eyes roving the room. The only sound was the creak of the rope bed as the old man's massive weight shifted in an attempt to rid himself of the torturing knife. Burr shoved his gun back into its holster and went quickly to Mack. He pried loose the frantic fingers, pulled out the knife, and let it drop to the floor.

"Who . . . who . . . ?" Johanna gasped.

Burr jerked his head toward the end of the room. In the semidarkness a brown bundle, much like a discarded rag doll, lay on the floor. Going a step closer, Johanna saw the ragged buckskin dress and the long matted hair of an Indian woman. She lay slumped against the wall where the bullet had slammed her.

A sound from old Mack brought her attention back to him. His eyes were open and bright.

"Goddam dog-eatin' bitch!"

"Was that Bucko's mother?" Burr asked insistently.

"Goddam dog-eatin' bitch!"

"I said, is she Bucko's mother?" Burr ground out desperately.

"Aye," old Mack whispered hoarsely. "You going to let me bleed to death, you . . . bastard?"

Burr straightened. "Get towels," he barked, "and whiskey."

Ben was standing in the door, and Johanna brushed by him on her way to the kitchen. She could hear the pounding of heels on the stone outside the house and the excited whispers of the men.

Grabbing some towels, the teakettle from the stove and the washbasin, she hurried back to Mack's room.

Burr cut open the old man's shirt and moved aside to make room for Johanna. She willed herself not to faint at the sight of the warm, sticky blood welling up from the hole in the hairy chest. Knowing there was no way they could stop the blood, she covered the hole with a cloth. Her anxious eyes sought out Ben's and he shook his head slightly. She looked down again to see the old man staring at her.

"Juanita," he whispered, "why'd you have to go and do that for?" His eyes closed and a bloody froth came out of his parted lips.

The doorway was crowded with men attracted by the sound of the shot, and Mooney squeezed his way into the room.

"Ain't nothin' out there, Burr."

"Didn't think there would be. She sneaked in here alone, but how in the hell did she do it?" Burr motioned for the men to move back into the hall, and he followed them out. "Codger still with Bucko?"

"Sittin' on him like a mama hen," Mooney said. "He ain't gonna let no one near. Got a shotgun on his lap."

"Mack's done for, there's no question about that, but we got to think about what to do with that woman."

"Who'da thought an Injun woman woulda come in here and done such a thing?"

"She was a woman wronged, Mooney. Bucko's mother. Indians have different ways from ours. She was cast down and made a slave after Mack ruined her."

"The poor little ole thing," Mooney said sadly.

Not a flicker of surprise showed on the faces of the men when they heard Bucko was old Mack's son, although they had all firmly believed Burr to be his father. Schooled in keeping their thoughts to themselves, they only nodded in agreement at Mooney's pitying words.

"Stay with Ben and Johanna, Mooney. Wrap the woman in a blanket and get her out of there. I'm going down to talk to Luis. Hate to disturb him on his wedding night, but this can't wait."

Mooney brought a blanket and laid the pathetically thin body of the Indian woman on it. His features softened and he shook his head sadly. Gently he wrapped her and carried her down the hall to the sitting room, then returned with rags to mop up the blood.

Old Mack was deathly white now, and his breathing laborious. He muttered the name of the Mexican woman several more times before Johanna questioned Ben.

"Who was Juanita?"

"Luis's mother," Ben said in hushed tones. "She might have been the only person in the world that Mack cared a whit for. She was a sweet, young, beautiful girl, and Mack ruined her just as he did my Anna and that poor Indian girl." For the first time Johanna heard a bitter note creep into Ben's voice. "Mack put Juanita in a shack down where Luis now has his ranch, and no one dared go near her but me. Not that she wanted anyone; she was so ashamed she shrank from contact with anyone except for me and Luis. She once told me that Mack would sit his horse, off in the distance, and watch her. He didn't go near the shack, but the sight of him scared her half to death. Luis was her life, and she lived in constant fear that Mack would harm him. He despised the boy and laid the lash on him every time he caught him away from the shack. Juanita wanted me to adopt him and gave me a letter to present to the court at the same time I presented Anna's letter, so I adopted both boys."

Old Mack almost reared up in bed, and his eyes opened. "Juanita, you shouldn'ta let the dirty greasers touch you. You was mine." The words were almost inaudible, his breathing hard.

Ben shook his head sadly. "He'd never admit, even to himself, that Luis was his son."

Johanna wanted to cry for Luis and his mother, for Anna, and for all the people whose lives had been affected by Mack Macklin's ruthlessness.

"He must have cared for Juanita," Ben said in wonder. "He didn't know she was dead until after we buried her. Then he went storming down to the shack and stayed there two or three days. Got roaring drunk. Luis hid out in the corrals till he left. I thought sure he'd kill Mack, but he had promised his mother he wouldn't kill him unless he was defending himself. A week after she died, Luis left the valley, and I didn't know whether he'd ever come back. Burr found him in El Paso and brought him home. I'll never forget the day Paco came riding in to tell me the boys were down at the shack. All the years I'd put up with old Mack's cussedness paid off. My boys had come home." Ben's faded eyes came alive, and he clasped Johanna's hand with surprising strength. "Now Mack will die and neither of my boys was the cause of it. Johanna, you don't know how it relieves my mind!"

She sat silently for a while, then asked, "I wonder what ever happened to him to make him the way he is."

Ben was thoughtful, then answered slowly, "Things affect people differently, Johanna. Recently I learned a little about Mack's past. Willard Risewick came to the valley with two missions—one to buy land and the other to find out as much as possible about Mack. It seems Mack has a half brother back East, the son of his father's Spanish mistress. His father was never able to marry the woman he loved because his wife went into a mental decline, just after Mack was born. She died many years later, hopelessly insane. The poor man was tied to her. He was a good businessman, however, and wanted both his sons to take over his iron foundry, but Mack would have no part of it if the bastard son was included. The father stood firm, and Mack left home. Rafael, Mack's half brother, is without family, and Mack is his only blood relative. He sent Risewick out to get the lay of the land and to find out what kind of reception he would receive if he came out for a visit. Of course, Risewick knew right away that any reconciliation was impossible, but he was able to take back to Rafael the news that he has nephews who would one day welcome him. It seems that possibility is closer to happening than we expected."

It took Mack several hours to die. While blood continued to ooze out of him, his tough old body clung to life. Burr came back and stood looking down at him, a blank expression on his face. The stone house that the old man had built in his younger days was quiet, except for the slight rumble of the tin roof as the night wind passed over it. Mooney moved quietly up and down the hall, his steps a muffled acknowledgment that death was near. Only Johanna and Ben were with the old man when he gasped his last breath. Ben stood up and pulled her to her feet.

"It's over, Johanna. Go to the kitchen and make coffee. Mooney and I will take care of things here."

Someone had filled the cookstove with wood and laid fresh logs in the fireplace. Johanna didn't realize how cold she was until she felt the warmth of the room. After she had filled the coffee pot and set it on the stove she eased herself into a chair and stared wearily into the fire. She couldn't bring herself to be sorry the old man was dead. She was sorry, though, that a man like Mack could live so many years and accomplish as much as he had accomplished here in the valley and still die without a single person to mourn him.

Burr was beside her before she was aware he had come into the room. He squatted beside the chair, his eyes on a level with hers.

"You all right?"

She nodded, surprised at his concern.

"There's no reason to be afraid. We've been out looking around, and as far as Luis and I can tell the woman came in alone. We think she got past the spring before Mooney went up there to patrol and hid somewhere near the smokehouse all day. She must have seen Mooney leave his post when I told him to go get some sleep. Mack's lamp was still burning, so she could see him through the window. The old fool was waiting to see if I took you to bed," he said dryly. "He must have been dozing or the woman wouldn't have got the knife in him before he shot her. He always kept the gun on the bed beside him, probably thinking he'd have to use it on me or Luis sometime." He took a deep breath, and his shoulders sagged. "Anyway . . . he's dead!" There was a bone-weary tone in his voice. "Luis is bringing Jacy up to stay, and he and Red will be on watch for the rest of the night. Mooney and I are going to get a couple hours' sleep. We're taking the wagon down to the Indian camp first thing in the morning, just as if nothing's happened."

Johanna raised stricken eyes to his. "You're going down . . . there?"

"I always take a load of stuff to the camp. They expect it."

Her hand reached out and clutched his arm. "But . . . they might kill you!"

"I don't think so." His eyes fell to her hand on his arm. She removed it quickly, and he stood up. Mockingly he said, "Don't tell me you wouldn't be pleased to be made a widow tomorrow?"

A look of shock crossed her face. "How can you say such a thing?" Her voice trembled and her lips quivered.

He stared at her, his eyes questioning, but he said nothing.

Johanna got up and stumbled past him. She glanced at him over her shoulder as she reached the door and saw, surprisingly, a look of concern on his face.

"Will you tell Jacy to be careful of the steep stairs? She's one of those people who can't see very well in the dark."

"Don't worry. I'll bring her up." His voice held a quality that, had Johanna been less distaught, would have made her wonder.

She was shaking all over, and felt so frightened and weak she could hardly walk. Burr might not come back from the Apache camp. She fought an impulse to run after him, to plead with him not to go. What was the matter with her . . . to feel this way about a man who only thought of her in terms of his physical needs? She was no better than a harlot! The very word stiffened her resolve.

"Goodnight," she said, her voice coolly composed.

CHAPTER SEVENTEEN

JOHANNA AND JACY walked down to the corral the next morning to watch the loading of goods that Burr would take to the Indian camp. There was a quantity of corn, tobacco, blankets, bolts of cloth, dried fruit, knives, and a small keg of powder. The Apaches were not a frivolous people. They were practical and wanted practical things. Mooney and Burr joked lightly about their mission.

"I'm sure a-hatin' to depend on these old clods to get me outta that camp fast." Mooney shifted his chew of tobacco to his other jaw. "Sure'd like to take that old pie-eye of mine along."

"They'd steal that old nag and have her butchered for the pot before you could spit, Mooney."

"I still think I should go with you, Burr." Luis lifted the large sack from his shoulder and threw it into the wagon.

"Things are different now, Luis. We got more than just ourselves to think about."

"I'll ride as far as my place and wait for you there," Luis insisted.

"Stay here. I'll stop at your place and see if things are right. You've got three men there, and if anything had happened we'd have heard the shots." Luis looked worried, and Burr laughed. "Cheer up, brother, you got that pretty little bride over there to

198

keep you company.'' When Luis didn't smile, Burr sobered. "If we're not back by the time you think we should be, you know what to do. Don't let them draw you away from the ranch. There'll be nothing you could do for me or Mooney. They're either going to take our goods and treat us as usual, or they're not.''

Mooney let loose a stream of tobacco juice, pulled his hat down on his head, and climbed up onto the wagon seat. Burr's eyes sought Johanna, who now stood behind the corral fence. He climbed over the railing and took her hand, leading her away from the group that had gathered to watch him set off.

"Guess I'd better kiss you, to make it look right.''

"Yes,'' she breathed, her eyes mute testament to the fear churning inside her.

He touched his lips to hers. Her arms went around his body and her lips clung. The kiss lasted for a long while, and when it broke she lowered her eyes in an attempt to hide her tears.

He put his arm around her shoulders. "If your luck holds out my hair could be hangin' from a belt by night,'' he said lightly.

Her eyes, now sparked with anger, came up to meet his. "You . . . you . . .'' she gasped, and drew back her foot and kicked him on his lower leg. "You make me so mad!'' She broke loose from him and ran to the house.

He stood with his hands on his hips and watched her go. The smiling, devil-may-care expression on his face vanished, and in its place came a look of puzzled frustration.

"Little silver fox,'' he muttered to himself and climbed back over the rails.

"Hee-yaw!'' Mooney shouted and cracked his whip over the backs of the team the moment Burr climbed into the wagon. "H'yaw!'' The yell echoed in the morning stillness. The mules strained at their harnesses, and the wagon moved out of the corral and through the gate. Burr's eyes clung to the slim figure standing by the back door under the dilapidated straw hat with its faded pink rose. He almost regretted nailing it to the barn after the wind had torn it from the peg.

* * *

Squinting his eyes under the pulled-down brim of his hat, he studied the terrain with care. Behind them and higher up were the ranch buildings and below them the Indian camp. The sun was at their back and not yet high enough to give warmth. A cool breeze drifted down from the mountains and waved the long grasses alive with small birds whirring up from under the feet of the mules. The trail ran alongside the rocky stream, and a startled deer bolted when they approached. The snow peak of the distant mountain glistened in the morning sun. It was all very peaceful.

The men hadn't spoken since they had left the ranch yard. Each was wrapped in his own thoughts. Mooney finally broke the silence.

"Ain't this a mite more stuff than you usually take, Burr?"

"Yeah, it is, but I figure they could take it all if they had a mind to." He glanced at Mooney and grinned. "We just might get our hair took today, Mooney."

The leathery-faced cowboy took off his hat and scratched his head. Wisps of sweat-drenched hair were plastered to the near-bald pate.

"I guess I got the least likely scalp any 'pache'd ever want," he said dryly. "Wouldn't be no pride in a-hanging that on a belt."

"Let's hope so." Burr took off his hat and threw it on the floor of the wagon. He was wearing the fringed Indian boots for which he'd bartered a few years ago, cord pants, and a dark cotton shirt. His only weapon was a hunting knife tucked in his belt. Mooney wore a gunbelt that held two heavy revolvers. In spite of the lightness of their talk, both men knew the seriousness of their mission. It could very well be that the Apaches would kill them and ride on to the ranch.

As the wagon rolled along, Burr thought of the woman, Bucko's mother. He decided she was probably insignificant enough to the Indians that she wouldn't be missed, except by the women she served. If Burr could remember right, the warrior from whom he'd bought Bucko was Black Buffalo. A surly, troublesome man, he just might think he could gain something from the woman's disappearance.

They stopped for a short time at Luis's ranch and watered the mules. Burr talked to the vaqueros left behind to guard the hacienda.

"Keep a sharp eye on the gap that goes into the lower valley. If a sizable force comes through, hightail it to the ranch and warn Luis. There won't be anything you can do here and there won't be anything you can do for us."

Quiet and grave, the vaqueros watched the wagon roll away.

The sun was almost straight overhead when the Indian camp came into view.

"Wheeeee . . ." Mooney whistled through his teeth. "That's a purty good-size camp!"

"Yeah, you stubborn old goat, I told you it would be!" Burr laughed without humor.

The wickiups formed a large circle within which there was still another ring of proportionately larger wickiups, and at the center of that circle, with a fire burning in front of it, stood the largest wickiup, that of the chief. An old man, he had three young, powerful chieftains. Burr had talked with them all, but found he liked one above all the others, the Indian called Geronimo. He realized the short, squat man would be a formidable enemy, but he also recognized in Geronimo a shrewd man. Geronimo was sure to understand the need to keep the white man alive so as to ensure future supplies for his people.

"Well, let's get on down there, Mooney, and see which way the wind blows. Don't let any hotheaded buck bait you into doing anything foolish."

"Don't you worry none. I ain't openin' my yap."

As they approached the camp they heard the noise of barking dogs and children. Unpleasant smells assailed their nostrils. From everywhere people came running to see the white visitors. A group of mounted braves charged forward, yipping, and encircled the wagon. They wore breechcloths and leggings, and their hair hung to their shoulders. Twisted bands of cloth were wrapped around their heads.

It seemed to Burr that all sound stopped as they entered the village. There was only the sound of a single dog barking frantically, and then it too became silent. Some of the Indians gathered around the wagon, others lined the route Burr and Mooney would take to reach the chief. Curious black eyes stared at the white men.

Burr and Mooney looked straight ahead, concentrating on the lodge in the middle of the camp. Mooney moved the mules to within a few yards of the big lodge and pulled them to a halt. Burr jumped lightly down, and the crowd fell back. He strode forward to meet the chief, and the two men shook hands. The Indian was large, with a muscular body and flat belly. His long hair was streaked with gray and fell unbound to his shoulders. His head was bare, but he needed no elaborate headdress. His majestic bearing alone distinguished him from the others.

"I greet my friend, chief of the Chiricahua Apaches," Burr said solemnly in Spanish.

"Greetings, Sky Eyes." The old Indian's voice held authority.

"I bring gifts from the house of stone, as I have done other times, in payment for the use of your land."

The old man nodded and went to the wagon to look at the supplies. The crowd moved back when he waved his hand. He grunted his satisfaction and raised his hand to beckon the three chieftains lined up in front of his lodge. They came forward, and Burr extended his hand. They shook it stoically. The chieftains talked together in low tones and poked and prodded the bags in the back of the wagon.

Burr stood at the head of the mules and tried to read the mood of the crowd. The women and children looked well fed, but there was a tenseness in the quiet faces, an attitude of expectancy. The warriors stood in groups. Those with rifles proudly displayed them in their folded arms. One cluster showed open hostility toward him . . . and one brave in the group more so than the others. He strutted back and forth spouting bitter words, his fierce eyes never leaving Burr's face. Burr looked at him boldly and allowed a flicker of contempt to show in his expression. The uneasiness he had felt all along escalated. Gray Cloud was showing too much resentment to back down. His pride would force him into action. Burr sensed what was to come. His muscles tensed and his mouth became dry.

One of the chieftains hefted the keg of powder from the wagon and pried open the lid. Smiles appeared on their faces, and they gathered about the small keg and talked in excited tones. On a word from the chief, a warrior came forward and carried the keg into the big lodge. He spoke again, and a group of braves started unloading the wagon, then came to stand in front of Burr.

"You brought no rifles."

"I brought powder. The bluecoats would chase me from your land if I came with rifles." Burr knew every eye was on him, and he looked straight into the fiercely proud eyes of the old man. "I have rifles to hunt food and to protect myself from Mexican *bundidos*."

The old man nodded and looked away at last, but the others continued to stare at him. "We will smoke," he said.

Burr moved over to the wagon where Mooney sat like a statue. He leaned over and made extra work of lifting a small bag from under the seat so he could speak.

"Stay on the wagon, but watch that bunch on your left. If they come at you, yell out like you're yelling at the mules."

Burr took the bag to the circle that was forming in front of the chief's lodge and handed it to the chief before he sat down. The Indian sniffed at the bag, and his eyes sparkled with pleasure.

"The tobacco comes from over the mountains. I will have more when you return in the spring."

A group of Indians came into the circle and lowered themselves cross-legged to the ground. Others sat close by and listened. The women and children dispersed, and the sounds of playing children, barking dogs, and scolding women could be heard once again.

The chief raised the pipe he was holding and after taking several long meditative puffs passed it to Burr, who puffed at it and passed it on. The pipe made a complete round of the circle. When it came back to the chief he carefully placed the long-stemmed feathered pipe before him. He looked directly at Burr and asked in fluent Spanish, "You bring people to our land?"

"No. I do not want more people to come and spoil your land."

There was an ominous murmur, but Burr kept his eyes on the old man. The chief raised his hand for silence, and all were instantly quiet. He lifted the pipe to his lips with dignity, puffed, and passed it again to Burr. After he passed it on, Burr searched the faces in the circle. The pit-marked face of Black Buffalo was there, and there was Gray Cloud, whose eyes burned with passionate hate. When the pipe passed, Black Buffalo he stood up, signaling his wish to speak when the ceremonial pipe completed the round.

When the pipe was returned, the chief once again placed it on the ground in front of him then nodded to Black Buffalo.

Black Buffalo spoke in the gutteral tongue of the Apache. He was enraged. The longer he talked the angrier he got. The chief listened without looking at him. He was handed another pipe, which he puffed for a moment before handing it to Burr. Black Buffalo continued to talk, and the men listened and smoked.

Finally the chief lifted his hand in an impatient gesture and Black Buffalo fell silent. The chief turned to Burr.

"Black Buffalo says you have stolen one of his wives. She has been gone from his lodge for two sunsets. He wants her back or you come with six ponies."

"Which one of his wives is missing?" Burr asked gravely.

"The most beautiful of all his wives," the chief said. "The one that gladens his heart the most. His third wife."

Burr looked straight into the dark eyes of the chief. "I have bartered with Black Buffalo and I have seen his third wife. If I steal a woman it will not be one who has been beaten until her spirit is broken, whose skin has been pierced many times and whose body has been starved until there is no fat."

Burr thought he saw a glint of amusement in the old chief's eyes. He gravely repeated the words to Black Buffalo. The Indian almost jumped with anger as he listened to the words of his chief. He opened his mouth to say something, but was silenced by a sharp word from the old man.

The warrior Gray Cloud, who showed such open hostility

toward him, sprang to his feet and began to talk. He addressed his words to all in the circle as well as the chief. His angry bright eyes and his sneering face often turned toward Burr, and he pointed his fist toward him and spat. Several men in the circle added remarks, and a few nodded in agreement to what the brave was saying. They were arguing about him; Burr knew this without understanding their words. The skin on the back of his neck tightened. He looked fleetingly at the chief. He was smoking calmly, his face expressionless.

Several braves behind the angry speaker got to their feet and began to dance. Burr's seemingly calm blue eyes found Mooney. The old cowboy sat stone-still, his coat pulled away from his weapons. The dancers began to chant.

"Heya . . . a . . . a . . . heya!"

An excited warrior leaped up brandishing a bow. The excitement was catching; more warriors jumped to their feet. Burr considered for a moment making a dash for the wagon and the rifle hidden in the compartment beneath Mooney's feet. He wished he knew what the chief was thinking.

Geronimo got to his feet. The speaker didn't wish to stop, but the chief raised his hand and the Indian stepped back, his face sullen and resentful. Geronimo spoke in dispassionate tones, his words rolling out of his mouth calmly and confidently. He talked for several minutes while the circle of men and the dancers grew quiet. The chief nodded his head as he listened. Geronimo stood with feet braced apart, and it seemed as if he had issued some sort of challenge to Gray Cloud, who drew himself up to his full height and looked contemptuously down at Burr. He drew his knife from his belt and sank the blade into the earth.

Geronimo turned to Burr and spoke in halting Spanish. "Gray Cloud wishes to kill all the paleskins in the valley. He has braves who will follow him. If you fight him and kill him you leave in peace to bring blankets and tobacco and powder when we come this way again. If he kills you we go to the house of stone and take what you have."

Burr got slowly to his feet. All eyes were on him. He felt a flash of elation. It was better than he had feared—at least they had a chance. He drew his knife from his belt and with one flick of his wrist sank it into the ground between Gray Cloud's feet. The Indian's eyes burned hotly.

Geronimo drew a large circle in the dirt with a stick. Gray Cloud stood proudly among his admirers, and Burr, after picking up his knife, went to the wagon.

"I'm going to fight him," he said, taking off his shirt. "If I kill him we can go and the ranch will be left alone. If he kills me they ride on the ranch." He grinned up at Mooney. "We got a chance. It's more than I thought we had a while ago."

"Gol damn, Burr," Mooney said, taking off his hat and wiping his face on his sleeve. "It's tight, ain't it?"

"Yeah, it's tight, Mooney, but I'm not too bad with a blade. Luis taught me a trick or two. The only thing I can tell you, old friend, is if it looks like I'm not going to make it you whip up them mules and try to get to the ranch." He didn't mention that it was almost certain he wouldn't make it, but Mooney knew that. He wrapped his neckerchief tightly about his right hand. "Give me a chaw of that tobacco, Mooney. I got to take every advantage I can get." Immensely glad he had chosen to wear moccasins that allowed him greater agility, Burr popped the tobacco into his mouth, took a tight grip on the handle of his knife, and walked into the circle.

The crowd closed in. Gray Cloud, obviously confident of his prowess with the knife, was enjoying the attention now focused on him. He was taller than the average Apache, broad in the shoulders and thick through the chest. His legs and arms were heavily muscled, and he moved on the balls of his feet like a cat. He stood legs apart, one ahead of the other, staring at Burr. He was supremely confident, having fought many battles with other Apache tribes, Mexicans, and the Yaqui Indians of Mexico.

Burr gripped his knife tighter as the Apache moved in, his blade darting and thrusting like the tongue of a striking rattle-snake. The point of the blade ripped a small gash in Burr's forearm. He sprang forward, then Gray Cloud leaped back to escape the thrusting knife. They fell into the dirt and rolled over, stabbing and thrusting. They came up facing each other. There was blood running down the Indian's shoulder. Burr was bloody, too.

"Shit-eatin' buzzard," Burr hissed in English.

He held his knife low, cutting edge up. They circled each other, ramming and stabbing. Another fleck of blood showed on Burr's forearm. The Indian was incredibly fast. His flat, hard face and cold eyes showed no emotion. He lunged forward. Burr moved and seemed to slip; the Indian sprang to the side, and Burr swung with his left fist, catching Gray Cloud on the side of the head, knocking him to the ground. Gray Cloud came up swiftly, thrusting low for Burr's crotch, but Burr knocked the knife aside and lunged. His blade sliced a path across the Indian's chest. Gray Cloud swung around, striking rapidly with his knife; it went into Burr's shoulder. Burr struck again with his fist, and they both fell. The blood from Burr's arm soaked the cloth tied around his knife hand.

The Indian was on his feet first and lunged. Burr side stepped and caught Gray Cloud's wrist, throwing him over. He moved in to step on the knife arm, but the Indian rolled and came up slashing. Burr circled to the right, forcing the Indian to turn. Blood ran down his chest, and he could feel it, wet, in the bottoms of his moccasins. He moved his foot forward, gaining a step, then crouched. The Indian feinted, then came in fast. Burr struck the knife arm as the blade entered his side. He grunted with pain and clamped his hand on the Indian's arm, his fingers seeking the funny bone, to find it and paralyze it so he would drop the knife. For a moment they fought, straining every muscle, then the Indian suddenly yielded and stepped back, throwing Burr off balance. He lost his grip on the knife when his fist hit the hard ground. The Indian sprang up, and Burr rolled over and came to his feet empty-handed.

Gray Cloud leaped at him, and Burr side stepped, his left forearm taking the tip of the blade, his right fist smashing into the face of the Indian. The second Gray Cloud hit the ground, Burr was on him, his powerful arm straining to hold the knife away from his body. Burr hammered the Indian with his fist while the clawlike hand grabbed for the soft parts between his legs. Wildly, bitterly, and desperately they fought, their bodies slick with blood. They rolled in the dirt, their faces close. Burr got his hand into the oily hair and jerked Gray Cloud's head back. The hate-filled eyes blazed up at him. It was the chance he had been waiting for. He spat a thick stream of tobacco juice into the blazing black eyes.

The Indian let out a yell, and Burr's two hands closed over the knife in his fist and plunged it into the Indian's throat. A well of blood gushed up, covering Burr's hands. Dazed, he looked at Gray Cloud, expecting him to spring up again. He got to his feet and backed away.

The shrill keening of the women made him aware the fight was over. He staggered to the wagon. Mooney reached down, grasped his hand, and hauled him up onto the seat.

"Hee-yaw! Heeee-ee-yaw!" Mooney shouted to the team and cracked the whip over their backs. The crowd parted and the wagon rolled out of the village.

Mooney walked the mules until they were up over the rise and out of sight of the camp, then he stood and cracked the whip viciously over their backs, whipping them into a run. Burr swayed dizzily on the seat, his chin on his chest, blood dripping from a dozen cuts on his arms, chest, and back. Realizing he could tumble from the seat, Mooney slowed the mules to a fast walk and held onto Burr with one hand. After a while he pulled the mules to a halt and tried to stanch blood coming from Burr's side.

"I'm all right. Go on," Burr said weakly. "Just let me . . . lie . . . down."

Mooney stood and eased Burr down onto the seat. "Hold on—we ain't far from Luis's place."

Still, progress was slow. Mooney was afraid to run the mules, afraid Burr might bounce off the seat. A rough ride might even cause more bleeding. The late-afternoon sun was low in the sky and Burr had been unconscious for some time before Mooney spotted a rider in the distance. He signaled by waving his hat, and soon the rider came at a gallop. It was Luis, and he let out an astonished oath when he saw his brother's ghastly pallor and ugly wounds.

"Get up here and hold on to Burr so I can whip up these mules," Mooney said. "Ain't more'n a couple miles to yer place."

Burr roused when Luis knelt beside him to lift his head.

"Tobaccy did the trick, brother . . . but God, I'm sick." He vomited.

"Swallered too much juice, I reckon," Mooney said.

When they reached the hacienda they placed a straw tick in the back of the wagon so that Burr would be more comfortable. They talked about leaving him there and having Mooney ride to the ranch for Ben and Johanna, but decided the needed care would come faster if they took him home.

Mooney filled Luis in on the happenings at the camp.

"Burr fought like a wildcat," he said with pride. "And that Indian buck was ugly—ugly as a mud fence. He shore did want to take our hair and ride on the ranch. Don't think we'll have no trouble now."

CHAPTER EIGHTEEN

IT WOULD BE the longest, most miserable day in Johanna's life. From the moment Burr's wagon rolled out of the corral she had a sick, uneasy feeling in the pit of her stomach. At first she was angry because of the flippant attitude he had taken about going to the Indian camp. After thinking about it she decided the flippancy probably was to conceal deeper feelings.

It was high noon when they buried old Mack and the Indian girl. Johanna and Ben rode on the tailgate of the wagon that carried the bodies to the small cemetery. Red drove, and Codger sat beside him. Bucko was left in Jacy's care. It was decided not to ask the padre to stay over for the burial, because Mack would have scorned a service. Under Ben's instructions a grave for Mack was dug at the far end of the burial ground, as far away as possible from that of Anna Englebretson and Juanita Gazares, although the resting place for the mother of Mack's third bastard son would be near that of the mothers of his two other sons.

They placed the woman's body in the ground first. Red carried the slight blanket-wrapped body and placed it in the grave. Johanna was pained as she looked down at the pitiful bundle. She wished she knew the woman's name. As the two men covered the body with earth, she softly recited the Lord's Prayer, knowing it would mean nothing to the woman, but somehow she felt better for doing it.

The men were sweating profusely by the time they got old Mack's huge bulk out of the wagon and into the grave. They stood with hats in hand while Ben read from Scripture, then shoveled the soft earth over the body, ensuring that his dust would remain forever in the valley he had loved.

Red and Codger went back to the wagon and waited while Johanna and Ben walked over to the other graves. She read the inscriptions on the board markers. Tears flooded her eyes. Anna had been only twenty years old when she died. She had been even younger than Jacy when she was introduced to Mack's cruelty.

Ben's hand reached out and caressed the top of the board marker on Anna's grave. Johanna looked at him through her tears and saw that his face was serene. His eyes had a faraway look as if he were seeing once again the fragile, golden-haired girl with enormous blue eyes. As she moved away to leave him alone, she heard him say softly, "It's going to be all right now, Anna."

On the way back to the house, Ben's words stayed with her. She clung to them for reassurance. If Burr lived to come back to her she imagined her own life would be a series of crises that would run from ecstatic happiness to the depths of despair. She loved Burr Macklin. She would be more miserable away from him than with him. She reached out and touched Ben's hand. She needed physical contact with someone who loved Burr.

"I'm scared, Ben."

He patted her hand. "I know. So am I, but it's going to be all right. I feel it. It's going to work out. It is working out."

Red pulled the team up in front of the house, and Johanna and Ben went up the dirt path to the porch. It looked different. The enormous cowhide-covered chair and the bucket old Mack used for a gaboon were gone, although the tobacco-juice stains remained. The door to his room stood open, an eerie silence emanating from it. In the kitchen Rosita was busy with the noon meal while another Mexican woman cleaned. They were laughing and talking, but fell silent when they saw Johanna standing in the doorway. Bucko and Harley, Rosita's little one, sat at the table stuffing themselves with warm bread smeared with butter and sprinkled with sugar.

"Señora," Rosita said, "Señor Burr tell me to come and bring Sofía, she have no family, she stay and help you, no?"

"*Sí*. I would like Sofía to stay and help."

The short, plump woman's face was wreathed with smiles. She dipped the mop into the bucket of water and scrubbed the floor vigorously.

Jacy and Luis were across the hall in the sitting room. Johanna stopped and stared when she saw her brother-in-law striding nervously the length of the room. It was undoubtedly the first time Luis had been inside the house.

Jacy jumped up from the comfortable chair. "Johanna, can't you feel the change in this house already? Oh, I don't . . . I know. It's wicked to be . . . not sad, it's not that I'm glad, but . . ."

Luis looked at her with an indulgent smile. "*Vida mía*, sit down and rest. You've been like a small drop of water dancing on a hot stove." He continued his pacing.

"When do you think they'll be back, Luis?"

"I do not know, *hermana*, perhaps not till dark."

It was comforting to hear him call her sister, but his anxiety mangled her nerves.

"Not before then?" The anguish in her voice brought Jacy to her side.

"Burr's going to be all right, Johanna." Her eyes sought those of her husband. "Didn't I tell you she loved him, Luis? Didn't I tell you Johanna wouldn't have married him if she didn't love him?"

"Yes, little one, you told me." He gazed at his wife with such love blazing in his eyes that Johanna felt a stab of poignant longing. "I think I'll ride out," he said abruptly.

Jacy threw her arms about his waist and buried her face against his chest. "If you feel you must go, my husband, be careful."

"Of course." He raised her face with gentle hands. "My first

212

concern is for you, my life. My next is for my brother and"—he looked at Johanna—"his wife."

They walked out of the room, their arms entwined, and Johanna slumped down in the chair. She sat for only a few minutes before jumping to her feet. She went out in the hall in search of Ben, passed the old man's room, then slowly went back and looked in. It was almost bare; only the rope bed, the table, and the bureau remained. Everything, including the floor, had been scrubbed clean, and it smelled of soap and damp wood. Johanna again felt sorrow for the man who had been so lacking in feeling for those around him that they couldn't wait to remove all trace of him. Deep in thought, she wandered out onto the back porch only to be startled by the sudden appearance of Isabella, on her way into Burr's room. Johanna felt a surge of anger that propelled her into the room in time to see the woman toss some freshly washed shirts onto the bed. Isabella turned to face her rival, her eyes challenging, her mouth curled in contempt. Johanna, however, was prepared to face her down. It was Isabella who finally lowered her eyes and then, with spiteful arrogance, attempted to sweep past Johanna. She did not get far before Johanna grabbed her arm. Isabella whirled, her eyes full of venom.

"You are never to come into this house again," Johanna said, with all the self-assurance she could muster.

"Only Señor Burr tell me what to do," Isabella hissed, confidence blazing in her eyes.

Johanna smiled coldly. "I am mistress of this house." The very words now brought with them a new confidence. "If you wish to remain in the valley you will do as I say."

Isabella, not unlike a brazen child, placed her hands on her hips and flaunted her body.

"Gringa!" she taunted. "You not woman enough for Señor Burr! He no want your pale skin and body sharp with bones. You go!"

Johanna's anger turned to wide-eyed disbelief. "I'm here to stay. You had better understand that right now. You are not to come here again. *Comprend?*"

213

There was such loathing and violence in Isabella's eyes that had Johanna been less angry she might have chosen her words more carefully. But Johanna was blinded by her own emotions. She was jealous of the woman who had obviously pleased her husband. Isabella spoke again.

"You never have the señor's *niño*! I swear it! Señor Burr my man! You know nothing of how to please him!" And as though to inflict further pain, "Luis not wed your *puta* sister if not for *niño* in her belly."

"That's enough!" Johanna said sharply.

"What I say is so, *gringa*." The Mexican girl spun around and was through the door before Johanna could say another word.

Johanna followed her out of the house, and from the porch watched her race down the path toward the adobe house. Calmer with Isabella gone, Johanna began to play back their conversation and realized Isabella's threat. But she refused to be cowed. She went back through the house and out to the front porch, where she found Ben looking off into the valley. He took the pipe from his mouth.

"I see Luis couldn't stand it any longer," he said quietly. "But don't worry, he won't do anything foolish. Sit down, lass, we'll wait together."

The afternoon wore on. Johanna strained her eyes toward the horizon, watching and waiting for a moving speck, a puff of dust, anything that would mean that Burr was on his way home. Neither she nor Ben exchanged a word. For once, the man beside her didn't wish to visit.

The shadow of the mountain crept down over the ranch buildings and the air became cooler. Rosita brought a warm shawl for Johanna, and Jacy, wrapped in a blanket, joined them on the porch, her usual exuberance dampened by worry. Across the porch, Sofía came out of Burr's room. She was lighting fires in the hearths to relieve the evening chill. Food smells wafted unnoticed from the kitchen, where Rosita was preparing their meal.

At first Johanna wasn't sure she had seen anything. She had moved to the edge of the house, all of her senses willing the image for which she hoped. The speck was too large to be a horseman; still she waited, scarcely breathing. The speck disappeared down an incline, and it was a long while before it appeared again, larger this time. It was the wagon, and her heart leaped with relief.

"They're coming, Ben!" She wrapped her arms about the heavy post supporting the roof, and her eyes clung to the wagon. As it drew nearer, her happiness dimmed. Only one man sat on the seat, and it was the unmistakable figure of Mooney. Oh, God, she thought, don't let him be dead! On numbed legs she walked out onto the path in front of the house. She could see Luis's horse tied behind the wagon and his black sombrero bobbing up and down behind the wagon seat. She stood very still, trying to fight the feeling of despair that threatened to swamp her.

Red's big sorrel horse sped by her. He was riding out to the wagon. He looked into the bed and talked to Luis, then wheeled his horse and rode to the house.

"They're all right," he shouted. He pulled his horse to a stop. The animal danced around while Red said, "Burr's been cut up some. You'll need hot water and lots of clean cloth."

Johanna's heart soared. The fact that he was alive galvanized her into action. She ran to the kitchen, calling out orders to Sofía and Rosita, then went swiftly to Burr's room to stoke up the fire.

Mooney pulled the wagon up to the edge of the porch and hopped down while Johanna waited anxiously, her eyes seeking her husband. It took three men to carry Burr's limp body into the house and place it on the bed. He was almost totally covered with blankets, so Johanna saw only the top of his head and the soles of his moccasins.

"Johanner," said Mooney, at her side, "he'll be fine as a fiddle in a day or two. Lost a parcel of blood, and you best wait here and let Ben and Luis clean him up a bit." Johanna would not be deterred. She was sure she could help.

Sofía bustled by carrying the teakettle and an armful of clean cloths. Rosita came along behind with whiskey and a large washbasin, and Johanna followed. It was Luis who barred her way.

"In just a few minutes, sister. No man wants his woman to see him so."

"What's the matter with him that you don't want me to see him?" Her voice rose in hysteria.

"He throwed up, that's what he done, Johanner," Mooney said. "Come and sit and I'll tell ya about it."

They were outside Burr's door, and the ranch hands, who would not have dared set foot on the porch while old Mack was alive, gathered around. Mooney was in his glory. They hung on every word he spoke.

"I tell you that Indian, the one that wanted to kill us and go on a rampage, was meaner than a steer with a crooked horn. He was big, too, and madder than a cow with her tit caught in a fence." Mooney described every gory detail, leaving nothing to their imagination, and the men, if not Johanna, enjoyed it all.

It wasn't until later that Johanna remembered that not a word about old Mack had been spoken all day. From outward appearances, at least, it was as though he'd never existed. Red took his family home and Mooney went back to the bunkhouse.

Jacy was sure Johanna would want to be near her husband, as much as she longed to be with Luis. She was so totally devoted to Luis, so very happy, that it colored everything around her and made her oblivious to the real situation between Johanna and Burr. She asked Johanna if she and Luis could use the room at the top of the stairs, as she was sure Johanna would want to stay near Burr. It was something Johanna hadn't expected, but she hadn't the heart to refuse. Ben offered his room to her, but she refused, saying she would sleep with Bucko, where she would be near if Burr should wake and need her. As it was he slept for twenty-four hours, and when he woke the house had been restored to some semblance of order.

Sofía was by now preparing the evening meal, tending the large joint of meat simmering on the stove. Meat, she knew, and thick broth, was the quickest way to replace blood.

Johanna had bent to place a small log on the fire when his voice came from the bed.

"I'm hungry."

The words were barely whispered, but she heard them.

"You're awake." She said no more, because her voice was so shaky and it wouldn't do to let him know how worried she had been, how glad she was to have him back.

"Yeah. Hunger is gnawing a hole in my belly."

"You've already got one hole in you, and you don't need another. I'll bring you some broth."

He pulled the cover back and lifted his head, his hand seeking the bandage on his side. He closed his eyes against the pain that shot through him and moaned. His head fell back on the pillow, and he looked up at her with the familiar, irritating, obstinate look on his face. Damn know-it-all woman! She was so damn confident, so . . . haughty, and so goddam . . . beautiful. He couldn't even look at her without feeling like an inferior dumbhead. He didn't like that feeling. It brought out the worst of him.

"I don't need any damn broth! I need meat. Where's Ben?"

With hands on her hips, Johanna glared down at him. He was back to his true self: demanding, ungrateful . . . and crude.

"I'll call Ben and Sofía will bring your . . . meat."

"You bring it. You're my wife," he called as she left the room.

She stuck her head back in the door. "Unfortunately, but not your servant."

In Ben's room, Ben and Luis were going over a stack of papers found in old Mack's bureau. They looked up when Johanna appeared in the door.

"He's awake," she announced, "and cross as a bear."

She walked brusquely down the hall and out onto the back porch. Her eyes found, instantly, the straw hat nailed to the top of the door. The unpleasant symbol of her humiliation brought an angry prick of heat. How would she ever manage to muster the strength to live here in Macklin Valley as the wife of so unfeeling a person as Burr Macklin? She looked out over the peaceful valley, felt the cool mountain air on her cheeks, and gradually regained her composure. Dwelling on the situation would not change it.

*   *   *

When the evening meal was over, she and Jacy settled down in the sitting room. Jacy had spent time with Burr while Johanna helped Sofía. Johanna hadn't gone near her husband since she had left his room shortly after he had awakened, and Jacy, although puzzled by her sister's behavior, didn't ask any questions.

Jacy and Luis were going to stay at the stone house until the Apaches left the valley, and having them there, so obviously in love, made Johanna more aware than ever that she was the wife of a man who did not love her. She kept thinking that had the wedding been scheduled for a few hours later there would have been no need for her to marry Burr. Old Mack was dead, and surely it could be established that Burr, Luis, and Bucko were his heirs.

Luis came for Jacy. He and Ben had been with Burr for over an hour.

"Come with me, *querida*." He pulled her up and out of the deep chair. "Ben wishes to talk with your sister, and you need to rest."

"Is he in his room?"

"No, sister, he's with your husband." His eyes flicked to Jacy to see if she had noticed the tightening of Johanna's lips.

Johanna picked up a shawl and draped it over her shoulders. The arrangement of the house, with all outside doors, is ridiculous, she thought, going out the door and along the darkened porch.

Two lamps were lit in Burr's room; one sat on the table beside the bed and cast a glow on his stern and forbidding features, the other sat on the wide mantel shelf. Burr said nothing to her, but his eyes met hers the moment she walked through the door.

Ben got to his feet. "Come sit here, Johanna. Burr and I want to talk to you."

Johanna advanced slowly, pulling the shawl closely about her, because although the room was warm, she suddenly felt cold. Burr was propped up on the bed, and several papers lay on the quilt beside him.

"We found a paper among Mack's things, Johanna, that concerns you." Ben cleared his throat.

Startled, she looked at him questioningly.

"Mack left a letter to let us know, in case of his death, that when Willard Risewick left the valley he carried with him a will making you his heir. You're to receive his land and his money." Ben finished speaking and looked at Burr.

The full import of his words did not at first take root in her mind. She was shocked and confused. Finally she gasped, "No! He couldn't have."

"He did," Burr said with a sardonic grin. "You played your cards right, little fox. He liked the way you stood up to him and told him how the cow ate the cabbage. You're rich. You can go to town and buy your own saloon. Only thing is, I'm not having my wife living in town. Old man kicked off just a bit too late for you, little fox. Just about a day too late."

"Burr . . ." Ben's voice was filled with exasperation. "I wish you wouldn't talk like this. Tell her all of it, or I will."

Johanna jumped to her feet. "I don't want it! I never wanted it! I'll go to town and sign it over to you and Luis. Ben . . ." She looked at him pleadingly.

"Don't get so worked up, little wife. You didn't get it all. You got a pile of money, but only a bit of land. The house is yours, and you can throw me and Ben out of it anytime you take a notion. We'll just go over a ways and build ourselves another."

"Burr, there are times when I wish you were small again. I'd take a stick to you."

"Let me have my fun, Ben. It's not often a little fox gets outfoxed."

"Johanna, come sit down, lass. I want to tell you something you should have been told long ago, and would have except for this stubborn boy of mine. As I told you before, I legally adopted the boys long ago. Well, back in 1853 the United States bought hundreds of square miles of land from Mexico. It was called the Gadsden Purchase, and this valley was included in the land that was bought. All title to the land had to be reestablished in Sante Fe. Mack went there and filed. A year later I went to Santa Fe and discovered Mack had filed on the number of sections the law would allow. I filed on an allotted number of sections and took out tentative title to sections in the names of the boys. That meant that if no one else filed on the land, when they became of age they could go to the land office and sign and the land would be theirs. The three of us own all the land surrounding Mack's. Mack never knew that. He assumed he owned the whole valley, and that lawyer of his let him think that. Probably too scared of him to tell him otherwise." Ben had been looking at the paper in his hand while he talked. Now he looked up. Johanna's face was coolly composed and it was impossible to tell what she was thinking. "I explained the situation to Risewick, Johanna. Now you see why he didn't push to buy the land."

Johanna's eyes swung toward him. "And there was no danger the valley would be turned into a battleground?" She said the words fatalistically.

"Not by . . . no, Johanna."

"And I need not have married to keep the valley safe for Jacy and to save the land for Luis and . . . him?"

"Ah . . . no, Johanna."

"I see." She got to her feet, and going to the end of the room, stood with her back to the men and closed her eyes. She wasn't angry. She felt betrayed, and she couldn't understand why Burr had done this to her. Turning back, she came to the foot of the bed and addressed her words to him.

"Why did you marry me? Why did you go to all the trouble of making up the lie about the land's being sold when you knew it would never happen?"

Burr grinned, but in no way was it an embarrassed or sheepish grin. He was enormously pleased with himself and wanted her to know it.

"I wanted your sister to be happy." The smile left his face. "If she is happy, Luis will be happy. I wanted you to stay and teach Bucko." He looked at her now with eyes that mocked, teased. "There's a couple more reasons. You're not a bad-looking woman, and I get tired going to El Paseo to visit the . . ."

Johanna interrupted. "I'll be leaving as soon as Jacy's baby is born." She spoke to Ben. "I'll see to it that the land is put in Bucko's name—he's more deserving of it than I am—and the money divided between Mr. Macklin's sons. I'll keep enough for myself to see me through to California and a teaching job. I'm entitled to that much. My main concern is for Jacy. I don't want her to know of my plans or about any of this . . . sordid affair. Distress at this time wouldn't be good for her."

"Lass, don't make plans just yet. Give yourself a little time. I know how you feel, but—"

"You couldn't possibly know how I feel. Being victimized by old Mack's son doesn't surprise me, but you, Ben . . . I'm disappointed in you."

"Hold on." Burr swung his legs off the bed and sat up with a grunt of pain. "Don't go blaming Ben for any of this. It was my idea."

Johanna didn't look at him.

"Yes, lass, he knew you wanted to leave, and he thought—"

"He was right, Ben." She started for the door.

"You're not going anywhere! You're my wife, by God, like it or not, and you'll stay here, damn you!" Burr's angry voice filled every corner of the room.

Without a backward glance Johanna went out the door. Dimly she heard Ben's raised and agitated voice talking to Burr.

When the Apaches dismantled their camp and started the long trek to the mountains of Mexico, Luis loaded Jacy's belongings into the wagon along with supplies from the storage shed and foodstuffs Johanna and Codger had boxed up from the root cellar and the smokehouse. Burr brought a milch cow from the barn and tied her behind the wagon. He had been up and about since the day after the fight, but moved slowly and painfully. At the last minute, while the goodbyes were being said, Mooney came from the bunkhouse proudly carrying a cradle. It was small, but expertly made. The bare wood had been rubbed smooth and a coat of wax applied. Jacy was ecstatic, and after Mooney carefully set the cradle in the wagon she insisted he come around so she could plant a kiss on his weathered cheek. He was all grins and embarrassment.

Johanna watched the slowly moving wagon for a long while, then went to her room beneath the roof. The minute she closed the door she gave herself up to the pain and confusion she'd kept locked inside her. The facade of cheerfulness that she'd held in place for Jacy's sake would surely have collapsed had it gone on much longer. Sofía had been a blessing, relieving her of much of the work, and giving her time to devote to Bucko. Thankfully, Burr made himself scarce as soon as he was able to be up and around. She hadn't spoken directly to him since the night Ben had told her about old Mack's will.

Johanna stretched out on the bed and stared at the tin ceiling. Whatever had possessed that old man, she asked herself for the hundredth time, to leave his land and money to her? Surely it was to spite Burr and Luis. It was clear to her now that Burr had married her, not to keep his land as she first thought, but to keep Jacy happy for Luis's sake and to care for Bucko. Her affection for the boy was obvious. And, of course, Burr himself would have the convenience of a whore right here in the valley. Hadn't he told her that when she had first arrived? That really wasn't true, she told herself bitterly. He already had one in Isabella.

She counted on her fingers. Jacy should have her baby in less than six weeks. Six weeks! How was she going to endure staying in this house for that long?

CHAPTER NINETEEN

THE DAYS SPED by faster than Johanna thought possible. The occupants of the stone house settled into a routine. Burr was up at first light and gone from the house, not to return until before evening. He had retreated behind a wall of polite silence. At times Johanna would search his face for a sign of softness, of real humanity. She saw only eyes hard as steel, a firm outthrust jaw, and an implacable mouth. Ben breakfasted early and either went to his room or over to the bunkhouse, leaving Johanna and Bucko to have their meal alone.

Johanna was constantly surprised by Bucko. The little boy was very bright and even witty. They spent the morning hours at the table in the sitting room working on reading, numbers, and penmanship, and in the afternoon, if the day was warm, they walked down to the Mexican village. Bucko seemed to be unaware of the tension between Johanna and Ben and Burr. Evening meals were pleasant enough as Ben and Burr discussed ranch work and Johanna encouraged Bucko to talk. He was opening up more and more, wishing to share his new knowledge with the others. His English was improving, and Burr seemed to be pleased.

One day he put down his book and asked Johanna the question she had been waiting for him to ask.

"Why did the woman kill old Mack?"

Johanna thought for a moment, then sat down and pulled the boy down on her lap. "Long ago old Mack did a cruel thing to the woman. She was young, a beautiful young Apache girl, and he shamed her. It's terribly hard to be shamed before your family and friends. She must have thought it right to kill him."

"What did he do to her?"

Without hesitation Johanna answered. "He put a baby in her stomach and went away and left her. She didn't have anyone to take care of her and she had to work hard so that she would have enough food to eat. She wasn't strong, and a lot of the time she was tired and hungry."

Bucko was quiet for a long while. "The baby was me, Johanna. I was hungry, too, before Burr bringed me here."

"The word is 'brought,' and yes, I'm sure you were hungry, too."

"I'm glad she kill him," he said fiercely. "She was brave."

"Yes, she was brave, but killing is never right, Bucko. I think in this case she thought it was the right thing to do." She hugged him close. "The woman was your mother, darling. Think about her, but forget about old Mack. You have two brothers who will take care of you now."

That evening at the supper table, during a lull in the conversation, Johanna encouraged Bucko to talk.

"We had a history lesson today. Bucko, tell Ben about Christopher Columbus."

Bucko looked proudly around the table. He was beginning to enjoy having everyone listen while he talked. He spoke in halting English.

"The woman kill old Mack for he put me in her stom . . . chy. She was tired with shame and hungry. She was very brave." His eyes searched the faces of the two men to see their reaction to his news. They were speechless.

Burr carefully sat his mug down and glared at Johanna.

Although as astonished as the men, Johanna said calmly, "Your English is much better, Bucko, but the word is 'stomach.'"

Some call it 'belly,' but I don't think it's as pretty a word as 'stomach.' We'll learn to spell it tomorrow, if you like."

Burr was waiting for her when she left the kitchen after helping Sofía. Somehow she had known he would be.

"Why did you tell Bucko a thing like that?" he demanded.

Johanna lifted her head and drew her dignity about her like a blanket. "Because he asked me, and I don't lie." She emphasized the word 'I,' and saw his face tighten with anger.

"I told you I didn't want him to know anything about that."

"You told me nothing of the kind, and if you had, I would still have used my own judgment."

"Another thing. He's liking you too much! You'll . . . go and leave him and he won't understand. So don't spend so much time with him."

"All right, but you tell him, Mr. . . . Calloway. You tell him to stay away from me. Try to explain that to him, if you can. As long as I'm here I'm going to teach him, and when I go, Jacy will take over the lessons. He's too bright a child to remain ignorant." She walked away from him and made her way up the dimly lit stairs to her room.

Aware that he stood below watching her, she firmly closed the door and felt her way in the darkness to the table and lit the candle. She heard the pounding of the boot heels on the stairs, and by the time she'd turned he'd flung open the door. He ducked his head and stepped inside the room.

"Don't walk away from me when I'm talking to you . . . like I'm . . . nothing!"

Johanna raised her brows. "You put your own value on yourself, Mr. Calloway."

"And don't, ever again, go to my men and ask them to take you away from here! I won't be shamed in front of those who work for me. Is that clear? When the time comes for you to go, I'll take you myself and be glad to be rid of you!" His loud, angry voice bounced into every corner of the small room.

"Very well. That sounds like a reasonable request." She moved out of the light. "Now, please leave my room."

He stood scowling for a minute, then ran his fingers through his unruly mop of hair.

"I asked you to leave." Every nerve in her body was screaming.

Burr stared at her as if mesmerized.

She put her hands behind her to hide their trembling and encountered the hairbrush on the table. Her tense fingers gripped the handle and her cool control broke.

"Get out!" she shouted and flung the brush. It bounced off his chest and fell to the floor with a loud clatter.

He looked at her searchingly for a moment, his eyes probing her angry ones. Then he backed out the door, closing it behind him.

She threw herself on the bed and sobbed. She hated herself for what she'd just done. She loved him!

It was the week before Thanksgiving and the weather had turned cold. Now Johanna spent an hour each morning with Bucko before sending him down to the bunkhouse or over to Rosita's. She did her best to explain to him that she was spending too much time on his lessons and neglecting her housekeeping duties. The little boy accepted the new routine, but seemed dejected and less happy and talkative than before. Reluctantly Johanna admitted to herself that Burr was right—Bucko was becoming too fond of her, too dependent on her company. It would be easier for him when she left the valley if she gradually weened him away from her now.

Jacy's baby was due to arrive in a few weeks. She had settled nicely into her new home and was so glowingly happy that Johanna was sure she would be content with Luis and the baby when she was gone. Two families had moved to Luis's ranch, and one of the women came in each day to help with the work and to be with Jacy while Luis was away. Johanna's heart was lighter each time she returned from a visit with her sister. It had worked out well. Their coming to the valley had been right for Jacy . . . but oh, so wrong for her.

It was afternoon. Johanna wandered about the ranch and paused at the corral to watch the cowboys break a dun-colored stallion.

A whoop went up from the men as she approached, and she climbed onto the rail just as the stallion broke away from the opposite fence and bucked his way to the center of the corral. His sharp hoofs stirred up a cloud of dust in his frenzy to rid himself of the man clinging to his back. One moment the cowboy was there, the next he was arcing high in the air before crashing to the ground. Seconds later he was up and scrambling over the fence, slapping his floppy-brimmed hat against his leg and enduring the good-natured joshing of his friends.

"I don't see you galoots a-tryin' 'em. All you're a-doin' is a-runnin' yore mouth and a-ridin' the rail." He climbed on the rail beside Johanna.

"That was a hard fall. I hope you're not hurt."

" 'Twarn't nothin', ma'am. Woulda been iffen he'da got a hoof on me. He's a wild un. Never lets ya get settled in, just takes off a-rompin'. He'll make a good un once he gets whipped in shape. He can turn on a dime and give ya a nickel to boot."

Several cowboys were still trying to rope the bucking horse. Finally they had the mustang caught between two ropes. They held him fast while a bowlegged Mexican vaquero ran to his head and tied a handkerchief over his eyes. He then grabbed one of his ears between his teeth.

"I feel sorry for him," Johanna muttered.

"Ma'am," the cowboy snorted, "that grulla ain't the one ter feel sorry fer. He's a heller, that un."

Paco called down from the fence, "Señora, your man, he gonna try him."

Burr settled himself firmly in the saddle, his long legs locked against the heaving sides of the animal and his feet planted in the stirrups. His work shirt was open to the waist, revealing his hard-muscled chest and a binding of white cloth about his middle. Oh, God, Johanna thought frantically, that wound isn't healed enough to take this kind of punishment! For a fleeting second his eyes locked with hers, then he wound the reins around his gloved hand and tugged at his hat. Not a flicker of surprise showed on his face at seeing her at the corral fence. He said something to the cowboy holding the horse's head. The cowboys leaped back and dived for cover. One had taken the blinder with him. The grulla stood for a fraction of a second, then exploded into the air like a coiled spring in release. The animal twisted in midair and came down on all four feet with a bone-jarring crash. With renewed frenzy he continued to buck. But Burr held fast.

A whoop went up from the cowboys on the fence. The longer Burr stayed in the saddle, the louder they hollered encouragement. With cold-blooded determination the mustang's body continued to jounce his rider. Johanna held her breath as Burr was whipped back and forth. Through the swirling dust she saw the horse leap up, his hind legs lashing out to splinter the rail behind him. He landed on the run and circled the corral, wheeled, and headed around once again before charging the fence. Burr yanked the mustang aside. The eyes of the beast were wild and rolling, and he screamed with rage and shot into the air again, then stood on spraddled, quivering legs.

Burr sat the horse for a moment, then called softly, "Come get me off."

Two loops were put over the horse's neck and pulled taut. Slowly and painfully Burr climbed down from the saddle. The white binding around his middle was stained with blood, and his jaw was clenched with pain. He squinted, passed Johanna without expression. The cowboys whooped and exchanged money. Not until the air escaped from her tortured lungs did Johanna realize she had been holding her breath.

She walked past the house and up the path toward the smokehouse. She needed a quiet place where she could gather her thoughts and calm her nerves. It seemed to her she had been living in limbo for the past few weeks. She and Burr did no more than barely acknowledge each other when they met for meals. At first, Ben had tried to heal the breach between them, but days ago he had given up and retreated behind a polite silence. Now it was the waiting period. Waiting for Jacy to have her baby. Waiting to know her sister was well and happy. Waiting to leave the valley and make some order of her life once again.

* * *

Isabella stood close to the walls of the smokehouse. She could hear the faintly audible shouts of the men at the corral. From here she could see the rising dust created by horses being broken.

Her heart pounded. The *gringa* was coming up the path. The pale *puta* who had taken her man was walking straight to her death, and she, Isabella, was glad. Let the bitch go unsuspecting to the stream and the Apache warrior who waited there!

Isabella's sharp, experienced eyes had seen the Indian, standing in the shadows, as still as the large boulders that lined the stream. Her eyes had passed over him twice before the outline of his head alerted her to his presence. Unconcerned, she veered off and circled back to the smokehouse. Her intention, at first, had been to report to Señor Burr, for since the Apache seasonal camp had broken up the vigilance had relaxed. Surely her discovery would make him proud of her, make him realize she was better fit to be his wife, have his sons, but . . . no!

She quivered with excitement as she watched Johanna approach. Señor Burr had scorned her, forsaken her, cast her out for the pale, haughty *gringa*! Señor Burr, the man she loved with all her heart, had even suggested she marry Paco, the wiry vaquero who had been making cow eyes at her for months.

She drew her rebozo closer about her shoulders and braced herself against the hurt as she remembered the warmth of the señor's kisses. That was all she had to remember, for never would he go farther, never would he enter her, always laughing at her insistence, at her passion for him, telling her she was but a child. A child! She was a woman, no longer a child, a woman not to be ignored and ordered away from the stone house like a *puta*. She laughed lightly to herself and her eyes gleamed triumphantly. Let the Apache kill the *gringa*! And then the heat in the señor's loins would force him to take her and to give her his *niño*. Then he would be hers!

Isabella hesitated, reluctant to leave the shadow of the building, yet unwilling to face the *gringa*. A small fear leaped into her mind. What if Señor Burr should find out . . . find out she knew the Apache was lingering by the stream and she had allowed his woman to walk, unwarned, up the path? His anger . . . his rage

. . . his fury would be terrible! She tossed her head. It was foolish to think he would know, but supposing he did find out she had been to the stream, he would never believe she was a traitor. Shoving herself away from the wall, she started down the path toward the woman who walked slowly toward her, her head bent as if in deep thought. Isabella's hatred burned deeply as she passed Johanna, her dark, smoldering eyes straight ahead, her chin defiantly lifted.

Johanna looked up and saw Isabella coming toward her. It was the first time she had seen the young Mexican girl since she had ordered her from the house. No doubt he was meeting her somewhere else now. Johanna was thankful she no longer had to suffer her presence. She looked directly at Isabella as she passed her, but the girl clutched her full skirt in her hand and swept past, her face set, her eyes never leaving the path ahead.

Going on down the trail, Johanna let her thoughts wander. She was legally married to Burr Engelbretson Calloway. Would he divorce her when she left the valley? She knew it could be done, especially by a man with money to pay the high court cost. She searched her mind, but could think of only one woman she knew that had been divorced. No respectable man or woman in San Angelo had had anything to do with her. Was that to be her lot in life? A divorced woman wouldn't be allowed to teach school, and so the only option open to her would be as a singer in a saloon. Of course, Burr had said he would never let her go . . . but now he had told her he would be glad to be rid of her. She closed her eyes as the pain of his words pierced her heart.

There was no movement and no sound that she could recall. Abruptly she was swept off her feet. A hand came from behind her and clamped over her mouth and nose, and a greasy arm tightened about her throat. She had only a moment of panic before she lost conscience.

Black Buffalo stood over the unconscious woman. It had worked out better than he had planned. He would do what Gray Cloud had failed to do; he would take the woman of Sky Eyes to be his slave. A look of gloating satisfaction crossed his face. Once again he had outsmarted the white man. His first victory over the white man was when he had demanded and received six ponies for Sha-we-ne's lame son, who was dead by now. The weak one could not have lived. Sky Eyes had stolen the slave woman thinking he, Black Buffalo, would swallow his pride and allow his possession to be taken. He would show all the Chiricahua Apaches that he was a man of pride, of vengeance.

Black Buffalo's dark eyes gleamed. His long wait beside the stream had paid off. He was glad the dark woman had not come on down the trail; he would have taken her, and missed the chance to get this woman with hair like a cloud. How envious the other warriors would be when they saw his white slave. He pictured her in his wickiup. He would forbid his wives to mark her skin and make her ugly, but he would allow them to beat her until she cringed before him. He would go inside her and she would give him many sons, all with eyes like the sky, to remind the Apache Nation of his brave and daring mission.

He nudged her with his foot. She would awaken soon. He cut off her air for only a short time, time enough to stuff her mouth so she would make no sound. He bound her hands with a thong, then looped the strong string of rawhide about her neck so he could lead her.

Johanna was now conscious. Her eyes flew open and she found herself staring into the pockmarked face of an Indian. Her head throbbed, and the hide that bound her wrists behind her back cut cruelly into her flesh. Her heart pounded with fear. The sound was so loud she felt sure the Indian could hear it. He didn't move, and she wished fervently she had not awakened. Why hadn't he killed her? If he was going to, why not now, and get it over with?

Several minutes passed. A frog croaked. Leaves crackled as a breeze stirred through the trees. The Indian stood as still as a statue, waiting. Johanna shifted about. Her mouth was dry and foul, tasting of the filthy cloth with which it was stuffed. She closed her eyes, feigning unconsciousness, but he kicked her in the side, seized her by the forearms, and hauled her to her feet. The Indian picked up her shawl and tied it tightly around her, binding her arms to her sides. He jerked viciously on the hide thong looped around her neck. It bit into her throat, and she frantically fought to breathe air into her lungs. He wrapped the end of the leash about his hand, then knelt and carefully removed all trace of their having been there. When satisfied their sign was erased, he tugged on the leash and jerked his head, indicating that she was to follow.

Slowly at first, the Apache moved out and down the rocky bank, looking back often to see if they were leaving a trail. Johanna followed on shaky legs, keeping within the distance the leash allowed. She had no doubt that if she couldn't keep up he would strangle her, leave her, and fade away into the distant mountains.

When they were some distance from the stream, the Indian increased his pace, and soon he was moving at a slow trot. Johanna staggered behind him, her lungs afire. She stood the pace as long as she could, then halted suddenly and let the leash jerk her to the ground. The Apache turned and kicked her in the side. The pain tore through her, and she felt herself fading. Suddenly he was standing over her, his knife in his hand. She closed her eyes in resignation as she felt the blade touch her cheek, and then swiftly the gag was gone. She breathed deeply and was revived, revived enough to plead with her eyes. He placed the flat side of his knife over his mouth, indicating silence, then drew the sharp edge of the blade across her throat, plainly telling her what she could expect if she made a sound. Johanna nodded and got to her feet, grateful the foul rag was out of her mouth. Now, breathing more easily, she was able to keep his pace.

Black Buffalo began to trot again. They were in the foothills of the mountains now. Grimly determined not to break stride, cry out, or fall, Johanna anesthetized herself with a rhythmic inner whisper of the name of the man whose arms would never hold her again, whose memory of her would not be with sweetness and love as Ben's was of his Anna. Burr . . . Burr . . . Burr.

For the rest of the day the Indian never looked at her or spoke to her. The emotional shock of the kidnapping had worn off, and Johanna, in the cool of the evening, appraised her situation. No one would realize she was gone until she failed to appear at supper, and then they would think she had gone to visit Jacy, although she had not been allowed to go that far from the house alone. She had to believe that she would eventually be missed and someone would come looking for her. If not Burr, perhaps Luis, for Jacy's sake, would search for her. She had to believe it.

Fatigue, physical and spiritual, struck with the setting of the sun. Each step was torture. Thirsty, hungry, and tired beyond her wildest nightmares, she doggedly held her pace. Her hair, pins long gone, streamed down her back and stuck to her sweat-covered face and neck.

Evening came quickly. In the semidarkness she stumbled often. She let herself imagine Burr's face, but now, when she wanted to remember each and every detail, his image was hazy. Her eyes focused weakly on the back of the Indian and she trudged on. A night bird whistled shrilly, and she heard the swish of his wings as he left his perch. The wish to fly with him moved fleetingly across her mind.

When Black Buffalo stopped, Johanna's mind and body were so numb that she did not register the action and stumbled into him. He put his palm over her face and pushed hard. She tumbled over backward, falling against a tree trunk. Her head seemed to explode, and for a few moments she whirled in a black void. She lay exhausted against the mesquite trunk until her vision cleared. Her legs and ankles throbbed; her wrists were rubbed raw by the hide. Her stockings hung by threads to her garters, and she tried to cover her scratched and bitten legs by drawing them up and under the now ragged skirt.

The Apache took a pouch that hung from his belt and with his eyes on her face lifted it and squirted water into his open mouth. Johanna's tongue was swollen and her mouth felt like a cotton ball. She would have given anything for a drink of water, but her pride would not allow her to beg. She curled her lips scornfully and looked away. Inside she prayed silently for strength.

She lay back, pride doing battle with thirst. There would be no water for her, she knew that now. Perhaps it was just as well; her ordeal would be over all the sooner.

Wiry fingers checked the bonds on her wrist and twisted the leash about his hand to shorten it. The rancid smell of the man almost sickened her. He settled himself with his back to a tree. She lay down in the grass and gratefully surrendered to sleep.

Johanna stirred in her slumber; sometimes she stayed half awake for a few seconds only, then dropped back into unconsciousness. Sometimes she would stir and imagine faces staring down at her. She saw Burr's face close to hers, willing her to get up; the next instant his face was far away, his voice calling her name. She dreamed of Jacy and her papa and mama walking around her, looking down at her, wondering why she was lying in the grass. She would try to get up off the ground, then she would drift back into darkness again.

She was in old Mack's room. He had locked the door and his back was to it. He was young and quick and the look in his eyes told her plainly what was in his mind. She backed away; the room seemed enormous, and she kept backing away, farther and farther away. Still he continued to stalk her, never letting his eyes leave her face. He reached out to her, and she eluded him. She heard Luis's voice. Was he cursing old Mack? Killing old Mack? There was a struggle beside her, and she opened her eyes and saw the Indian grasp his chest, a look of startled anguish on his face. His eyes bulged and gurgling noises came from his throat. The thong about her neck was jerked cruelly; she fought for air, then . . . blackness.

Johanna opened her eyes. Someone was holding her, cradling her against his chest. Her arms were free and she tried to raise them, but they fell lifelessly to her side. Her face was wet and her mouth full of water, delicious water, running down her parched throat. She wasn't dreaming, because she could taste the water and smell the familiar tobacco-y smell and hear the beloved voice of Burr.

"Johanna! Johanna! Oh, God, I thought you were dead!" His hoarse words vibrated in her head. He was kissing her hair, her lips, her face, wiping dirt from her eyes.

She pulled back to look at him, but her eyes flooded and she couldn't see.

"Don't cry. You're safe now. You're safe with me and Luis." His voice was strained and his face blurred.

"I can't stop!" she said. His arms held her so tightly she could hardly breathe.

"I was afraid." His arms relaxed a little. "I was just so afraid you'd gone off and left me."

"I'll never." Johanna tried to put her arms around him. "I'll never leave you unless you want me to go."

He kissed her again, burrowing his face into her hair, mumbling unintelligible words. The stubble on his cheeks and chin scratched her skin as he kissed her. "You don't hate me? Say you don't hate me!" He lifted his face to search her eyes for the answer.

"How can I hate you when I love you so?" Her arms reached out toward him, and held her close.

She must have drifted back to sleep again, for suddenly he was carrying her, trying to kiss her eyes open. His voice was strange, as though he had been crying.

"Help me on the horse, Luis. We've got to get her home."

Other arms held her for a moment, and she heard the creak of the saddle. Then she was lifted up and she lay against him again, feeling the strength of his arms as he took the reins. Every part of her body throbbed with pain. "How did you find me?" she asked.

"Luis tracked you. Didn't you know I'd come? I told you you'd never get away from me." His arms tightened around her. "Are you all right? Do you want more water?" His questions were anxious, loving.

"I'm all right, now." She snuggled her face against him. "But . . . the Indian?"

She felt his arms tense. "Dead. Nothing will ever hurt you again. I swear it."

CHAPTER TWENTY

THEY WERE APPROACHING the stone house. She knew it the second she opened her eyes, for light seemed to shine from every window. As her eyes began to focus properly she could see two figures standing on the porch and two coming across from the bunkhouse. The place was alive with activity. Anxious voices called out to Burr.

"Is she all right?" Ben's voice was trembly.

"She's worn out," Burr called, "but all right."

"By gol, Burr, we been mighty itchy. It didn't seem right, us jist a-sittin' here waitin'."

Johanna looked down into Mooney's worried face and began to cry.

"What's the matter?" Burr whispered.

"I'm just so . . . glad to be home."

Arms reached up to help her down. Her body ached all over, and her legs were too weak to hold her. Burr was by her side almost as soon as her sore feet touched the ground. He picked her up in his arms as if she weighed no more than a feather. She let her head fall to his shoulder, and he cradled her to him. He started walking very slowly, then stopped.

"Son of a bitch 'bout run her to death," he said huskily. "Sofía," he called sharply, "bring water to wash her and a gown of some kind. She's got to have something to eat, too. Ben, I promised Bucko I'd not come back without her. If he's sleeping, wake him and bring him in."

"He fell asleep about a half hour ago, Burr—he just couldn't keep his eyes open any longer."

Burr carried her into his room and lowered her onto the bed. Her eyes questioned his.

"Our room and our bed, Mrs. Calloway," he whispered in her ear.

Johanna sank into the soft bed, hardly aware that Burr worked to remove the shoes from her swollen feet. Her eyes rested on the curtainless windows, the stark walls, and the crude pieces of furniture. A well of pity surged up within her. This poor house! This poor, sad house was just sitting here waiting to come alive. Too exhausted to move, she gazed into the corners of the room. The sadness of the house and those who lived in it, the gentle ministerings of the crude, hard man bent over her, suddenly overwhelmed her. Johanna turned her face into the faded quilt and wept silently.

"Johanna." Burr's hand was on her shoulder.

She looked up to see Bucko standing beside the bed, his big, solemn eyes bright with tears. She held her arms out to him, and he clutched her tightly, burying his face in the warmth of her body.

"Bucko, darling, don't cry."

"I saw the bad Indian hit you, Johanna. I saw him tie you up and kick you. I was by the tree and I stood so still, so he couldn't see me. Then I run to tell Burr. Isabella saw the Indian, but she didn't tell. I hate Isabella!"

"Bucko's been following you ever since . . . well, for days now." Johanna's eyes moved to Burr. "He's been like your shadow, trailing you everywhere. Thank God he did." His voice became husky. "When he told me about the Apache I sent Paco for Luis, and as soon as he got here we were on your trail. If it hadn't been for Bucko, Johanna, it would have been hours before we discovered you were missing."

"Thank you, Bucko. I'm proud of you and I'm proud of the

part of you that's Apache. It was your Apache blood that let you stand so patiently and wait until it was safe to go to Burr.'' The boy beamed and looked up at Burr, wanting to share his newfound pride.

Later when Johanna was washed and in a clean nightdress she drew the quilt up to her chin and stretched her legs in sheer luxury. The kindness and concern of everyone made her realize how fond she had become of them all. It was pure heaven to feel so wanted, so cherished and loved.

When she awakened, evening was approaching once again. She could hear the ring of boot heels on the stone porch and Sofía's high musical voice talking to the men. Through the window she could see that almost all the light had gone from the sky. It was the gold time of day, as her papa had used to say.

"Do you feel better?" Burr came through the door and stood by the bed. He reached down and tucked the quilt about her shoulders. He spoke gruffly and did not look at her.

"Burr . . . about Jacy . . ."

"Luis didn't tell her," he said quickly. "On the way back he turned off so he would be home before she awakened."

"I'm glad." Johanna reached up and took his hand in hers. "Sit by me and tell me about finding Bucko in the Indian camp."

He sat on the side of the bed and studied her with an intensity that puzzled her. He dropped his eyes for a moment to look at her hand now resting so naturally in his, then met her eyes again, willing her to understand what he was about to say.

"When I first saw Bucko he was lying alone under a scrub oak on a piece of dirty blanket and making a weak, mewing sound. Camp dogs surrounded him, sniffing at the wretched mess." Johanna drew in a trembly breath and tightened her fingers on his. The compassionate tone of his voice affected her as much as his words. He continued, "I thought, Oh, God, how can they treat their little ones like this? Then it occurred to me that this one was an outcast, a less than perfect one in body. When I got closer to him he looked up at me with big blue eyes and I almost fell off my horse.'' Burr stopped speaking; the telling was painful to him. He looked down at the slim hand engulfed in his, then met her eyes and spoke firmly. "It didn't seem possible he could belong to one of us, but I had to get him and give him his chance." Johanna would never love him more than at that moment. He went on to tell her how he had traded ponies to Black Buffalo for the boy. "He'd not have made it if not for Rosita and the other women. I didn't know anything about how to take care of him, and Luis and Ben didn't know much more."

He sat silently, his fingers gripping hers. Johanna hesitated to interrupt, but she was compelled to ask: "Why didn't you say you were not his father?"

"It was a matter of not knowing, Johanna," he said simply. "Ten, twelve years ago, Luis and I were just a couple of young scutters and we were just finding out what it was all about. Mack took me to El Paso and turned me over to a couple of women . . . you know the kind. I came back, and, boylike, I told Luis all about it. Now, when I think about it, I know I didn't have any more brains than a flea." He lowered his head and looked at the floor. "The Apaches came down that year. They were a small friendly bunch. We were out one day and came onto these two girls down by the creek . . . and they were willing. Both of us regretted what we did. The next year we saw them again and they didn't seem no different, so we figured nothing happened. We swore then that we'd never father a bastard." He got up and went to the fire. Johanna followed him with her eyes. His voice lowered on a sigh. "Thank God the old man lived long enough to admit that Bucko was his."

Johanna's heart went out to him, and she wished she could think of something comforting to say, but the right words wouldn't come. The man was a curious mixture of compassion and bitterness. He had carried the guilt all these years not only of looking like the man who had raped his mother, but perhaps of having done the thing he had sworn not to do—father a bastard.

Burr sat in the chair and stretched his long legs out to the fire. It seemed hours, but could have been only minutes before he broke the silence.

"Isabella will be leaving the valley." He paused as if that was all he was going to say. "Paco wants to marry her, and I'll see to it they have a start somewhere else." Johanna started to say something, but he was speaking again. "I'm right sorry you don't like it here, Johanna. I realize that because Luis and I think it's the best place to be don't make it so for everyone." He cleared his throat nervously. "What I want to say is . . . well, what's done is done. We're wed and . . . I want my wife with me."

He looked at his feet, shifted them from side to side nervously, then, for the lack of anything else to do, he drew the makings of a smoke from his pocket. His fingers were shaking so badly he spilled some of the tobacco on the floor.

"You know," he said, trying to roll the smoke, "there's never been a woman in this house before, except my mother. It's been good having the house like it is and a meal ready . . . and knowing there'd be a pretty woman to look at while you ate it."

"Now that Mack's gone there's no reason why one of the Mexican women can't come and clean the house, and Sofía is an excellent cook." The words were softly spoken. He glared at her impatiently.

"Goddammit, that's not what I mean, and you know it!"

Johanna got up out of bed, fully aware that only a thin nightdress covered her naked body. On sore, bare feet she walked around behind him and stood near his chair. Her glance found the crushed paper and tobacco in his tight fist. She closed her eyes tightly in an effort to still her pounding heart.

"Have you ever wondered why Jacy is so open with her expressions of affection, Burr?" Once she started talking the words came easier. "She learned it from Papa. Every day, from the time she was old enough to understand to the day they died, Papa would tell Mama he loved her. Sometimes it was at the supper table, or when she was working about the house. He would say, 'Have I told you today that I love you?' and she would say, 'Yes, *querido,* but tell me again.' " Burr sat rigidly in the chair, the only movement his big fist opening and closing. Johanna hurried on before she lost her nerve. "If love is nourished it will grow strong. Fail to feed it and it will wither and die. Burr, I cannot stay here as an unloved wife.''

Boldly she moved around to the side of the chair, so she could see his face.

"Unloved? What are you talking about?'' His voice was strained, husky.

Her taut nerves made her voice almost a shout. "Do you want me to stay and keep your house and care for Bucko, or do you . . . love me? You acted as if you did when you brought me home last night.''

Silence ensued, and Johanna colored as the enormity of her words hit her. Slowly his expression changed from shock to wonderment and his eyes and mouth became tender. His voice, when it reached her, was deep and sincere.

"I want you to stay because I love you.'' His hand came out and clasped her arm, pulling her onto his lap. "If loving you means not being able to sleep without seeing your face and not being able to eat unless you're at the table and not speaking to you unless I'm either sore at you or acting the fool . . . and being crazy out of my head when you . . . were gone!'' He leaned his head back against the chair and studied every feature of her face, his eyes lingering on her softly parted mouth. "The first day I saw you standing in that cluttered kitchen I thought you were a vision. You were too beautiful to be real. Too beautiful for the likes of me.'' He gave her a tender, apologetic look. "I wanted you to take to me like Jacy took to Luis, but you didn't, and . . . I told myself I didn't care. Then the idea fell right in my lap . . . the way to get you to marry me, for Luis's sake, I told myself, so Jacy would be happy in the valley.''

Johanna tried to speak, but failed. She lifted trembling hands and stroked the hair back from his face, then with palms against his cheeks she leaned forward and tenderly kissed his lips, before resting her head on his shoulder. His arms adjusted her on his lap and he cuddled her close. She snuggled in his arms, and felt his heart beat as wildly as her own.

"I love you,'' she whispered. "Love you, love you.''

Her voice was the softest of sounds. He searched her face for reassurance, and when she smiled radiantly up at him he saw the love in her eyes and believed it. All that mattered was being close to each other, being together, and more whole because of it. He nestled his warm mouth close against her face with a gentle reverence that turned her heart over.

"That time in my room . . . I hated myself for what I did to you. Can you forgive me?" With restrained passion, far removed from his earlier onslaughts, his hands caressed her face and he threaded his fingers through her hair. "I've been such a fool," he breathed huskily. "Tenderness is much better."

Her arm tightened and she moved her mouth to his. "Not all the time, darling."

He chuckled and his lips found hers in a kiss that was at once a joy and a promise. She knew they would always be together. And her happiness was so overwhelming it seemed akin to pain. She moved her head to kiss the still tender scars on his chest, and thankfulness flooded her heart.

"Burr," she said softly, "can you imagine what our children will look like?"

The chuckle came from deep in his chest. She could feel the vibration against her heart.

"I know what they'd better look like," he growled.

She caressed his face with her fingertips. "We'll have a wedding fiesta at Thanksgiving and invite everyone."

She sounded so amazingly like Jacy that Burr laughed and kissed her nose.

"I can see I'm going to be clay in your hands, Mrs. Calloway. How many turkeys do you want?"

She laughed. "You'll never be clay in anyone's hands, Burnett Englebretson Calloway." She clutched his face between her palms. "You're a fraud! That's what you are. You're not one bit as churlish and unfeeling as you pretend to be."

EPILOGUE

AROUND HER WAS silence, utter and complete except for the wind that raced down the valley and stirred the tall grasses, and whispered through the pine trees causing a cone to fall now and then without a sound to the grass-cushioned earth. It was a beautiful morning and this was a beautiful place. Johanna walked slowly through the gate and approached the graves reverently. For the past twelve Septembers she had made this pilgrimage to the cemetery. Not only did she enjoy the serenity of the place, but it was one of the few places where she could look down on the ranch house.

Turning now, she saw the stone house, surrounded with its split-railed fence, and shrubs, flowers and hanging baskets trailing their bright blossoms. The morning sun shone on the tin roof of the new addition, on the sparkling, curtained windows, and on Grandpa Ben sitting on the porch. A smile played around the corners of her mouth as a small, blond-haired figure raced out of the house and climbed up onto his lap. Dear, dear Ben, she mused, how he loves his grandchildren! She should hurry on back before the scamp had him worn out.

There were scarcely more than a dozen graves inside the piled-stone enclosure, but at one end three markers stood straight and solid. Johanna walked over to read the inscriptions.

ANNA MARIE ENGLEBRETSON

1827–1847

Farewell, my love, your life is past,
My love for you through life will last.
I'll grieve for you and sorrow take,
And love your child, for your sake.

B.N.C.

Through the years the headboard had weathered, but dabs of stain outlined the letters and they were as easy to read as the day they were put there.

She walked a few feet away to the other headboard.

JUANITA GAZARES

1828–1860

Beloved mother of Luis Gazares

Kind angels watch this sleeping dust,
Till Jesus comes to raise the just,
Then may she wake with sweet surprise,
And in her Savior's image rise.

The markers were identical, except one was much more seasoned than the other. The thought crossed Johanna's mind that Mack Macklin had probably never come to this cemetery and read the inscriptions. He would have scorned such sentiment.

Johanna stood beside the Indian woman's grave for a few minutes. Before Bucko had left five years ago to go back East to school he had carved a headboard. The words were his. It simply read:

MOTHER

Shamed in life
Brave in death.

It was proven that Bucko had a brilliant mind. When Uncle Rafael Macklin had come to the valley for a visit he had taken Bucko back East with him. The young man had finished his studies at the university in record time and joined his uncle in business.

Johanna passed on to another grave. The headboard was as neatly carved as the others.

O. MOONEY

1825–1875

Dear Mooney, Johanna thought with a smile. No wonder he had always said, "Just call me Mooney." It was after his death they had discovered his name was Only. Mooney had died with an arrow in his back, but he had lived long enough to fire warning shots that alerted the roundup camp where Burr and the men had been working.

Several times during the last few years there had been small Indian raids in the valley. Geronimo and another colorful chief, Victoriano, were raiding and causing havoc in southern New Mexico, Arizona, and southeastern Texas, but they had kept their word, so far, and had left Macklin Valley in peace. Burr still took supplies down when the Indians came to the valley, but now they came in small pitiful groups, made up mostly of women, children, and old men.

Johanna went toward a small mound. The marker was newer than the others.

NATHAN CALLOWAY

son

3 months 2 days

Tears filled her eyes. Four years had failed to dull the pain of loosing her second son. She and Burr had had a daughter the first year of their marriage and three years later a son. Both children were naturally blond, with blue eyes and bounding energy. Little Nathan was born with a dark tinge to his skin, and they had known almost from the first that he would never grow up to be as healthy as his brother and sister.

Two weeks ago Johanna had presented her husband with a third son, and from the way he pulled on her breast when she fed him this morning she was sure he was going to be as robust as her other two children. She had left him with Anna, her eleven-year-old daughter, who was fascinated with him and had vowed she was going to have dozens and dozens of babies.

Luis and Jacy had three children and another on the way. Tiny Marietta was almost a year older than Johanna's Anna, yet barely came up to her shoulder. She had long, shiny black hair and large black eyes and was as shy as Anna was daring. Both girls suffered the same lament: overprotective fathers.

Johanna passed Codger's grave and that of Red and Rosita's little one and moved on to stand beside the grave at the far end of the cemetery. At her insistence a marker had been placed there.

MACK MACKLIN

He found the valley.

She never lingered beside the old man's grave, but passed on as if by going by she had somehow done her duty. Looking down toward the ranch house, she saw a rider come out of the corral and head up toward the hill. She knew who it was before he took off his hat to wipe the sweat from his forehead and the sun glistened on hair yellow as cactus blossom. She leaned against the stone fence and waited for him.

From her vantage point the land fell away, sweeping down to the sparkling stream whose waters threaded their way across the valley carpeted with waving, knee-high grasses. She let her glance wander to the mountain peaks where the green timber gave way to rocky, snow-covered towers. She remembered Burr's words on that night, so long ago, when they had declared their love. " 'Cause Luis and I think this is the best place to be don't make it so for everyone." It *was* the place she wanted to be, she thought. The only place in the world she wanted to be.

"Johanna." Burr's voice drifted up the hill.

She waved to him and laughed with utter abandonment when she saw the scowl on his face and knew she was in for a scolding. The instant he got off the horse she hurried to him, and his outstretched arms welcomed her. He kissed her tenderly at first, then roughly, almost savagely.

"I've missed you," she whispered.

He held her away from him and looked down with a mocking sternness. "Don't be trying to get around me with honeyed words. You shouldn'ta walked all the way up here. It's only two weeks tomorrow since you had the babe. You're not strong enough yet."

"I've missed you," she said again with sparkling eyes.

"What am I going to do with you, woman? You don't have the brains of a flea, but I . . . love you, love you, and I've missed you, too." He folded her to him lovingly, and she raised her mouth for his kiss.

"How much longer?" He breathed the words in her ear.

She drew back and laughed up at him. "Two weeks."

"Two weeks!" He groaned. "I'll have to go to El Paso and visit the—"

She drew her foot back and kicked him on his lower leg.

"You just try and get out of this valley without me, Burr Calloway!"

He laughed happily. "Come on, you mule-headed shrew. I'll give you a ride home."

He lifted her up onto the saddle, placed her hands on the pommel and cautioned her to hold on tightly, then jumped up behind her. She leaned back against him, feeling loved and protected, and loving the strength of his arms as he took the reins. The horse moved on down the slope.

"Have I told you today that I love you, Mrs. Calloway?" The soft familiar words were whispered in her hair.

"Yes, *querido*," she murmured, "but tell me again."